HER DEADLY BETRAYAL

BonzaiMoon Books LLC
Houston, Texas
www.bonzaimoonbooks.com

Editing by Kelly Hartigan of Xterra Web
http://editing.xterraweb.com

1

The Woodlands, Texas
Carlton Woods Gated Community

Sione walked into the master suite, a spacious area as big as a one-bedroom apartment with a sitting area, reading nook, and a wall of French doors leading out to a large terrace. With a quick intake of breath, he stopped short, staring at the woman who'd stolen his heart, the woman he was falling more and more in love with day by day. The brazen and beautiful woman who had come into his life more than a year ago.

Spencer Edwards.

The first time he'd seen Spencer, perched on one of the divans in the lobby of his resort, the Belizean Banyan, he'd known he would, eventually, fall in love with her and the exhilarating descent would change his life—for better and not for worse, which was what his family believed.

From the first moment he'd met her, Spencer had been sexy and full of secrets, not exactly honest and forthright about her real reasons for visiting Belize. She'd lied to him about so many things, too many things, but the lies she'd told him more than a year ago no longer bothered him. He had stopped wondering if the lies might be stronger than their love. He decided to forget about the lies, and the truth, and the worries about whether or not he would ever be able to trust this woman he'd fallen in love with—and whether or not she would be able to trust him.

His mother's assertions notwithstanding, Sione wasn't convinced their love had been built on deception, something fragile and fractious, something that could fall apart easily and might collapse or implode.

There had been a time when Sione had wondered if their relationship could survive the dishonesty. He'd doubted if love would really be enough to overcome deception, and thought the lies between them might have the potential, or the power, to destroy them. He'd feared the truth would come out despite his efforts to suppress it, or ignore it, and when it did, the truth would not make them free—it would arrest them, binding them in unbreakable chains.

Those suspicious, unfounded fears had been fostered by his family, who'd tried like hell to make him believe Spencer was a lying bitch who couldn't be trusted. Over the past year, as their love for each other had grown and deepened, Sione realized he couldn't allow his family's doubts to influence his feelings for Spencer.

He loved her, couldn't imagine his life without her, and had decided he wouldn't live without her.

Spencer was sprawled across the king-sized bed on her stomach with her legs in the air, ankles crossed, wearing a skimpy pair of purple lace panties and matching camisole. She had a piece of paper, maybe a crossword puzzle, propped on the pillow in front of her and was twirling a pencil between her fingers.

Sione gazed at her ass for a while, entertaining enticing thoughts of being with Spencer forever, for better or worse, in sickness and in health, until death.

Spencer turned over, a slow, languid, tempting roll and then sat up, arching a little so he could see her nipples straining against the sheer fabric.

"Hi, John." She smiled. "How was work?"

"It was...okay...how was your day?"

She shrugged. "All right."

"What you got there?" he asked. "Crosswords?"

"Yeah, but I'm so bad at crosswords." She tapped the pencil against her bottom lip, grabbed the paper, and perused it. "Like I'm stuck on this one...a four-letter slang word for copulation."

He smiled, knowing she was teasing him.

"Oh, well..." She tossed the paper in the air, then moved onto her knees, and inched toward him, a playful yet salacious look in her brown eyes. She jumped off the bed, walked to him, and slipped her arms around his waist. "So, John, are you interested in a four-letter slang word for copulation?"

"I am..." Sione stared down at her, mesmerized by how pretty she looked, how he could feel her nipples, as hard as pearls, and how he wanted nothing more than to swirl his tongue around those nipples before taking them into his mouth. "But, I'm more interested in an eight-letter word which symbolizes love, devotion, and commitment forever..."

———

The clothes were discarded quickly, as usual, and they tumbled onto the bed.

Settling back against the pillows stacked against the tufted headboard, Spencer tried to ignore the hint of apprehension threatening to put a damper on her desire. As John loomed over her, Spencer reflected on his words, relishing and reveling in his heartfelt sentiment. She couldn't take what he'd said to heart even though his intentions made her heart soar.

An eight-letter word which symbolizes love, devotion, and commitment forever.

Spencer had just smiled and kissed him, unable to respond when she realized the word he was referring to—marriage.

Did John want to marry her?

The thought filled Spencer with joy, but the happiness would be short-lived. If she married John, things between them would change. Especially in the bedroom. As his wife, he would expect her to accommodate him every time he was rock hard and ready to go. There would be no more slow, sexy, teasing foreplay. He would want her naked as soon as possible. He would always be in a damn hurry to be inside her. And, truthfully, Spencer figured she would be in a rush, too, because marriage would have turned her into "that wife" who would behave like a lust-stricken bitch in heat at the sight of her husband. She would crave him like a drug, aching to be filled to capacity.

Spencer struggled to focus. She couldn't entertain wayward thoughts of John as her *husband*. He wasn't her husband, and he never would be. Marriage wasn't on the agenda—wasn't one of the items on their list of things to do as they fell in love. Marriage wasn't what she had in mind when she thought of happily ever after with John. She didn't need to marry John to live together forever with him. All they needed was love and commitment.

The road to happily ever after wasn't paved with gold—or good intentions. There were cracks in the foundation and potholes. Sometimes, that sunset they were riding off into seemed so far away she felt as though they would never reach it; other times, it seemed too close, scorching and bright, with the power to expose everything she'd fought so damn hard to keep hidden away in the dark. But, she wouldn't give up. She couldn't because—

You're so close to getting what you want.

The memory came out of nowhere, like a seemingly random attack, quick and brutal. Ben's voice. His sarcastic advice, his condescending tone. *Don't blow it now, sweet girl...*

Abruptly, she felt his mouth on hers and his tongue slipping between her lips, swirling slowly. Moments later, he pulled back and stared at her, his dark eyes mesmerizing and menacing.

Spencer gasped and tried to push him away.

"What's the matter?" John asked.

Her heart pounding, Spencer stared at the eyes gazing at her, focusing on the swirls of green and light brown flecked with gold. Hazel eyes, beautiful and intoxicating, comforting. As John stared at her, his desire increasing, she forced herself to think of all the things she loved about him and all the reasons why, for her, he was the perfect man. He was loving and kind and compassionate and protective and supportive. John was the man of her dreams, the fantasy that had come true. He was—

Not what you think, sweet girl. You think he's your knight in shining armor, but the truth is, we are more alike than we are different. Squeezing her eyes shut, Spencer tried to will Ben's voice and his image from her mind. What the hell was he doing in her head anyway? Why the hell was she thinking about him now? Why was she thinking about him *at all*?

"You okay?"

"Yeah…" she said, trying to smile, trying to think of something dirty and nasty to say, but a strange, ominous feeling had taken up residence within her, like some unwanted houseguest, and she was having a hard time getting it to leave.

Gently, John teased her with soft, lingering kisses, but Spencer was impatient, desperate to have him inside her, and didn't want to wait a second longer. She wasn't really interested in foreplay. She needed vigorous thrusts, hoping the frenetic pounding would drive away the errant, intrusive memories of Ben Chang, his dire prophecies, and his terrorizing gaze.

John's fingers delved inside her, sliding and probing, and soon, he was finding spots she didn't know existed, sending her over the edge several times, soaring and crashing…

Before she could recover, he was burying his face between her legs, licking around her clit, slipping his tongue inside her, flicking and sucking, as his hands reached up the length of her body and grabbed her breasts.

Panting, she arched her back, circling her hips as he took her over the edge yet another time.

Soon, the sheets beneath her were soaked.

Even after all that, there was resistance when he tried to thrust. The vagina that had been so welcoming moments ago closed ranks, refusing the head of his penis. Despite how wet she was, there was a refusal to accept him within her without struggle…

Frowning, John asked, "You okay?"

Spencer nodded, trying to relax and ignore the panic fluttering in her chest.

John pushed, and insistence met resistance again, but for Spencer, it was like exquisite torture, and soon, the defenses began to break down, the barriers allowed them to be broken through, and full access was granted.

As soon as his entire massive length and width was inside, she didn't think she would get enough; she wanted it to last forever.

With the first full thrust, she was moaning and panting.

Teasing her, John withdrew entirely and then battled his way back in, past the decreasing resistance, so each time felt like the first time, over and over again, a constant ebb and flow, sending a surge of pleasure through her, flooding her, drowning and drenching...

Finally, John found a pace, sliding in and out with velocity, but he didn't commit to it. She hooked one leg over his shoulder as he entered her slowly, so she felt him inch by inch, and it was intense and delicious, but she was still impatient.

He withdrew and entered her again. With the retreat and surge forward, she went over the edge, crying out as she went limp beneath him, panting and groaning. But, it wasn't enough. She wanted more. Forcing him to switch their positions, she climbed on top of him and guided him inside her. Sliding up and down his long, thick length with vigor and determination, she moaned as she went over the edge again.

Moaning and writhing, she kissed him, swirling her tongue in his mouth. Spencer sunk her nails into his shoulders as her moans grew louder as she moved up and down on him, wild and maniacal. Each time she rose, she squeezed him as hard as she could, and when she moved down, she was grinding against him, taking him in all the way.

And it wasn't long before she was thrashing, and when she came, she was screaming his name.

2

The Woodlands, Texas
Carlton Woods Gated Community

Sione stood at the island in the kitchen, whipping egg whites in a glass bowl as conflicting thoughts divided his attention.

Sex with Spencer last night had been satisfying but not as spectacular as it could have been, as it usually was, and he had a feeling she'd been troubled about something. Whatever had been on her mind caused a disconnect between them. It was disconcerting, but he wasn't sure he wanted to know the reason for her distraction. Speculation, of course, had run rampant, right out of his control, leading him toward disturbing conclusions. He hoped his suspicions were unfounded. But, the possibility that his suspicions might be true unnerved him and made him reluctant to ask questions.

He stopped whisking, realizing he was seconds away from making a meringue instead of an omelet.

Cursing, he stared at the egg whites as the foam began to dissipate. His thoughts shifted, pivoting toward memories of his most recent trip to Belize. Two weeks ago, he'd traveled back to his birthplace—after being away for the past three months while Spencer spent some time with her sisters and grandmother—to deal with an issue concerning the luxury tree houses. The ambitious endeavor had quickly become a headache with all sorts of problems and issues he hadn't foreseen from bad weather to construction workers threatening to strike and unionize to misguided tree-huggers creating human chains to protest what they considered his "rape" of the natural environment in the name of greedy capitalism.

Beyond weather and employment concerns, the most pressing issue was always money, and his presence had been required in San Ignacio because he needed more funds. Raising capital wasn't easy, particularly when the bank was a bit squeamish about loaning him more cash. He'd had to do a bit more leveraging of his property and liquefying of his assets than he'd been comfortable with, but it couldn't be avoided. He didn't want to put the project on hold, but he was starting to question his decision.

Initially, the idea for the luxury tree houses had convinced Sione that he just might deserve the legacy his uncle had left him—the sprawling five-star Belizean Banyan resort. But the money problems and the uncertainty about whether or not he would be able to successfully solve them had shaken his confidence.

Following a long, exhausting, somewhat successful meeting with the bank, the last thing he'd wanted to hear was his family nagging him about Spencer being the wrong woman for him, especially when those warnings were coming from Jared, who usually stayed out of Sione's love life. Normally, Sione could shrug off his family's dire predictions, but Jared was a calm, calculating detective, not prone to melodrama or histrionic hand-wringing. Jared was all about facts, and he had presented his case against Spencer in a logical, rational manner that was sobering and hard to dismiss.

"Listen, I know you don't want to hear this," Jared had said after a few beers and some trivial banter. They were sitting out on the terrace behind the owner's casita, watching the sun go down.

"Then don't say it," Sione advised.

"I think I need to," Jared said, sitting his beer bottle on the ground. "I think you need to know the truth about Spencer."

"You been talking to DJ?"

"No," Jared said. "I've been talking to William Bermudez."

"William Bermudez?" Hearing the name, Sione almost flinched, remembering the sweat-soaked son of a bitch, remembering things he hadn't wanted to believe, things he'd tried to forget.

"The guy who told you where to find Spencer when you insisted on risking your life to look for her."

"What about him?" Sione asked, trying to keep his tone bored, with a trace of annoyance, but his heart was pounding.

Sione nodded, trying to ignore the effects of the name that still had the power to infuriate him. What enraged Sione even more was Spencer's connection to Ben—an indirect connection through Bermudez, who'd been her contact when she'd arrived in Belize to do Ben Chang's bidding. Spencer had never met Ben, but Sione hated that Ben had been the reason for Spencer's trip to San Ignacio. Like some sadistic puppet master pulling the strings, Ben had forced Spencer to do favors for him, deadly instructions given to her by Bermudez, assignments that had resulted in the twisted, ritualistic murders of three women.

"You know Bermudez worked for Ben Chang, right?"

Sione nodded and took another sip of the beer, wishing he had something a lot stronger.

"You ever wonder how Bermudez knew that Spencer had been kidnapped and was tied up in that shack?"

"All I wanted to know was where Spencer was so I could go get her," Sione said. "I wasn't really interested in how he knew where she was."

"Maybe you should have been interested," Jared suggested.

Sione had stared at his cousin. "What the hell does that mean?"

Leaving the center island, Sione walked toward the breakfast nook, an airy, sun-splashed octagonal space with wide windows overlooking the expansive backyard.

He didn't want to think about what Jared had told him or how the information had led his cousin to believe Spencer was a liar who shouldn't be trusted. Not because what Jared had said couldn't possibly be true, but because it could. Spencer might have lied to him about more things than Sione had initially thought. Which wouldn't really be so shocking. He knew she hadn't been truthful with him about her trip to Belize. But—some lies were worse than others. Some lies were impossible to recover from.

"Morning."

Sione turned. Dressed in a short silk kimono, Spencer headed toward the refrigerator, shuffling across the tile floor in fluffy slippers and rubbing her eyes.

"Good morning," he said. "I'll get some coffee started."

"Don't want any coffee," she mumbled, opening the refrigerator.

"You don't?" That was odd. Usually, Spencer needed a large cup of straight black Sumatra blend to start her day.

"No, I don't," she said, and when she left the refrigerator, closing it with her foot, she was holding the remaining two-thirds of a key lime pie he'd picked up for dessert earlier in the week.

Chuckling slightly, he said, "Key lime pie for breakfast."

Shrugging, Spencer got a spoon from a cabinet drawer, took a seat at one of the stools around the island, and scooped out a large hunk of the pie.

Sione went back to the bowl of egg whites he'd abandoned. "Are you okay?"

"Why the hell wouldn't I be okay?" she asked and shoveled another spoonful of pie into her mouth.

"Because you're eating pie for breakfast."

Rolling her eyes, she carved out another scoop.

Sione cleared his throat, picked up the whisk, and whirled it around half-heartedly. "And because last night..."

"What about last night?"

"Just didn't seem like..."

"Didn't seem like what, John?" she asked, licking the back of her spoon.

"Didn't seem like you were in the mood to make love."

———

Spencer coughed as the pie she was about to swallow lodged in her throat.

"Want some water?" John asked.

Nodding, Spencer managed a few more fake coughs. As John walked to the refrigerator, she took a deep breath, thinking about how to respond to him. She had to be very careful even though his comment pissed her off. She had to watch her tone, though, because she didn't want to lose the love of her life.

"It wasn't that I wasn't in the mood," she said, hoping to sidestep the issue. "I was just..."

Memories of the intimacy issues seized her. Last night, the

intrusive thoughts of Ben had threatened her lovemaking with John. For a moment, Spencer had worried she wouldn't be able to take him all in, and it would have been Ben Chang's damn fault. Somehow, she knew Ben would have mocked her if he knew his patronizing advice had almost derailed her desire for John.

Sione would never forgive you if you made a mistake, sweet girl. He would never understand your choices, and he would condemn you for them.

Spencer shook her head, wary, desperate to get Ben out of her thoughts. She didn't want to think about the mistakes she'd made. There had been so many, too many. Starting with her decision to have dinner with Ben Chang when she'd first met him, lifetimes ago. It had been a somewhat mercenary decision, based on the designer shoes she'd noticed him wearing. She'd thought he might be a good prospect to "date" even though he wasn't a dirty old geezer, her usual mark. As she'd enjoyed the duck confit, microgreens, and sweetbreads, she chose not to slip a few drops of GHB into his wine or to steal from him.

Not dating Ben that night had been a stupid mistake.

Her decision to date Ben several months later had been another stupid mistake. Of course, now she realized the ultimate mistake had been not getting up and walking away from Ben when he'd sat next to her on that park bench in front of the Houston City Hall reflecting pool.

"Spencer...?"

Jolted, she glanced at him. John was giving her a skeptical look, waiting for an answer. She had to come up with something to get him off the subject. Something that wouldn't invite further conversation about an issue she didn't want to deal with right now —marriage and how to explain why she didn't want to get married. She didn't know how to explain why she *couldn't* get married.

"I was just tired," she said, the only lame excuse she could come up with.

"You sure that's what it was?" he asked.

"Well, if it wasn't," she said, "then what do you think it was?"

"I was hoping you would tell me," he said. "Hoping you would be honest with me."

"You say that like you think I wouldn't be honest with you," she said. "You sound like your mother."

"What does that mean?" he asked.

"Like you don't trust me," she said, and finished the last of the pie, still craving the sweet tanginess. "Like you think I'm going to lie to you. That's what your mother said, I'm a liar and—"

"My mother said that? When?"

"Last month, when I went back to Belize with you," she said, her voice rising. "I came down to the kitchen, and she starts telling me that I'm not good enough for you. She said you're only interested in my looks."

His frown deepened, turned to a scowl. "What?"

"She said our relationship is just about sex," she said, struggling to manage the wayward, escalating emotions and failing miserably. "You like me because I look good. But, one day, you're going to wake up and realize that you're no longer interested in these tits and this ass."

Shaking his head, he said, "You know that's not true."

"Your mother said I should leave before you kick me out and I end up depressed and feeling like a damn fool," she said, feeling even more irrational as she thought, incongruously, about licking the residual graham cracker crust and smears of key lime filling from the glass pan.

"She said ... *what*?"

"Your mother is not the only one who thinks that," she said, her voice rising again, in volume and volatility. "All of your cousins think that. And your aunts and uncles. And that's just your Belizean relatives. I'm sure if you took me to that island where you grew up, your Tongan relatives would take one look at me and think the same thing. After all, what else is a girl with big boobs and a nice ass good for except—"

"You really believe that?" John asked.

"I don't really know what to believe," Spencer snipped.

"Maybe you should believe me," John said. "Maybe you should believe what I say instead of—"

"Maybe you should tell me what you like about me besides the big boobs and nice ass." Spencer dropped the spoon into the empty glass pie pan, wincing at the cacophony of metal against glass.

———

Pulling Spencer into his arms, Sione kissed her and then said, "My uncle Siosi told me to find the woman God wanted me to be with, and I did when I found you."

"Are you sure?" Her tone was dubious.

"You don't think you're that woman?"

"The woman God wants you to be with?" She shook her head. "I know I'm not. I can't be."

"Why not?"

"Because..." She looked away.

"Don't let my mother upset you," he said. "She's wrong."

"Or maybe she's right," Spencer said.

"Why do you think you're not good enough for me?"

"Because you're, like, the perfect guy." She gazed up at him. "You know you are."

"What makes you think I'm so perfect?" he asked. "You think I haven't done stuff that I regret? You think I haven't done things that I'm ashamed of?"

"What?" She gave him a skeptical gaze. "You mean you broke some girl's heart or something?"

"No, I…"

Not some girl's heart, Sione thought. Her neck. Maybe. He still wasn't sure. *Multiple gunshot wounds to the face. Throat slit. Stabbed several times in the chest.* Sione had wanted to end Moana's miserable life. He'd hoped he had killed her. Knowing he might not have been responsible for Moana's death filled him with an emotion he couldn't identify. Maybe regret? Possibly relief?

"John?"

Ignoring the disturbing memories, Sione said, "What I love about you, even more than the big boobs and nice ass, which, trust me, I absolutely love, is that you are courageous, tenacious, resilient, supportive, loyal, compassionate, caring—"

"You don't have to say things you don't mean to make me feel better about myself."

"Why do you think I don't mean it?"

"I don't know," she said. "Maybe you do, but…"

"But you don't think you deserve to be loved or that anyone could ever love you because of how your mother treated you?"

"I don't want to talk about my mother," she said, pulling away from him.

Sione pulled her back, tightening his arms around her. "I don't either. I want to talk about the eight-letter word which symbolizes love, devotion, and commitment forever."

Sighing, Spencer squirmed in his embrace, her expression furtive and frustrated.

"Wait, I didn't tell you what else I love about you besides the big boobs and nice ass."

Glancing up at him, she seemed suspicious but willing to listen.

"I love you because you are a loving woman who cares about other people," he said, and then stopped for a moment to kiss her forehead, her nose, and finally her lips. "You're smart and you definitely have your own opinions, but you're not judgmental. You're someone I can trust, someone who will help me be a better person."

"You know that's not me, John," she said, frowning. "That's who you want Mrs. Tuiali'i to be."

"And that's who you are," he said, staring at her. "You are who I want to be Mrs. Tuiali'i."

3

———

The Woodlands, Texas
Carlton Woods Gated Community

"Did she tell you about the key lime pie for breakfast?" Rae asked, laughing as she took a swig of her mimosa.

"Yes, and I couldn't believe it," Shady said. "He had to have been suspicious."

"He was distracted," Spencer said. "The night before, we'd had sex, but it was more catastrophic than cataclysmic. Took a while for the earth to start moving. And then he confronted me about it."

"And you just wanted to eat some damn key lime pie," Rae said.

"Absolutely!" Spencer said, laughing a little. "I was, like, can I just eat this pie in peace? I mean, practically every night, I'm Cowgirl Spencer, in the saddle."

Shady giggled, and Rae rolled her eyes.

"I don't know why he wants to bitch because I just happened to not be in the mood to have that damn elephant trunk shoved up my twat," Spencer complained and then grabbed another honeydew melon cube, wrapped a strip of prosciutto around it, and popped it in her mouth.

"Oh, Spencer," Shady admonished, shaking her head as she picked up the glass of lemonade on the coaster in front of her and then took a sip.

"What do you mean, '*Oh, Spencer*'?" Rae gave Shady a pointed stare.

"Don't have to be so vulgar," Shady said.

"Whatever, Shady," Rae said, rolling her eyes.

Ignoring Rae, Shady looked at Spencer. "What did he say when you asked him what he liked about you besides your looks?"

"He said everything I wanted to hear," Spencer said. "And then he said something that I couldn't believe."

"What did he say?" Rae asked.

"He didn't say it explicitly." Spencer amended. "But I could read between the lines. I think he wants to marry me."

Shady squealed and clapped her hands. "I knew it! I knew he was going to ask you to marry him."

"Did you say yes?" Rae asked, her gray eyes dancing with a delighted excitement.

"Were y'all listening? I said I think he wants to marry me," Spencer said. "I didn't say he proposed."

"Well what exactly did he say?" Rae asked.

"He said that I was who he wanted Mrs. Tuiali'i to be," Spencer said, her heart pounding just as it had yesterday, when John first said those words. She hadn't really known how to respond and was thankful when John kissed her, scooped her into his arms, and took her upstairs to their bedroom. As he made love to her, she couldn't help thinking John was wrong about her. She couldn't be Mrs. Tuiali'i. She didn't know how to be the wife John deserved, and she couldn't stomach the thought of disappointing him.

What terrified her even more was the fear of becoming like her mother.

She didn't want to get married and turn into "that wife".

"He's going to propose," Shady said. "I just know it. I can tell he's crazy about you."

"Well, if John asks me to marry him, then …" The thought of a proposal filled Spencer with panic, made her feel dizzy and faint.

"Then you better say yes," Rae commanded.

"What else would she say except yes?" Shady asked.

"I would say that I can't," Spencer said, shaking her head.

"What do you mean you can't?" Rae asked.

"You have to," Shady insisted. "You love him. He loves you. Marriage is the next step."

"I don't believe in marriage," Spencer said. "Y'all know that. And you know why."

"Yeah, and it's a very stupid reason," Rae said. "What the hell is "that wife" anyway?"

"Spence, you can't let the past dictate your future," Shady said.

"Enough about marriage, okay? It's not going to happen," Spencer said. "Besides, I have bigger problems."

————

Standing in the butler's pantry, Sione stood still, listening.

He felt like a spy and a sneak, like some paranoid jealous boyfriend, trying to catch his girlfriend admitting she'd cheated on him. Which Sione wouldn't have been worried about, and probably could have handled, if that was what Spencer was hiding from him.

He doubted it. Still, he wanted to know what she and her sisters were talking about.

Minutes ago, he was heading into the kitchen when he'd heard them. Just before he stepped over the threshold, Spencer had said something about an elephant trunk, and he'd stopped, amused and curious about their conversation.

When things turned to marriage, his heart had sped up a bit. He didn't want to eavesdrop, but he was anxious to get more insight into Spencer's thoughts about marriage. From their conversation yesterday, Sione had started to suspect she was against the idea. Those suspicions had been confirmed when Spencer had told her sisters she couldn't marry him. But why? Her sisters seemed to know, but they hadn't elaborated or expounded on Spencer's issues with holy matrimony. He'd been hoping Spencer would explain her views, but instead, she'd mentioned some "bigger problem."

"A cell phone?" Shady was saying.

"No, not just a cell phone. A burner." Spencer said.

"When did you get it?" Rae asked.

Sione was wondering the same damn thing. Who the hell would send her a burner? And for what?

"It came a week ago," Spencer said. "Courier service."

Shady said, "And you're sure it's from—"

"Who the hell else would have sent her a burner phone?" Rae cut Shady off.

Shady asked, "Has he contacted you?"

"Not yet," Spencer said. "But I wish he would."

Sione's stomach twisted a bit. Shady's and Rae's responses had suggested they knew who'd sent the burner, but Spencer's reply had confirmed it. Spencer knew exactly who the sender was, and she was waiting for him to get in touch with her.

Rae asked, "You do?"

"I'm ready for him to be out of my life for good," Spencer said. "That's not going to happen until I give him—"

Shady interrupted with, "But you can't give it to him unless he gives you—"

"Right," Spencer said. "I know that."

Rubbing his jaw, Sione took a deep breath, not sure he wanted to hear any more. Not sure he needed to hear anything else. He had a feeling he knew who'd sent the burner to Spencer, but he didn't want to be right. He was praying he was wrong, praying she wasn't waiting to hear from the man who had blackmailed her and taken advantage of her, forcing her to do favors to pay off a debt she owed him.

Slowly, Sione let out a breath, feeling pathetic for eavesdropping, but he couldn't bring himself to walk away. He had a feeling Spencer was talking about Ben Chang. Somehow, the bastard had contacted her, maybe because he wanted her to do another favor. More deliveries of fake passports and money to another group of women stupid enough to get involved with Ben. Women who could end up like the three women Spencer had made deliveries to in Belize—dead. Each of them murdered, shot in the head and—

His cell phone vibrated.

Cursing under his breath, Sione removed the phone from the inside pocket of his sports coat and stared at the screen. His banker in Belize. What now? he wondered, hoping nothing was wrong as he turned and headed out of the butler's pantry.

––––––––

"You can't worry about that envelope until Ben calls you," Rae said. "So let's get back to more important matters."

After popping a melon ball in her mouth, Spencer asked, "What's more important than that damn envelope?"

The envelope was the key to her freedom from Ben Chang.

Ben had blackmailed her into traveling to Belize to look for the envelope—that was the "favor" he'd forced her to do, but she hadn't really done the favor; she hadn't completed all the "steps" Ben had required her to take. The final, and most important step, had not been completed.

Spencer hadn't delivered the envelope.

She would have to, one day. When she least suspected it, Ben would make his way back into her life, sly and insidious, like the slimy snake he was, and demand that she take the final step. Spencer would be ready for him. She still had the damn envelope in the bottom of that bright blue Hermes Birkin bag. Easily accessible, it was hidden in the bottom drawer of the bureau in one of the guest bedrooms that no one had ever used.

Spencer was willing, and anxious, to complete the final step. But only if Ben would hold up his end of the bargain and give her the evidence he'd used to blackmail her into doing the damn favor—the surveillance tapes which clearly showed her stealing Rolex watches and stacks of cash from a drawer in his closet.

"Spence, did you really just say that?" Shady asked. "That envelope is not more important than—"

"Shady, please, okay? I don't really want to talk about it."

"Girl, you have to talk about it," Rae said. "But not to us. You have to discuss it with Sione."

"I can't do that," Spencer said.

"Why not, Spence?"

"Because I'm not sure how I feel about it myself," Spencer said. "It's going to change our lives."

"Yeah, but in a good way," Shady said.

"You don't know that," Spencer disputed. "Who knows if we're ready? I mean, John and I are still trying to figure out this relationship. Don't forget, there are things about me that he doesn't know, things I can never tell him. Things that, if he found out about them, would make him hate me."

"Girl, whatever," Rae scoffed. "You think that mofo ain't got no secrets? You think he's told you everything about himself?"

"Nobody tells anybody *everything* about themselves," Spencer countered. "I know that there are things John hasn't told me. John and I are still getting to know each other. So, yeah, there are things I don't know about him. But what I don't know isn't anything bad."

"How do you know that?" Rae asked.

"Remember what Ben said?" Shady asked. "Something about Sione isn't really what you think?"

"Ben said that he and Sione were more alike than you thought. Don't you wonder what he meant by that?" Rae asked

"Ben was just trying to trick me. He didn't want me to trust John because he was pissed off that I'd fallen in love with John," Spencer said.

Lips pursed, Rae said, "Well, I think—"

"I don't care what y'all think," Spencer snapped. "John is nothing like Ben, okay? John is kind and decent and caring. He's not some blackmailing criminal who probably murdered three women."

"You really think Ben killed those women?" Shady asked, skeptical.

"Girl, that don't make no sense," Rae said. "Why would Ben tell you to deliver money and fake passports to them if he was gonna turn around and kill them?"

"I don't even want to understand Ben," Spencer said. "Who the hell knows what goes on in that psycho's twisted mind?"

"All right, whatever," Rae said, sighing. "You still haven't told us what you're going to do."

Frowning, Spencer pushed her empty plate away. "Because I don't know what I'm going to do."

"You're not going to be able to keep it a secret forever," Rae said. "Sione is eventually going to notice."

"I know that," Spencer snipped, exhaling her annoyance.

"Spence, you have to tell him," Shady said.

"I know that, too." Spencer dropped her face in her hands for a moment and then trailed her fingers down the sides of her cheeks, trying not to cry as she looked at her sisters. "I don't know how I'm going to do it, but I'm going to have to find a way to tell John that I'm pregnant."

4

———

The Woodlands, Texas
Carlton Woods Gated Community

Spencer was in the shower, and since she'd made it clear she didn't want company, Sione figured he might as well look at some budget reports his assistant manager had emailed him. After grabbing a file from the desk in the study nook, a circular alcove to the right of the terrace doors, he crossed to the bed.

Settling against the pillows stacked against the headboard, with his legs stretched out toward the tufted footboard, he opened the file and scanned the latest projections, paying close attention to the budget variance. The numbers weren't making sense. Sione suspected his confusion was due to something he'd been trying to ignore for the past week—the things he'd overheard Spencer talking about with her sisters. Or, more importantly, the things he *hadn't* heard.

"I'm ready for him to be out of my life for good," Spencer said. "That's not going to happen until I give him—"

Shady interrupted with "But you can't give it to him unless he gives you—"

The him Spencer wanted out of her life was Ben Chang. Sione was sure of that. What exactly did Spencer have to give Ben to get him the hell out of her life for good? Sione doubted there was anything Spencer could give the bastard to make him go away forever.

The situation bothered him.

He was sick of Spencer thinking she had to be tough and fierce, never admitting or acknowledging fear. She was still keeping things from him. She still didn't trust him. He'd tried like hell to convince her that he would protect her and fight for her. He would be on her side even when everyone was telling him he should break up with her because he deserved better than some beautiful liar.

The pillow rumbled beneath Sione, and he sat up, confused.

What the hell?

He heard a faint buzzing, then picked up the pillow, and saw a cell phone wedged between several accent pillows Spencer had stacked against the headboard. Frowning, Sione picked up the phone and glanced across the bedroom toward the short hallway leading to the en suite bathroom. The shower was still going.

Staring at the phone, his confusion quickly turned to clarity as one particular speculation captured his thoughts, refusing to allow him to think of any other conclusion. He was holding the burner phone he'd overheard Spencer talking to her sisters about last week.

Conflicted, Sione debated whether or not to answer the burner or check the text message or the voice message or whatever the vibration indicated. He didn't want to snoop or pry into her business.

Sione sat up, turned the phone on, and glanced at the screen. It was a text. Glancing toward the en suite, he listened to make sure the shower was still running and then read the message. *We'll make an even exchange, sweet girl.* An even exchange? What the hell did that mean? Sione took a deep breath. There were more messages, several texts sent days before. Scrolling to the first message, from two days ago, he read through the messages.

We need to meet, sweet girl

When? Where?

next Thursday. Toyota center after the basketball game.

After the game? It'll be too crowded. How will I find you

Don't worry, sweet girl. I can pick you out of a crowd.

Fine

Bring what you owe me

And you'll bring what you promised me?

We'll make an even exchange, sweet girl

Heart pounding, Sione read the chain of text messages several more times, trying to rationalize it, trying to pretend it couldn't mean what he knew it meant, what he was hoping it didn't. There was no way he could fool himself into thinking he didn't know who the text message was from...

Ben Chang.

The bathroom door opened. Wary of being caught holding the burner, Sione leaned over the side of the bed and tossed the phone under the nightstand. Rising quickly, he grabbed the file and opened it. Spencer came into the room, wearing one of the silk kimonos she liked to wear, showcasing those fabulous breasts, swaying and bouncing beneath the thin fabric.

Instantly, he felt himself growing stiff as a board.

"Well, I made a mistake." Spencer hurried to the bed, then crawled across it, and curled up next to him, resting her head on his chest.

"A mistake?"

"You were right." Placing her palm on his chest, she walked her fingers from the right pec to the left, reaching to touch his biceps. "It was no fun being in that shower alone."

He eased an arm around her and picked up his report again. "I tried to tell you, but you didn't listen."

"John…" she started. "I, um…"

He looked down at her, wondering why she'd trailed off. What was she about to tell him? Maybe the truth about the burner phone? Curious, he prompted, "What is it?"

"Nothing." She squirmed a bit, and he sucked in a quick breath as her nipples pressed against him, making his groin tighten.

"Nothing that you want to tell me?"

"Nothing that you would understand," she said.

"How do you know I wouldn't?"

Spencer angled her head to look up at him. "Because you'll probably think I'm worrying for nothing."

Wary, he asked, "What are you worried about?"

"I'm worried that you think I didn't want to make love the other night…"

Sione leaned back against the headboard, half-listening as she went on about how she really had been tired. Part of him thought about bringing up the subject of marriage and her issues with the institution, which he believed was the real reason why she'd been distracted during sex. Another part of him, a more demanding part, was still wondering about the burner phone and the texts.

"John?"

Startled, Sione glanced down at her, his heart pounding.

"Did you hear me?" Spencer asked.

Embarrassed he hadn't been paying attention, Sione pulled her closer. "What did you say?" He shifted, pissed he'd allowed the past to make him lose awareness of his surroundings.

"Are you upset that I was tired the other night?"

"What I'm upset about is that..." He put the file on the bed table and then pulled her on top of him so she straddled his hips. "I didn't get to have any fun with you in the shower, so..."

"So you want to have a little fun in bed?" She leaned forward, kissing him.

"I want to have a lot of fun in bed," he struggled to say, while he still could, before the desire he felt for her overtook him.

5

The Woodlands, Texas
Carlton Woods Gated Community

On her hands and knees, Spencer had her head low to the ground and seemed to be peering under the nightstand.

Sione stopped near the foot of the bed to watch her, wondering what the hell she was doing.

Minutes ago, he'd walked into the bedroom and stepped out of the driving shoes he'd been traipsing around in all day, listening to a hard sell from a guy anxious to unload several apartment complexes he owned in the Greenspoint area. Sione was interested, but it wasn't a good idea to seek investors for a new acquisition when the situation with the tree houses was tenuous.

Tired and slightly frustrated, he shrugged off his jacket, remembering how he'd slid the phone under the nightstand two days ago, hoping she wouldn't catch him with the burner. She was looking for the phone, he figured. Probably, sometime within the past few days, she realized she didn't know where it was, probably concluded she must have misplaced it. Most likely, she'd been searching for it and hadn't found it, even after retracing her steps over and over. Now she was frantic, panicking because she needed the burner.

Bring what you owe me

And you'll bring what you promised me?

We'll make an even exchange, sweet girl

Sione exhaled, rubbing his jaw. Since finding the burner phone and reading the chain of text messages, he'd thought about almost nothing else. The more he turned it over and over in his mind, deducing and examining it from all conceivable angles, the more he was absolutely certain that Ben Chang was behind the scenes, pulling all the strings.

The way Sione figured it, Ben planned for Spencer to meet with one of his associates. Probably some low-level triad enforcer, like that bastard Tommy Fong, the son of a bitch with the green snake tattoo who'd followed Spencer to Belize to terrorize her. Fong had been given orders to attack Spencer, but those sadistic directives hadn't come from Ben Chang, it turned out.

Pushing the thoughts of Fong from his mind, Sione cleared his throat. "What are you doing down there?"

Spencer gasped and then stood, using the nightstand to help her get up. "Oh, I was, um..." She faced him, pushing errant tendrils of hair back into her loose chignon. "I was looking for my earring."

"Looking for your earring?" he repeated, wishing he wasn't so suspicious.

"Yeah, I was taking it off," she said. "And I dropped it and I thought it rolled under the bed table."

"Oh..." he said. "You want me to move the table so you can—"

"No, that's okay," she said, her response quick but not enough to make him suspicious. "It wasn't under there."

"Was it the earrings your grandmother gave you?" he asked. "Those pearl ones you misplaced when you were staying in my casita at the resort?"

Her eyes narrowed imperceptibly, a slight hint at possible suspicion of his question, but then she shook her head and walked away from him. "No, not those..."

Sione turned around.

Spencer stood near the settee at the foot of the bed, pinching her right earlobe. "The diamond hoops you bought me a few months ago."

Sione knew the earrings—a fifteen-thousand-dollar "just because" gift he'd purchased on a whim. Removing his blazer, he tossed it on the bed, went to the settee, and sank down onto the plush cushion. Spencer sat on his lap, snaked an arm around his neck, and kissed him. "So, how was your day?"

"Encouraging," he said.

"Encouraging?" She kissed him again and smiled.

"I may have a new investor."

"That's great news!"

"Hopefully," he said. "It's a *potential* investor."

"I have no doubt that you'll convince this potential investor to become an actual investor," she said.

"I'm taking him to dinner Thursday night," he said, waiting for her reaction, wondering what she was thinking. Was she afraid he might ask her to come with him to the dinner? Was she desperately thinking of some half-assed excuse just in case he asked her to accompany him?

"Thursday night?" she asked, her voice just an octave lower than shrill with a hint of worry. "Where are you taking him?"

"I told him he could pick the place," Sione said. "Since I don't know anything about Dallas."

She frowned. "You're meeting him for dinner in Dallas?"

Sione nodded, irritated by her obvious relief. "And since you hate Dallas—"

"Most Houstonians hate Dallas," she interjected

"Right," he said, remembering. "So, I won't ask you to tag along."

"Well, I would, if you wanted me to," she said, giving him a few more quick kisses. "But, I can't."

"Why not?" he asked. "You got plans for Thursday night, too?"

"Oh, I um…" She glanced away. "Just going to a Rockets game with an old friend from high school."

"An old friend," he said, annoyed by the easy, flirty banter between them, as though every word wasn't a lie; they were both lying to each other, pretending, trying to hide their lies. "Should I be jealous?"

"No, silly. My old friend is female, and she's married to the love of her life," Spencer said. "But if she met you, she'd be jealous of me."

"Well, the game should be fun."

"Maybe." She shrugged. "I'm not a huge basketball fan. Mainly, we just wanted to get together, and I think her boss gave her the tickets and her husband couldn't go, so she invited me, and I haven't seen her in forever, so…"

He nodded again, hating how easily the lies rolled off her tongue and how plausible they sounded. "Well, it's been sort of a long day, and I'm going to take a shower. Wanna join me?"

"Of course, I do," she said and then gave him a kiss that made him forget about all the lies and deception, a kiss that almost made him want to abandon the plan he'd concocted in order to find out exactly *whom* she was meeting with on Thursday to make the exchange.

Pulling away, she said, "But you go ahead. I want to look around for the earring for a few more minutes."

Ten minutes later, she joined him beneath the steamy, hot spray falling from the large, rectangular ceiling-mounted shower head. "I found it," she said, smiling as she tilted her head back, allowing the water to rain on her skin. Placing his hands on either side of her face, he stared at her, amazed by her beauty.

While waiting for her, he had thought about his plans for Thursday night. The dinner meeting in Dallas was a lie he hadn't wanted to tell, but he thought it might be better if Spencer wouldn't be looking over her shoulder, afraid he might accidentally discover her schemes. If she thought he was four hours away, in Dallas, she probably wouldn't bother to cover her tracks or employ any stealth moves designed for confusion and misdirection.

Now she was with him, naked and exquisite, her arms wrapped around him, and once again, the lies didn't seem to matter, didn't bother him so much. Still, as he bent his head to kiss her, he wondered if all the old doubts and the suspicions would return.

He picked her up and she wrapped her slick legs around his waist. Lowering her onto him, he hoped they wouldn't be destroyed by the truth she hid from him or the secrets he could never tell her.

6

"This is a nice car," Peter Rios exclaimed, impressed by the Italian sedan as he settled into the plush leather seat of the Maserati. "You gotta let me drive this bitch."

"That won't be happening," Sione said, steering away from the passenger pick-up lane at Hobby Airport. An hour ago, Peter had landed in Houston, via Southwest Airlines. "Traffic in Houston is brutal. You wouldn't be able to handle it."

Peter laughed.

Leaving the airport, Sione took a side street toward the interstate.

Accelerating into the brutality, he sped around several slower moving cars and then found an opening between an SUV and a Ford F-350, slipping through it and onto the entrance ramp that fed into I-45.

His plans for tomorrow night called for precise execution. Sione knew he couldn't pull it off alone. Thinking through the logistics, he'd realized he would need help. His cousin, Peter Rios, wasn't the best choice, but Sione's only other option had been DJ's little brother, Micah, who couldn't hold water in a bucket, so asking him was out of the question. Last thing Sione wanted was a call from DJ, and possibly Jared, demanding to know why he was following Spencer. Because unlike Peter, who wouldn't be able to put two and two together and come up with four, Micah was sly and nosy and would most likely figure out the reason for the surveillance job Sione needed done.

Micah was persistent and didn't respond well to threats, but Sione knew he could intimidate Peter. The promise of a thorough and complete ass-kicking would keep Peter from asking too many questions and guarantee his silence regarding the assignment.

As Peter checked his iPhone, Sione accelerated into the flow of chaotic traffic on the interstate.

"Hey, I wanted to ask you…" Peter started.

"What?" Sione maneuvered around a slower car and then changed lanes.

Peter asked, "Have you heard from Moana?"

"Moana is dead." Sione gripped the wheel and focused on the traffic, but his heart felt like it was trying to escape his chest through his mouth. "I thought you knew that."

"She's not dead."

"What do you mean, she's not dead?" Sione asked, trying to sound skeptical, hoping his tone didn't betray any guilt or fear. "She was stabbed during a prison riot."

"That's what the prison guards thought," Peter said, a hint of conspiracy in his voice, slightly lowered. "But now they're not sure that it was Moana who died. Didn't Jared tell you?"

"No," Sione replied. Jared had been too busy warning him to stay away from Spencer, too busy suggesting some relationship between Spencer and Ben. A connection some desperate, lying criminal had been able to convince Jared was true because his cousin wanted to believe the worst about Spencer.

"Well, the prison thinks her cellmate was stabbed," Peter said. "They think Moana escaped."

The whole 'Moana gets stabbed to death in a violent prison riot' plot was Richard's bright idea.

"The prison officials are trying to track her down," Peter went on. "They talked to everybody who had visited her before she supposedly died in that prison riot."

Richard came to visit me in prison. He wanted me to steal an envelope for him.

"And I was on the list," Peter said, grudging contrition in his tone.

"Yeah, I know," Sione said, still upset.

Peter cleared his throat. "Look, about that—"

"Peter, I don't care, okay?" Sione said. "I didn't ask you to fly down here to discuss Moana."

Nodding, Peter asked, "So, what's this job you need me to do?"

"Need you to follow someone," he said before he had a chance to think about what he was doing, and the absurd hypocrisy of it, and before he had a chance to change his mind and convince himself that Spencer's meeting at the Toyota Center tomorrow night didn't matter.

Peter said, "So, who's the person you want me to follow?"

Sione sighed. "Not sure yet."

"You're not sure?"

"The way I'm hoping it will work is that when I figure it out I'll follow this person to their vehicle, which will probably be parked on a surface lot, or maybe in a garage, near the Toyota Center," Sione said. "Once I determine the make and model of the car, you need to be ready to go, following that vehicle to its final destination. Once you determine that, you text me the location. Then, you can drive to Hobby Airport, leave the car at the rental company, and fly back to Sarasota."

"I can handle that," Peter said. "So…this person you want me to follow? It's not Spencer, is it?"

"I said I don't know who the person is yet, remember?" Sione said. After a moment of silence that felt a bit too tense, he spoke again. "Let me ask you—why do you think I would want you to follow Spencer?"

"Don't know." Peter shrugged. "Guess 'cause Aunt Carmen and my mom think Spencer's a liar and a gold digger and she's going to use you. Aunt Carmen thinks Spencer is going to get pregnant, and—"

Sione scoffed. "Spencer is not going to get pregnant."

"But she could," Peter said. "I know you gotta be hitting that every night."

Sighing, Sione said, "She's on birth control."

"Birth control don't always work," Peter said, as though he knew a thing, or three, about it.

"Peter, shut up," Sione said. "Spencer is not going to get pregnant, my mother is worrying for nothing.

After a few moments of silence, Peter asked, "You wanna have kids?"

"What?" Sione hesitated, not sure how to answer. He hadn't really thought about having kids. But he wanted children, and he wanted to have them with the woman he planned to spend the rest of his life with—Spencer. "Yeah. Someday. Why?"

"Just asking because you and Spencer would probably make a

good-looking kid," Peter went on. "That's what my mom said. I think Aunt Carmen slapped her for saying that."

"Anyway," Sione said, pushing thoughts of pregnancy and kids from his mind, "I booked you a room at the Marriott near the Toyota Center. Tomorrow morning, I'm going to bring over a rental car. We'll drive around so you can familiarize yourself with the streets around the Toyota Center. The streets downtown are all one way, so you will need to know what street you can turn on but you can't turn down, stuff like that.

"That's cool," Peter said, nodding. "I can actually get started tonight. You know, take a walk around the place."

"Good idea," Sione said. "In the morning, we can check out the surface lots and parking garages near the Toyota Center."

Disconcerted, Sione exited the freeway, taking the curving ramp into downtown Houston.

Peter's question about Spencer having his child had rattled him. Sione knew why though he tried to pretend he didn't. He didn't know how he felt about starting a family with a woman with so many secrets. How could he have kids with a woman he was keeping secrets from? How could they bring a child into the middle of all the secrets between them?

7

———————

Houston, Texas
Interstate 45

As the cab sped along I-45, Spencer sat rigid against the leather seat and placed her palm over her abdomen, trying to relax. "Well, little one," she whispered under her breath, glancing out the back passenger window at the dusky, indigo sky, "Mama found the burner phone, thank God. The evil, twisted monster had sent her a text with instructions on where to meet him, but Mama couldn't remember the time, place, or date because Mama has pregnancy brain."

At least, Spencer thought she did. But maybe not. Was it too early in her first trimester to be so spastic and forgetful? She couldn't remember. She'd read something about it on some pregnancy website, after her fourth home pregnancy test had turned out to be positive, but there had been so much information on the site, too much.

Overwhelmed, and still in shock, Spencer hadn't been able to deal with what to expect now that she was expecting. *Pregnant.* The word nearly made her knees buckle. Spencer still couldn't believe it. Didn't seem real. Or possible. Or plausible. How the hell had she gotten pregnant? She was on birth control, took the pill every day, and never skipped or forgot it. But she and John didn't use condoms, and he never pulled out, so she supposed that one of those times they'd fallen into that one percent.

Rubbing her stomach, Spencer sighed. She needed to find out how far along she was. Finding a doctor, and making an appointment, was on her list of things to do. She also wanted to get some prenatal vitamins, and…

And, most importantly, she had to tell John about the little one growing inside her.

But how could she? She still wasn't sure how *she* felt about being pregnant, becoming a mother. One moment, she was frazzled and terrified at the idea of another person living and breathing within her, and the next, the astonishing miracle of it would flood her entire body with joy and love.

Spencer cradled her stomach. Could she actually be a mother? Could she take care of a baby? Could she raise a child? It wouldn't be like the time she spent with John's second cousins. She loved those little girls like they were her own, but she wasn't responsible for them. They weren't depending on her for love, affection, nurturing, and everything else her own baby would require and deserve.

"Time for Mama to finally get the monster out of her life, and once he's finally gone," she said, "Mama can tell Daddy about you and…"

She stopped, tears threatening. She didn't know how to tell John about the baby. She knew she couldn't keep it from him. She would, sooner rather than later, have to let him know she was carrying his child. But she was hesitant, reluctant, and terrified because…what would John think?

She and John had never talked about wanting kids. He had always been very loving and affectionate with his little second cousins, the caramel faeries. But that didn't mean he wanted his own kids. And really, the question wasn't did John want children. The question was did John want kids with *her*? Did John want *her* to be the mother of his children?

Would he be upset about the baby? His family thought she'd been planning all along to get pregnant and trap him into marriage. And what if, after they were married, she turned into her mother and become "that wife"? What if—

Pushing the troublesome thoughts away, Spencer grabbed the blue Birkin and put it on her lap. "One thing at a time," she said to herself. First, give Ben the damn envelope and get him out of her life. Then, find a way, somehow, to tell John about the baby and pray that he would be happy and excited and not upset with her.

"Don't worry, little one," she said, leaning her head back and moving her hand across her stomach as the cab continued down the freeway. "I know Daddy will love you as much as I do…"

The Toyota Center, one of the city's main sports and entertainment complexes, loomed impressively at the intersection of Polk and La Branch in downtown Houston, dominating the entire southeast corner with glowing red neon signage and bright lights casting wide swatches of illumination across the four-lane streets.

Sione turned the SUV into a surface lot, diagonally across from the venue, on the northwest corner. After paying the attendant twenty bucks, he steered the SUV around the lot, careful to avoid the potholes and cracks in the concrete, searching for a space. Sione pulled into a slot on the first row of spaces and then killed the ignition of the SUV, a rental he'd picked up earlier in the day, about an hour after he'd kissed Spencer goodbye…

Dressed in business casual attire, he'd stood in the foyer, one hand clutching the handle of his Hermes briefcase and, the other planted on Spencer's ass as he bent his head to press his mouth against hers. A Judas kiss, he couldn't help but thinking, knowing she thought he was heading to the airport to fly to Dallas. His guilt was tempered, though, because she was lying to him, as well.

True, she was going to a Rockets game, but it wasn't to meet some old high school friend.

From the glove compartment, Sione took out a pair of small binoculars and then opened the driver's window. Sounds of revelry floated across the street, wafting on the humid breeze. Pressing his skull against the headrest, he closed his eyes, trying to come to terms with his current situation.

How the hell had he gotten to the point where he was sitting in an SUV in the dark, clutching a pair of binoculars, spying on his girlfriend like some jealous fool? But he wasn't hoping to catch Spencer with some secret lover. The plan he'd orchestrated didn't have anything to do with a public confrontation, complete with cursing and wild accusations, a shameful spectacle that people would hold up their smartphones to video and then later post to a dozen different social media sites.

Opening his eyes, Sione took a breath. Trying to combat the surreal feelings and frustration, he thought about the events of the day from the moment after he'd kissed Spencer and walked out of the house.

Despite a pounding heart and a twisting stomach, he'd managed to get into his Maserati and navigate out of the neighborhood. Heading away from the interstate, he drove to a parking garage near Woodlands Square, an upscale shopping village. He headed toward a Starbucks, sat at one of the small bistro tables outside, and called a rental car service. Twenty minutes later, he was behind the wheel of a mid-sized SUV, his head pounding as he drove back to the gated community.

He parked about fifty feet away from the house he shared with Spencer. It wasn't a secluded place to wait, but the SUV was a Range Rover, and he figured he wouldn't raise any suspicions with the security detail that regularly patrolled the neighborhood.

About an hour later, just after the sun had set, a cab pulled into the curving, circular driveway, and Spencer walked out, wearing a form-fitting tee shirt, jeans and a baseball cap. Rockets attire, he noted, so she'd blend in with the other fans.

Once downtown, the cab pulled up to the curb directly in front of the entrance of the Toyota Center. Spencer had gotten out, clutching a large purse, the blue Hermes bag. According to the AM station broadcasting the game, four minutes remained until the end of the fourth quarter. The game wasn't officially over, but lots of fans had already begun the mass exodus, streaming out of the venue in an effort to get ahead of the traffic on the major highways heading out to the suburbs.

More than once, while Sione followed the cab along the interstate, the urge to stop the cab came over him. He struggled to remain behind the bright yellow van, wrestling with thoughts of somehow speeding alongside the cab and forcing it over to the shoulder. After jumping out of the SUV and into the yellow cab, Sione imagined himself coming clean with Spencer, convincing her that she needed to let him help her.

If he did that, he would have to tell her the truth about his own connection to Ben.

He might have to tell her how he planned to deal with the situation. He wasn't sure if she would go along with his plan. Spencer wouldn't like his idea, which involved confronting whomever Ben was sending to meet her and stealing the item she owed Ben. Then Sione would demand a meeting with Ben. He saw himself saying something like you tell Ben Chang that if he wants this, he needs to come and get it from me.

The item Ben wanted would be used to lure the bastard into a trap. Sione had no doubt that Ben would meet him, and when they came face to face, Sione was going to kill him.

He still wasn't at peace with the decision he'd come to, but he wasn't willing to change his mind. The plan was ambitious and dangerous. Something he had to do.

Carrying out the plan would require him to give up part of himself, he knew. The part he'd fought hard to obtain, and even harder to hold on to, but he would find a way to make peace with what he would lose.

After all, it wouldn't be sacrifice if it didn't demand blood.

8

Walking in a semi-circle, Sione watched as Spencer continued to wait, smiling every now and then as people passed her, getting lots of attention.

Maybe too much attention, Sione thought, irritated. He should have been used to the second looks she received. Her beauty couldn't be ignored. It always demanded a response. But he didn't like the roving eyes following her everywhere they went—out to dinner, to the movies, grocery shopping.

Spencer gravitated toward a bench near a cluster of trees cordoned off by a low stone wall and took a seat, placing the blue purse on her lap, curling her fingers around the handles.

Lowering the binoculars, tense and anxious, Sione found himself struggling, once again, with his decision to kill Ben Chang. It wasn't a decision he'd arrived at with haste and little forethought, an idea born from a spontaneous spark of rage. The idea had sprouted in his mind years ago, the first seeds having been planted the day he'd caught Ben in bed with Moana.

It had been a nice spring day. The air crisp and hopeful. Nothing about the expansive blue sky or the brilliant white popcorn clouds or the mild breeze had foreshadowed disappointment and disillusionment. Sione had arrived at the small house they shared early, thinking he would surprise her with a gift, a delicate anklet she'd admired weeks before during an excursion to San Pedro. It was an effort to make her feel more loved and appreciated and maybe to convince himself they did belong together. He wanted to do for her the things a husband would do, or should do, even though he had begun to question his decision to ask her to marry him—and her acceptance of his proposal.

Moana had always been wild, not the kind of woman anxious to settle down and attach herself to one man. When she'd said yes after he'd popped the question, Sione had been shocked and more relieved than ecstatic.

Minutes after entering the house, he'd heard the moaning and the rhythmic thumping of two solid objects against each other—the headboard banging into the wall behind the bed, he would find out.

He'd walked down the hall to the bedroom, curious about the strange noises, trying to convince himself it wasn't what he thought and yet knowing it would be worse than he could have ever imagined.

And it had been so much worse.

His fiancée and the man he thought of as a brother were banging their brains out. Frozen, he'd watched, enraged and yet entranced. Something about their slick, sweaty bodies both fascinated and irritated him. Maybe it was the contrast of their skin tones as they moved in frantic desperation. Moana's dusky tan and

Ben's darkness looked like a kaleidoscopic swirl of undulating lust. Or maybe it had been the look she'd given him when she had glanced over her shoulder, seen him standing in the doorway. There was no shock, no guilt, and no excuse. There was only a sly smile and a salacious invitation in her glazed, dark eyes. He'd had a feeling that she wanted him to join them, and a year ago, the last time he'd seen Moana, she'd confirmed that suspicion.

I never came between you and Ben…I wish I had come between you two, but you weren't down for that.

Sione raised the binoculars.

Across the street, Spencer was standing again now. She walked a few feet from the bench, cradling the blue Hermes bag in her arms, and glanced toward the doors of the venue. Raucous, rowdy, half-drunk fans poured out of the stadium, a steady stream of people, a diverse body representing the city's multifaceted culture. Most of them were clad in "Rocket Red," sporting T-shirts, jerseys, and hats, proudly displaying their team spirit and support for the local franchise.

As Spencer paced in a short arc, her posture rigid and tense, Sione went back in time to the moment he'd caught Ben making love to Moana. He regretted not killing Ben that day. Through the years, he'd often chided himself for just turning and walking away.

Of course, if he had wrapped his hands around Ben's throat and choked the breath from his body that crisp spring day, he never would have met Spencer. People said you couldn't miss what you'd never had, but he had a feeling he would have gone through life knowing she should have been with him. He would have missed her like something essential to his existence, as crazy as that was. He would have always wondered if—

Jolted from his grim reverie, Sione sat forward, his heart slamming.

He couldn't see Spencer anymore. Someone was standing in front of her. Some guy was blocking Sione's view. Who the hell was the guy? Some asshole hitting on her? Or maybe…

The guy started to walk away, and Spencer followed him over to the bench near the trees. Together, they sat on the bench, the guy turned at an angle so Sione couldn't see his face, just his back, as he lounged in a relaxed pose with one arm hanging casually over the back of the bench. Spencer was perched on the edge of the seat, as though she was seconds away from fleeing. This was the guy Ben had arranged for her to meet, Sione realized, his heart kicking up a few notches as he sat forward, the binoculars pressed against his face.

9

The night was balmy, customarily warm, even in October, but still, Spencer shivered as she stood among, but apart from, the groups of Rockets fans exiting the arena, laughing and talking, some of them engaging in good-natured jostling and horseplay.

Through the large, wide windows of the venue, she could see the activity on the main concourse level, where fans milled about in their Rockets attire, and could hear the faint roar of cheers.

Spencer sighed as she walked across the courtyard, gazing absently at the memorial brick pavers beneath her feet, hundreds of six-inch square stones spread across the plaza of the main entrance into the arena. Purchased by fans before the construction of the venue, they were engraved with personalized messages, names, businesses, and special dates.

Spencer read a few of the bricks, trying to calm down, but she couldn't focus, couldn't concentrate, and couldn't pretend she was some fan waiting around for a group of friends who were still inside or maybe for a ride to pick her up.

There was no escaping the real reason why she was loitering in front of the arena, trying to appear serene and inconspicuous, when what she really wanted to do was let out the howling scream that churned and roiled in her gut.

More than anything, she wished she were at home, preparing for John to return from his business trip to Dallas. He would be back early tomorrow morning, and she would be waiting, lying naked across the bed, in the beautiful Mediterranean-villa-inspired mansion where they were building a life—a wonderful version of their very own happily ever after, a life that, ironically, Ben had encouraged her to pursue.

But she was at the Toyota Center because Ben Chang wanted to meet here.

His text a few days ago, demanding the Thursday night *tête-à-tête*, after almost a year, sent a jolt of panic and disappointment and fear through her.

Bring what you owe me

Sighing, Spencer wandered aimlessly toward a bench.

She'd always known Ben would contact her again. The text had been like an assault upon her happiness, a threat to her hopes and dreams of being with John.

Earlier, after John left for the airport, Spencer had found the frangipani she had pressed between the pages of a book of love poems. John had given her the flower more than a year ago, a gesture she'd found ridiculously romantic, filling her with an overwhelming euphoria. Spencer had never believed in being on cloud nine before, but when John gave her the frangipani, happiness had expanded in her, making her feel airy and ephemeral, like she was floating in pure joy.

John had wanted her to think about their relationship, how she felt about it, and what she wanted to happened between them. Spencer hadn't needed to think about it. She'd known exactly what she'd hoped for the two of them and had immediately placed the flower behind her left ear, announcing to John that she was taken.

She'd always known that the frangipani belonged behind her left ear. Despite her doubts and issues, she'd realized that, secretly, she had always wanted love and romance and a soul mate and...

A baby?

Part of her wanted children of her own, the part who believed wishes could come true, but the realist within her wasn't sure about the idea of bringing a child into the world. She worried about being a good mother. She'd had the absolute worst example. A woman who had abused, neglected, and then ultimately abandoned her only to come back into her life, claiming to be a changed woman. That had been true, though. Her mother had returned as some kind of Stepford wife.

Pushing the disturbing thoughts away, Spencer glanced at her watch, wondering if Ben would suddenly appear out of the throng of fans milling about in groups of various sizes. What would she do when she saw him again? What would she say to him? What would he say to her? Was there really anything they needed to say to each other? The envelope was their only reason for meeting, and yet she felt as though there was some unfinished business between them. She sensed there was something other than the envelope that they needed to resolve before they said goodbye forever.

Goodbye forever. Spencer shivered. Why did the thought of never seeing Ben again make her feel...what? How did it make her feel? She didn't know. She couldn't articulate the feelings, which bothered her. What she felt for Ben shouldn't be vague or ambiguous—something hard to define. Spencer exhaled, frowning. She shouldn't have any feelings for Ben other than fear and loathing.

"Hey, sweet girl..."

Gasping, Spencer spun around and looked up, heart pounding. Ben stood in front of her, tall and handsome, giving her a mysterious smile as he stared down at her. She couldn't accurately describe what she felt as she stared up at him. A strange combination of apprehension and excitement gripped her.

Ben took her hand, brought it toward his mouth, and pressed his lips against her palm, somewhere close to her love line. Spencer thought of snatching her hand away and slapping him. But a few yards away, a large group of people was walking past them, and a few of the rowdy, fist-pumping fans glanced over at them. She didn't want to give them a show.

And, if she was honest, she was somewhat intrigued by Ben's gesture.

Maybe a part of her was still somewhat intrigued by him. It wasn't that she was still interested. She was completely, absolutely, over those ridiculous fantasies of being with Ben. But something residual remained between them.

"How have you been?" Ben asked.

"I've been waiting for you to call me so I can give you this damn envelope," she snapped, ignoring the tingling feeling on her palm where he'd kissed it. "And then you can give me the evidence you have against me, and we can finally go our separate ways and never see each other again!"

"Never say never, sweet girl." Still holding her hand, Ben led her toward the bench, and they sat.

"Are we going to make this exchange or not?" she demanded,

shaken by his words, which seemed a bit too plausible, too prophetic. "Do you have that DVD of me? Because if I don't get the evidence you have on me, then you are not getting the envelope."

"Is that a threat, sweet girl?" He smirked and released her hand. "Or a promise?"

"I am a threat to you, Ben," she said, feeling strangely, almost chaotically, emboldened. "And I promise you, if you rat on me, I will rat on you. Don't forget, I know what you did to Maxine Porter, Karen Johnson, and Carla Garcia—"

"I didn't kill those women," Ben said.

"But they're dead because of you," she said. "And so is Tommy Fong."

"He deserved to die for what he did to you," Ben said.

Spencer looked away from him. Ben was responsible for Fong's charred remains, and she hated that she had to keep quiet about it or he would ruin her life. But even worse was his explanation, which wasn't explicit, but implied, and the implications worried her.

Spencer didn't like the idea of Ben killing for her. Such an extreme, heinous action suggested he harbored feelings for her, feelings that might destroy the life she was trying to build with John.

"Are we going to do this damn exchange?" Spencer asked.

"Of course."

"The envelope for the evidence against me," she said, feeling the need to make sure. "That's what we agreed to."

"I am aware of the terms of our agreement."

"We don't have an agreement," she said, rolling her eyes. "I didn't agree to any of this. I was forced to do it, remember? Because I owe you?"

"Yeah, you do owe me," he agreed. "But I'm paying for it."

Spencer looked up at him, not sure what he meant and not wanting to ask. There was something in that enigmatic gaze that worried her, made her feel as though Ben's prolonged absence had been due to some trials and tribulations of his own.

"So, here you are, sweet girl," Ben said, handing her a DVD.

"You didn't make any copies of the video?"

"It's depressing enough that I even had one video of you stealing from me," he said. "Why would I need another copy of that sad travesty?"

"Leverage," she told him, determined to not let him make her feel like a pariah. "You might want something to blackmail me with later. Maybe when you need another favor."

"I assure you, sweet girl," he said, "I won't be asking you to do me any more favors. You've already done enough."

She detected some hidden meaning in his words, a veiled insinuation, but she wasn't in the mood to figure him out, and really, she didn't care. All she wanted was to get back to the mansion and move on with her life.

With John.

And their little one growing inside her.

Hopefully.

"Okay, so," she said, preparing to stand. "Goodbye. Take care of yourself."

"Not so fast," he said, pulling her closer.

She tried to pull away, but he held her firm. "I have to go."

"Before you do, tell me something, sweet girl," he said. "How is happily ever after with Sione Tuiali'i?

"What the hell do you care?" Spencer asked.

"Is it everything that you hoped it would be?" Ben asked, his smile a bit too sly. "Has it lived up to your expectations? Or have you started to notice the chinks in your knight's shining armor?"

Heart slamming, she said, "Happily ever after has exceeded my expectations."

"Has it now?"

"You sound disappointed."

"If I'm disappointed, it is because I know that soon you will be disappointed," Ben said. "The dreams that you think have come true will turn out to be your worst nightmare. Don't forget, sweet girl, that Sione Tuiali'i is searching for a specific kind of woman."

"And you think I'm not that woman, right?" She glared at him. "But you're wrong. I am that woman. John loves me, and I love him."

"Sweet girl, you shouldn't have to subject yourself to a man who will force you to jump through hoops of fire to please him," Ben said. "You deserve someone who will accept you for who you are, someone who won't condemn you for the mistakes you've made."

Wary, she stared at him. "Are you trying to say you're that someone?"

"You sound like you think I'm not."

"Ben, how the hell can you imply that you wouldn't hold my mistakes against me?" she asked, confused. "You sent me to Belize because you were holding my mistakes against me. You forced me to do favors for you, and you expect me to think that you would accept me for who I am? You don't trust me. You condemned me. You made me jump through hoops!"

"But I still wanted you in my life," he said. "I couldn't let you get away with what you did, sweet girl. Stealing is wrong."

"So is murder." She glared at him.

He leaned closer to her. "You want to know why I killed Tommy Fong?"

Spencer looked away, not sure she wanted him to say it though she had a feeling she already knew his reasons. Ben had murdered

Tommy Fong in retaliation, because Richard had told Fong to kidnap her in some twisted attempt to teach Ben a lesson.

"I wouldn't want a man to burn alive," Ben said, deep voice lowered, the lyrical Island lilt vibrating through her. "I wouldn't want a man to experience hell on earth, unless…"

"Unless?"

"Unless he tried to go after something very important to me," Ben said. "Maybe if he tried to hurt someone I cared about, someone who means the world to me, then he would have to pay with his life."

Staring up at him, she knew without a doubt why Ben had killed Fong.

"Sweet girl, Sione Tuiali'i is not the man you want to give your heart to," Ben said, redirecting the conversation. "He'll smash it into a million pieces."

Staring into his dark eyes, Spencer tried to see past the pretense. His concern about her feelings and her heart was disingenuous. Ben was just jealous and trying to scare her, but he wasn't going to make her doubt John's feelings for her. She was going to believe John's hopes for them were true and they would last; she was going to trust that John had been honest about his feelings and they wouldn't change.

"Listen, sweet girl," Ben said, his gaze piercing. "If you want to be with Sione, I won't put up a fuss. I won't stand in the way of what you think will be happiness. But, when he finds out who you really are, he'll cast you aside and leave you broken and disappointed."

10

Houston, Texas
Toyota Center

From what Sione could tell, Spencer and the guy hadn't made the exchange yet. They were talking. The conversation seemed intense but not confrontational. What the hell were they talking about? Sione wondered, his heart beating faster.

Spencer and the guy had been talking for almost fifteen minutes, a conversation that seemed... He didn't know what it was and couldn't really describe it. Or maybe, he didn't want to describe it. There was a weird chemistry between them and in their body language. It disturbed him. The guy was sitting a bit too close to her, and when he responded to something Spencer said, he would lean toward her, casual and comfortable, and Spencer didn't shrink back from him.

From the SUV, Sione had a vantage point of not quite forty-five degrees, and even from the passenger's seat, the view was no better. He could only see the guy's left side, his shoulder, and most of his back. His face was an obscured silhouette.

The guy put his hand on her cheek, and Sione felt as though something in his chest was expanding, threatening to explode. He took deep breaths, trying to calm himself, but it was hard as hell not to jump out of the SUV, run across the street, grab the guy, and slam him down to the concrete. Who the hell did the guy think he was, touching Spencer like that, so…intimately.

That was the word in his head. *Intimate.* A word that worried more than angered him. They reminded him of two people who had once been involved; former lovers who weren't friends but maybe not enemies either.

Spencer removed the guy's hand but not in an aggressive way. She didn't push his hand back, but instead, for some reason, she allowed the guy to hold on to her hand. She knew this guy, Sione realized. Whoever the hell he was, she knew him. But that didn't make sense. How could she know the guy Ben had sent to make the exchange? Who the hell was he? He wasn't some triad thug, like Sione had expected he would be. This guy was black. Maybe from Jamaica? Ben had connections to gangs in Kingston, so maybe the guy was some criminal associate. Sione exhaled. He wasn't in the mood to deal with some Caribbean gangbanger, who would probably have a gun—something stolen, unregistered, and loaded with hollow points.

He'd have to disarm the guy. Pistol-whip him with his own weapon and then use the methods Richard had taught him to render a man unconscious in three to five seconds. Then Sione would steal whatever Ben wanted and leave his gangster associate with a note, which would say something like *I have want you want. Contact me to get it.* He wouldn't bother signing it. Ben would know that—

Spencer stood abruptly and quickly disappeared into the crowd, allowing the crush of fans to swallow her. The guy leaned against the slatted back of the bench, obviously watching Spencer as she walked away. Sione kept the binoculars trained on the guy on the bench, an odd feeling of familiarity settling over him. Did he know the guy?

Sione lowered the binoculars.

No, that was impossible. It didn't make sense. He and Ben had run in different circles and hung with different crowds after Sione had left Belize to live with his Tongan relatives in the South Pacific. Still, there was something about the guy, he thought, as he peered through the windshield. Sione leaned forward, trying to make out the guy's features, which weren't a blur but still undistinguishable.

Cursing his own stupidity, Sione glanced at the binoculars clutched in his right hand and then raised them to his eyes. It took him a few seconds, but he located the guy again. The guy was standing now, still facing the direction in which Spencer had gone when she walked away from him.

He was tall with a muscular frame, similar to Sione's build. The guy wouldn't be easy to take down. But Richard had taught him how to get a man to the ground in a matter of seconds, and once the guy was flat on his ass, Sione would—

The guy turned, facing the direction of the surface lot where Sione sat in the SUV.

The face in the binoculars, magnified, hit him like a punch in the gut.

Sione jerked back, his chest tight, restricting his breathing. His stomach twisted as the binoculars fell from his trembling hand, sliding across the plastic mat on the floorboard beneath him.

Panicked and confused, Sione reached for the binoculars, fumbling them several times before he was finally able to grab them and press the lenses against his eyes, desperate to find the guy he'd seen with Spencer, to prove he'd been wrong about what he'd seen. His mind had to be playing tricks on him. It had been some kind of crazy optical illusion because it couldn't be…

Ben Chang.

11

___

Houston, Texas
The Third Ward

With shaking hands, Sione sent a text to Peter, giving him the direction in which Ben was heading. Less than a minute later, Peter responded, confirming he'd spotted Ben and was ready to follow the bastard.

Don't lose him! Sione texted.

He would have to kill Ben Chang. Ben's death was the only way they would be free. Richard had once told him *all threats must be eliminated, or they will eventually be carried out against you.* His father had been right.

As long as Ben was alive, he would always be a threat to their happiness.

As long as Ben was alive, Spencer would never be able to satisfy the debt she owed Ben. The burner phone was proof of that. The assignments Ben had forced her to do in Belize were supposed to have been good enough to forgive her debt, but Ben had lied to her and tricked her into thinking she would be free of him.

Ben had never planned to hold up his end of their agreement. He'd always intended for Spencer to be one of his puppets, using the debt she owed him to control her, pulling the strings, forcing her to obey his sick, sadistic commands.

His cell phone vibrated. Sione stared at the display screen. Peter had texted him an address to a house near the University of Houston. According to Peter, Ben had parked in front of the home, gotten out, and had gone inside.

Sione programmed the address into the SUV's GPS. From the map on the display screen, the house was located in Houston's Third Ward. Southeast of downtown and east of the Medical Center, it was a predominantly black neighborhood that, centuries ago, had featured some of the finest Victorian homes in the city. Those homes had been abandoned by their upper crust occupants after various modes of public transportation gave undesirables unfettered access to the area. The grand houses still stood; however, some had deteriorated over the years due to various economic depressions, becoming flop houses and then crack houses.

After several deep breaths, Sione started the SUV, pulled out of the parking space, and followed the directions from the GPS. His pulse raced as thoughts of how he would kill Ben consumed him.

Sione imagined he would break Ben's neck.

Wouldn't be hard to do. Crush the trachea. Richard had taught him how to do it; he had wanted it to be Sione's patented move. When a body was found with the throat crushed, his father had once told him, men would immediately know by whose hands death came to whatever bastard was sent to hell where he belonged.

Sione had been fourteen when Richard had revealed his grand designs for Sione's life. Much like Richard, Sione would be a businessman with a side hustle in death. The gentleman killer, as Richard liked to think of himself. In the mercenary world of wet work, his father was known as the suave assassin, tall, well-built, handsome, and hazel-eyed.

Despite Richard's gruesome penchant for cutting off the hand of his victims, his father was respected, and highly sought after, for his civilized, sometimes elitist, approach to murder. And though he could be sanctimonious, he was often forgiven when he went off on judgmental rants, declaring that those he got rid of were heathens who had been damned because they had rejected God.

By the time he was fifteen, Sione had become accustomed to his father's brutality—and annoyed by his hypocrisy—which terrified and fascinated him. Even more horrifying than his father's "side business" was the conflict he wrestled with—he knew his father was a cold-hearted killer, but he loved Richard fiercely and was often impressed by his homicidal exploits. Richard had never hesitated to describe his kills in graphic detail with grandiose sermonizing and editorializing. Most of the time, Sione believed his father's heinous business was entirely justified.

Making sure to observe the traffic laws, staying just a bit under the posted speed limit, Sione drove along the feeder road and then made a right, following the instructions of the disembodied female voice. Each side of the street boasted a mix of cracked and crumbling urban blight with abandoned buildings with boarded-up windows and overgrown, neglected lawns. As he approached the University of Houston, which encompassed several blocks in all directions, things brightened up a bit, but as he continued on, away from the college, darkness ensued, punctuated every now and then by an anti-crime street light. The street was full of shadows and mystery with side streets cloaked in inky blackness, roads that seemed to lead to nowhere.

At a traffic signal, he slowed for the yellow light and stopped when the light turned red.

Sione took a deep breath and pushed the thoughts of Richard to the far recesses of his mind where, hopefully, they wouldn't haunt him. Thinking about justification for murder brought up an old internal debate he had yet to settle—was he more like his father than he wanted to be, which was nothing like his father, at all.

At sixteen, when Sione had left Belize and traveled to A'arotanga at the request and expense of his uncle, Siosi, he'd slowly, steadily allowed his uncle's influence to win him over. He had never liked the idea of being a smooth, good-looking mercenary with a heart of gold, twisting Scripture so he could feel okay about taking a life.

But he no longer lived on a remote Pacific island where an army of aunts had acted as shepherds, offering spiritual guidance and making sure he went to church every Sunday. And, worst of all, his uncle had passed away several years ago.

There was no one to stop him from crossing the line.

There was nothing to prevent him from turning into his father.

12

————

After driving back and forth along the street several times, Sione decided he was familiar enough with the layout of the house and was ready, if not anxious, to make his move. The old two-story Victorian towered proudly on the corner of Birchdale and Fawn Streets with a well-kept lawn that extended from the front of the house and around to the side of the house, which he'd figured was the best approach for a breach.

The right side of the house, which faced Fawn Street, featured basic landscaping, mainly a large cluster of hedges, clinging to the lower lever of the home. A long concrete driveway ran the length of the back of the house, sloping up to a two-car detached garage with an L-shaped open breezeway leading to a back door.

After parking the SUV two streets away, Sione got out and headed up Fawn Street back to the house. The neighborhood was dark with only a few houses illuminated by porch lights. Staying close to the curb, he took brisk, purposeful strides through the shadows. Except for the faint bark of a dog and the occasional swish of tires on some adjacent street, the night was quiet and still, the temperature mild, slightly humid. The calm atmosphere was a stark contrast to the raging tumult within him, but he tried to take deep, measured breaths and tried to stay focused and relax his muscles.

Nothing could ease the tension that had him coiled so tight he thought he might explode.

Coming abreast of the house, he cut right and hurried up the driveway toward the breezeway. The back door was wood with a glass insert covered by mini blinds. The door was locked, which he expected. Turning, he followed the L-shaped breezeway to the garage door. It, too, was locked, but when he kicked the splintered wood just above the knob, it flew back, and he lunged forward, using his shoulder to stop the door from slamming against the wall.

Sione closed the door behind him and then removed his phone from the front pocket of his jeans, where he'd shoved it, and accessed an app that functioned as a flashlight. He splashed light around the interior of the garage until he found what he'd been looking for, something he could use to break into the back door.

Walking to a tool shelf on the opposite side of the garage, he grabbed the hammer, left the garage, and went back to the back door. With the hammer head, he broke a section of the glass near the bottom of the frame and then reached into the jagged opening. Ignoring the sting of glass shards scraping his skin, he found the lock, turned it, withdrew his hand, and then opened the door.

He stepped inside. Allowing his eyes to adjust to the darkness, he realized he was in the kitchen. The refrigerator hummed, and somewhere to his left, a clock ticked, the long hand counting the seconds. Anxious, and yet wary, Sione stood still, wondering if he'd lost his advantage, waiting for some surprise attack from Ben, who might have surveillance cameras around the house and might have already seen him kicking the garage door in and breaking into the back door.

There was no way to know for sure, but he would have to be ready for anything and everything. From the kitchen, he passed through a small butler's pantry and then into a large dining room. Out of the dining room, he headed down a hall to the foyer, where a flight of stairs ascended in a straight line along the wall.

Sione crept up the stairs, careful and stealth. He wasn't really planning a sneak attack, but he didn't want to give Ben the heads up, an opportunity to set a trap or execute some offensive strike, like a gallon of gasoline tossed at his face, neck and chest, followed by a flaming match.

He wasn't going to underestimate the dragon.

Continuing up the stairs, he thought about how his uncle used to always say that he and Ben were like Cain and Abel. One was bound to end up killing the other. *Well,* he thought, *it won't be my blood crying out from the ground.* But wearing the mark of a killer, even though no one would be able to see it and only he would know what he had done, was a burden he wasn't certain he could bear.

At the top of the stairs, Sione walked down a short hall, toward a door that was slightly ajar. Three strides and he was pushing the door open, peering into the room.

Ben sat at a rickety wooden desk, holding a small piece of paper, his head bent slightly, as though he was studying it.

Driving to the address Peter had texted him, Sione had imagined what he would say to Ben when he saw him for the first time in more than a year. Staring at him, Sione realized there was nothing to say; words didn't matter. The feelings screaming through him could not be put into words.

The feelings demanded blood, not conversation.

Sione slammed the door behind him to break the silence. Ben didn't flinch. He didn't seem to give a damn even though he had to know that he was no longer alone.

Sione tried to breathe but couldn't seem to catch his breath. Abruptly, Ben stood, and a dull roar began in Sione's ears. Time seemed to slow and then stop for a moment, during which dozens of emotions swirled in his head, like a kaleidoscope: guilt, anger, fear, grief, and some emotion that steadily eclipsed all others—anticipation laced with excitement.

He was anxious to kill Ben.

He'd waited years for the chance to get rid of Ben Chang for good, forever. Trepidation threatened his excitement. Wariness rushed in, and for a split second, he worried that things might go from bad to worse. What if he couldn't handle being Cain? What if the blood crying out would haunt him? Forcing himself to focus, Sione tried to push the doubts away.

Ben faced Sione. "Well, well, old friend," he said. "It has been a long time."

"Hasn't been long enough," Sione said, his stance relaxed, as though he had stopped by to sit a spell, as Spencer's grandmother would say. He was trying to read Ben, looking for slight, imperceptible muscle movements, trying to discern how Ben would begin his attack. Ben stood calm and relaxed and even had a trace of a smile. Richard had taught them to appear oblivious, or bored, until the first strike. *Never telegraph your attack. Don't give the enemy a chance to devise a counterattack before you rush him.*

"So, old friend," Ben said. "What do you want?"

"I want you gone for good," Sione said. "I want you dead."

"Is that so?" Ben cocked his head. "And how do you plan to accomplish that?"

The question worried Sione, more than it should have. He wasn't sure he knew the answer. All he knew was Ben had to die or—

Ben lunged.

Sione had messed up. Much like Richard, Ben was good at allowing the enemy to think he had the advantage, tricking the opponent into believing they were winning the battle. *Not always about strength. Most times, it's about deception, misdirection, misguided perception.*

Slightly off guard, Sione sidestepped and then kicked Ben in the hand. Another quick kick in the knee knocked Ben's feet from beneath him. On the floor, Ben grabbed Sione's foot, twisted, and yanked. Sione exhaled and rolled when he crashed to the floor, but it still knocked a bit of the wind from him. Before he could push himself to a sitting position, Ben executed a leaping crawl and was quickly on top of him. Shit! The fight had gotten to the ground too quickly. Sione had been hoping to avoid a floor fight—he wasn't his best on the ground.

The enemy will always try to get you to the ground because that's the best place to kick the shit out of you. Avoid that situation, if possible. But it won't always be possible. So get the son of a bitch off you, then get back on your feet, and finish him off. Remember, the battle ends when the enemy has stopped breathing.

Ben's hands were around his throat, thumbs and palms pressing against his windpipe. Trying to render him unconscious, Sione knew. *Once the enemy is no longer conscious, you can finish him off as you please,* Richard had taught them. *I prefer a nice, clean shot between the eyes, close range.*

Ben's preference was to shoot the unconscious victim in the

legs, kneecaps and feet and then douse the body with gasoline and set it on fire. Not willing to experience hell on earth, burning alive and unable to move, Sione jabbed several fingers into Ben's eyes.

The pressure on Sione's throat relaxed. He yanked Ben's hand from his neck and shoved his knee into Ben's chest, sending Ben stumbling back into a wall. Pushing himself to his feet, Sione rushed at Ben. A quick, swift kick in the gut and then another to the sternum put Ben down.

Breathing hard, Ben stayed on the ground. Sione figured the bastard was waiting for him to make some dumb move, something designed to get Sione on his knees and then back on the floor, where Ben would have the upper hand.

"Get the fuck up," Sione demanded, scanning the bedroom for a weapon. *When in doubt, allow a blunt object to help you out*, Richard would say. Focused on the desk, his eyes were drawn to the item lying on the polished dark wood, an item that seemed familiar, sparking a memory.

An arm snaked around his throat, pressing against his windpipe.

Options to break the hold sped through his mind, too quick for him to remember how to execute them. Think, don't panic. Remember what Richard had taught him. Ignore the slamming heart and racing pulse. Forget about Ben, grunting and growling in his ear, whispering promises to kill him.

"Maybe I'll shoot you between the eyes, old friend," Ben panted as they struggled. "And then cut off your hand and send it to your father!"

Sione slammed his elbow into Ben's gut and then stomped on his foot. Ben grunted but maintained his hold. Still trapped in Ben's headlock, Sione struggled to plant his feet, confused as he wrestled to free himself. Ben dragged Sione out of the bedroom and into the hallway.

Sione reached his arm back and grabbed Ben's shirt collar. Forcing his chin into the crook of Ben's arm, Sione bent forward at the waist and then pulled Ben over his shoulder, slamming him to the ground.

Ben scrambled to his feet and came at him with fists flying. Countering Ben's punches, Sione crashed his fist into the center of Ben's chest, trying to knock the breath out of Ben's lungs. He smashed his fist into Ben's face and then landed two quick blows to his temple and ear.

Ben punched Sione in the ribs and then followed with a knife-hand strike to the neck. The blow stunned Sione for a few seconds, long enough for Ben to grab him by the shoulders and head-butt him. Sione wobbled and ducked, avoiding Ben's wild swing. Ben rushed at Sione, and they wrestled like uncoordinated animals, grunting and panting as they grappled down the short, narrow hallways. Banging into walls and turning in circles, they abandoned the style and form of martial arts. Reduced to dirty street fighting, they punched and kicked and shoved.

On the landing, Sione pushed Ben away and then kicked him in the chest. Arms flailing, Ben lost his footing. Falling backward down the stairs, Ben tumbled head over tail and landed at the bottom in the foyer, sprawled on his side.

Sione ran down the steps and then took a knee next to Ben, checking for a pulse. Seconds later, he felt the vein jump beneath his fingers. Ben was unconscious but still breathing. It would be easy to kill him. The perfect opportunity to take Ben out for once and for all, for good—forever.

And yet, Sione found himself glancing back up toward the stairs, thinking about what he'd seen on the desk. As though compelled by some gravitational force, Sione stood and then headed back up the steps. At the top of the stairs, he looked down. Ben hadn't moved. Quickly, Sione turned and strode down the hall and into the bedroom.

His steps slow and measured, he approached the desk, memories returning as Moana's voice floated into his head…

Richard came to visit me in prison. He wanted me to steal an envelope for him. It belonged to Ben. Really fancy, made of lambskin with a red wax stamp on the back to seal it.

At the desk, he grabbed the envelope. Turning it over, he stared at the red wax stamp.

13

"How did you get this envelope?" Sione demanded, seconds after splashing a glass of ice water in Ben Chang's face.

Ben's eyelids fluttered several times, and then his eyes opened. Pupils unfocused, he stared at Sione as though he was confused and disoriented, trying to figure out what the hell was going on.

"Wake up!" Sione slapped Ben.

Head snapping back, Ben gasped and then coughed, and Sione could tell the bastard was slowly becoming aware of his situation—he was in the kitchen, tied to a chair, his hands bound behind him at the wrist and his ankles tied to the chair legs.

"You tied me up?" Ben coughed and then gave Sione that vicious smile. "You son of a bitch."

Sione backhanded him across the face, just hard enough to wake him all the way up. "How did you get that envelope out of my casita?"

"What envelope?"

"Don't pretend you don't know what I'm talking about. This envelope," Sione said, pulling it from the back pocket of his jeans and waving it in front of Ben. "How did you get it?"

Ben laughed. "Get these ropes off me and maybe we'll talk."

"You tell me how you got this envelope," Sione said, "or, I swear, I will burn it."

Glaring at him, Ben said, "You burn my envelope and I'll cut your fucking head off."

"Wow, you'll cut my head off," Sione said, his tone casual, though Ben's vehement threat infuriated him. "This envelope must be very important to you."

A year and a half ago, Sione had first learned about the envelope from his cousin Peter. In a convoluted scheme Sione still had problems understanding, Peter had been hired to steal the envelope from Ben Chang's house in Jamaica. Although, according to Peter, technically, he hadn't broken into Ben's place because he'd had a key. Moana had given Peter the key after persuading him to steal Ben's envelope.

Sione took a breath, trying to combat the memories of his ex-fiancée and what had eventually happened to her. Though, he wasn't quite sure what had happened. Sione still didn't know if he had killed Moana or not. He knew Moana had directed Peter to hide Ben's envelope in his casita.

"You told Kelsey Thomas that this envelope was in my casita, and you sent her to search for it."

"Kelsey Thomas didn't find it, unfortunately," Ben said. "Kelsey Thomas was supposed to be a direct hit. But that's the problem when you drop bombs, sometimes, you miss your target. So, I was forced to find a girl to replace Kelsey."

"What girl to replace Kelsey?" Sione felt his heart start to kick again.

"After Kelsey Thomas messed up, I decided on a different approach," Ben said. "A sneak attack. I decided to send another girl behind enemy lines to work undercover, like a Trojan horse."

"A Trojan horse?"

"A woman who could get under your skin and, if necessary, into your bed," Ben said. "A woman so enticing you could not help but be enchanted by her false charm, and while you were foolishly falling in love with this treacherous bitch, she would be busy looking for my envelope."

"Who did you send to replace Kelsey?" Sione demanded.

"A beautiful woman I had the misfortune to meet," Ben said. "She didn't do right by me."

"What does that mean?" Sione asked.

"She was deceitful and treacherous," Ben said. "And that is how I knew she was the perfect woman. I knew this woman would be able to accomplish what Kelsey Thomas could not. I knew this woman would be able to get close to you."

"Who was this woman?"

"She was my Trojan horse," Ben said. "I sent her to make a fool of you. There were specific steps I told this treacherous woman to take."

"Steps?" Sione echoed, feeling something plummet to the pit of his gut.

"This treacherous woman was supposed to get close to you," Ben said. "And then she was supposed to get you to have dinner with her, and then while you're at dinner, she was going to pour you some wine, and then when you were not looking, she would add a little something to it."

"A little something like what?"

Smiling, Ben said, "She was supposed to slip you a mickey."

Blood roared in Sione's head. "She was going to drug me?"

"She was going to use the date-rape drug," Ben said. "GHB."

"And then what?" Sione managed to ask, his voice hoarse, strange thoughts invading his head, crazy thoughts, ideas that couldn't possibly be true. Ridiculous bullshit about who the Trojan horse had been, the treacherous woman sent to get close to him and drug him.

"Once you were knocked out," Ben said, "she would have all the time she needed to look around your casita."

"And she would be looking for that damn envelope..." Sione found it difficult to breathe, hard to fathom what Ben was saying and what it meant.

As Ben's dark eyes focused and became clearer, Sione felt a sort of bitter self-recrimination, a burning regret churning in his gut. He should have killed Ben already, but he was beginning to think he'd missed his chance. Again, he'd let the opportunity slip through his fingers, and for what? He'd squandered the chance so he could find out about that damn envelope because he wanted to know the truth, had to know why the hell that envelope was so damn important. If he killed Ben now, what would it matter? Ben might be dead, but his lies would live forever.

"I don't have time for your fucking games," Sione said. "Who was the Trojan horse?"

"I suspect you already know the answer, but maybe you want me to confirm your suspicions," Ben said. "Or, more likely, you want your suspicions disputed because you don't want what you are secretly thinking to be true?"

"What I want is the truth!"

Ben laughed. "Why? Do you really think the truth will make you free? Do you think you can handle it? The truth will destroy you, but I suspect you know that as well, whether you want to admit it or not."

"Tell me who gave you this envelope, or so help me God—"

"I got it from that treacherous bitch I sent to Belize to find it," Ben said. "I got it from Spencer."

"You're lying," Sione said.

"I'm not the one telling lies," Ben said. "You're the liar."

Sione glared at him. "I'm the liar?"

"You're lying to yourself, old friend," Ben said. "You said you wanted me dead, but that's not true. You and I are brothers. We have a bond that neither of us is willing to break through the shedding of blood. Despite what your uncle told you, we are not Cain and Abel. We are more like Jacob and Esau. You are loved and I am cast aside because of my own foolish decisions, but you are the real trickster, the deceiver. You tricked Richard into thinking that you were the son he wanted you to be, just like Jacob made Isaac believe he was Esau."

Sione shook his head. "More Bible study lessons?"

"Spencer is a lying bitch," Ben said. "But you know that she has deceived you. That's what she does. That is her specialty. That is why she was so effective against you. You're easy to fool, old friend."

"Spencer didn't fool me," Sione said. "I know why you forced her to go to Belize. I know about the loan she couldn't pay. And I know that to satisfy the debt you forced her into some kind of devil's bargain."

"I'm not the devil." Ben smiled. "That's your father."

Pissed at Ben's judgment of Richard, Sione said, "You forced

Spencer to deliver fake passports and money to three women who helped you launder money, women who ended up dead."

"Not by my hands," Ben said, shaking his head. "I was trying to help those women, trying to get them away from your sadistic father. Richard wanted them dead."

"You really think their blood is not on your hands?"

Ben smiled, but there was no amusement in the dark, vengeful gaze. "You really think Spencer told you the truth about why I sent her to your resort? You really think you know everything?"

Sione braced himself, knowing Ben would launch a blitzkrieg of veiled accusations and innuendo carefully crafted to make him suspicious, make him doubt what he knew was the truth.

Ben said, "Spencer did not tell you that I sent her to look for that envelope, did she?"

Sione thought about it, and no, she hadn't. She'd omitted that part, but he wasn't shocked. He'd known she had secrets, hidden truths she never wanted him to know. He understood the secret, but he didn't like it and couldn't stand that her secrets put him at a disadvantage with Ben. Her secrets made him feel like a damn fool, duped and scammed. Worst of all was the smug, superior smile on Ben's face.

"Okay, she lied to me," Sione said with an indifference masking the indignation spreading through him like poison. "I know she's not perfect. She's made mistakes. Bad choices."

"Quite generous of you to be so forgiving of her blatant duplicity," Ben said. "Old friend, you are better than me. I was not so compassionate and understanding when that sweet girl lied to me."

Sione stopped him. "When did she lie to you? You mean when she agreed to pay back the loan, not realizing that you would charge five hundred percent interest?"

Ben laughed. "Old friend, I am afraid that you are about to learn the true extent of that sweet girl's treachery."

Sione glared, waiting.

"Spencer has deceived you, old friend." Shaking his head, Ben said, "Don't turn your back on her. She will put a knife in it."

The words sounded like an omen, some warning Sione should heed, but it was a false prophecy.

Dragging a hand down the side of his face, Sione stalked toward the back door, where he'd shattered a section of the glass to break into the house. Ben was lying about Spencer. The bastard was trying to get into his head, trying to mess with his mind. For some reason, Sione imagined he could feel the stinging point of something sharp pricking his spine. A knife in his back, sinking between his vertebrae.

Ben said, "The same way she put a knife in mine..."

"You deserved it," Sione said, pivoting and walking away from the door, his gaze on the kitchen counters to his left. He needed a knife, something sharp to stab into Ben's neck.

"I didn't deserve what she did to me," Ben said, head lolling to the right and then to the left, eyes blinking as though he was struggling to focus. "I was good to that sweet girl. I loved her. Maybe I still do..."

Sione stopped a few feet from Ben and stared at him. "What the hell are you talking about? You don't even really know Spencer. She was just another woman whose life you tried to ruin. You took advantage of her desperate situation. You tricked her and you used her. How the hell can you love her?"

"I know that sweet girl better than you think," Ben said. "Did she tell you that we don't know each other? Well, that's a lie, old friend."

Sione sighed, and turned from Ben, facing the sink. A dull ache throbbing at the base of his skull seemed to be steadily creeping up the back of his head. He couldn't seem to make sense of anything. He was confused and couldn't think straight. It was impossible that Spencer and Ben knew each other, and yet …

She had met with Ben tonight at the Toyota Center.

Ben was the guy who'd texted her, obviously, requesting the meeting so they could make some kind of exchange.

"I know Spencer very well," Ben said, a sly taunt in his slurred tone. "I knew her first."

A jolt went through Sione, and his eyes darted back and forth from the sink to the refrigerator, scanning the counters for a weapon. All he saw was a toaster and a blender. Nothing he could use to stab Ben.

"Before she was with you," Ben said, "she was with me. And if I had not sent her to Belize to look for my envelope, she would still be with me, old friend. She is only with you because I decided I didn't want her. True, I did love her, but she told me too many lies."

"You're lying," Sione said, hoping it was true.

Ben said, "I get the feeling she didn't tell you about our relationship."

"Your relationship?" Sione scoffed. "What relationship?"

"Spencer and I used to be in love," Ben said. "Well, I was in love. She just wanted my—"

Sione punched him.

Ben shook his head, cursed, and then laughed. "The truth does hurt."

Sione grabbed the toaster and yanked it, pulling the cord from the wall. Spinning to face Ben, he slammed the toaster against the side of Ben's head, compelled by rage and fear. Momentum and force caused the chair to topple and tilt to the left. Seconds later, the chair crashed to the floor, and Ben's head slammed against the tile.

14

The Woodlands, Texas
Carlton Woods Gated Community

Sione leaned back in the leather chair behind his desk in the home office and took another sip of the aged malt scotch.

The Blue Label went down smooth, filling him with a lazy warmth.

Midnight had come and gone. He sat mostly in the dark, the only source of light a faint illumination from the outside terrace lights.

He'd arrived at the mansion an hour ago and had slipped in quietly, not wanting to announce himself. He needed to be alone so he could think. There were decisions to be made. Choices which would most likely be irreversible. He couldn't afford a hasty reaction. He had to be logical and rational. Mercenary and methodical.

Something had to be done about Spencer.

The drive from the Third Ward area had been too long and yet not long enough.

He'd spent the entire time trying to make himself believe Ben had lied to him about Spencer's involvement with that damn envelope. He didn't want to believe Ben had sent Spencer behind enemy lines to accomplish what Kelsey Thomas had failed to do. He couldn't believe it.

There had to be some other explanation.

The Trojan horse was supposed to make Sione like her, get herself invited to dinner, and get close to him, but Spencer hadn't done any of that. From the first day Sione had met her, Spencer had been bitchy and abrasive. She hadn't come on to him, hadn't really flirted with him. Even when she'd jumped in his lap and kissed him, it seemed more like a rash reaction than a scheming seduction. She'd been quick to kick him out as soon as he'd mentioned her bedroom.

Sione took a drink, remembering when they'd made love for the first time. They'd had a few glasses of wine, but she hadn't drugged him.

Sione sipped more scotch, trying to manage the wild, wayward thoughts whipping through his mind.

Spencer couldn't be the Trojan horse...could she? Ben had sent her to Belize to deliver fake passports and money, not to make a damn fool of him. And yet—

"John, why are you sitting in the dark?" Spencer's voice floated through the darkness toward him, slipping around him like a caress.

Glancing up, he saw her standing in the doorway to his office. Backlit from the wall sconces in the hallway, she appeared as a sly, seductive silhouette.

Staring at her, he took another sip of the scotch.

"I didn't know you were back," she said, venturing into the office. "When did you get home?"

She walked to his desk and turned the lamp on. The room brightened to a cozy glow. She looked beautiful without any makeup on and her hair piled on top of her head with loose tendrils framing her face.

She looked like the prettiest girl in the world, just like she had with the frangipani bloom behind her ear. Sione could hardly breathe as he remembered the flower he'd given her and how the velvety white petals had curved around her left ear, where he'd hoped she would put it.

How could he be with her now, knowing what Ben had sent her to do? Knowing that their entire relationship was built on lies?

"How was the game?" Sione asked as she settled onto his lap, slipping an arm around his back.

After giving him a few kisses on the mouth and one on the cheek, Spencer said, "Exciting."

"Did the Rockets win?" Sione asked, trying to ignore the effect of those intoxicating kisses, trying to remember that every touch, every kiss, every caress, and every smile was all a lie.

"Yeah," Spencer said. "They played really well."

"And you had a good time with your friend from high school?"

"Yeah, it was great to see her," Spencer said. "So, did your dinner with the investor go okay?"

"Everything went fine," he said. "I was just sitting here thinking…"

"About what?"

"About us," he said, glancing at the bottle of Blue Label. "I was just remembering when I first saw you. I had this feeling about you. I thought you were so beautiful, I couldn't believe it, just breathtakingly gorgeous. I couldn't stop thinking about you."

"I felt the same way," she told him.

She sounded so sincere Sione almost believed her.

"All I wanted was just to be around you." He cut his gaze to the bottle of Blue Label and then glanced at Spencer again. "Everyone kept trying to warn me, but I wouldn't listen. They kept telling me not to have anything to do with you."

Smiling, she said, "I'm glad you didn't listen to them."

"I should have," Sione said. "Or maybe I should have talked to William Bermudez."

"Why would you want to talk to William Bermudez?"

"Well, I am curious about something," Sione said, stroking his chin and staring at her. "Bermudez said that he told Ben Chang that Fong had kidnapped you and was keeping you in that shack. He told Ben Chang where to find you."

Spencer said, "Bermudez lied to you. Ben wasn't at that shack that day."

"Well, you wouldn't have known anyway, right?" Sione said. "Because you have never met Ben Chang, right?"

Spencer said, "No, I've never met him."

"Are you sure?"

Spencer asked, "What do you mean?"

"I'm just asking because I'm remembering something that Bermudez said."

Spencer said, "You need to forget all those lies he told you."

"Bermudez said Ben Chang cared about you," Sione went on, "but at the time, I thought that makes no sense. How could Ben Chang care about you? He doesn't even know you."

Spencer said, "Exactly. Ben doesn't care about me. I mean nothing to him."

"You sure about that?"

Spencer frowned. "What?"

"You mean more to Ben Chang than you think."

Spencer shook her head. "I'm just some dumb girl he used."

Shaking his head, scoffing, Sione said, "And I'm just some dumb fool who should have listened to those people who told me not to trust you."

Her smile waned a bit as confusion and wariness clouded her features.

"If I had listened," he went on, "then I never would have gotten involved with you."

"Are you upset about something? I don't understand why you're saying these things. Are you mad at me, or—"

"Am I upset? Am I mad at you?" He pretended to consider her questions, trying to quell the rage he felt surging through him. "Upset and mad would be a gross understatement of the way I feel right now. But, yeah, I am upset and I am mad because I have been lied to and tricked and made a fool of, and I have no one to blame but myself for being so goddamn gullible and stupid."

"What are you talking about?" she asked, rising from his lap. "Who tricked you and made a fool of you?"

"Who tricked me? Who made a fool of me?" He glared at her. "Are you going to pretend that you didn't lie to me about your relationship with Ben Chang? Are you going to deny that Ben Chang didn't send you to Belize to get close to me so you could find his envelope?"

"What are you talking about?" she asked, staring at him. "Who told you that?"

"Someone who would know told me."

"Did you talk to Bermudez? Did he tell you that he sent me to Belize to scam you?" she asked, and though a spark of anger flashed in her brown eyes, Sione still heard the fear in her voice. "He lied to you, John, I told you why I came to Belize."

"You didn't tell me the truth!" he said. "You lied about why you came to my resort, and you lied about your relationship with Ben Chang."

"You can't believe anything Bermudez says!"

"I can't believe anything you say!" His voice became even louder. "You said you never met Ben Chang. You said all you know about him was that he owned the payday loan business that you borrowed money from. You said you didn't even know his name. You said the owner didn't want to meet you because if you got arrested delivering fake passports, the owner wouldn't want you to be able to tell the cops about him. You said the loan manager was acting as some kind of liaison between you and the owner, but you insisted that you never met him face to face!"

"John, please!" Spencer said, her voice shrill. "Will you just let me—"

"But that wasn't true," Sione said. "The truth is that Ben Chang is in love with you."

"What?" Her voice rose several more octaves as she stared at him, several shades of horror passing across her face. "No, that's crazy! I don't know why Bermudez—"

"The truth is that you and Ben used to be together," Sione said, taking a step toward her. "You would still be with him if you hadn't—"

"I was never with Ben Chang!" Spencer shrieked, taking a few wobbly steps back. "I would never be with him. I couldn't be with someone like him."

"But you were with someone like him," Sione said. "You were with a man who sent you to trick me, and I have to admit, you did fool me. You made me think you wanted to be with me, but really it was just a trick, and I fell for it and you—"

"How can you think that I don't really want to be with you?" A tremor entered her voice, and Sione heard unmistakable traces of fear and panic. "Why would you believe Bermudez's lies? John, don't you remember the frangipani flower you gave me? As soon as you gave it to me, I put it behind my left ear to show you and the whole world that I was taken!"

"Yeah, taken by Ben Chang."

"No, taken by you!" she insisted. "I'm with you, John!"

"You and I are not together. You are not with me and you never were. You just made me think that because that's what Ben Chang told you to do!"

"You have everything wrong!"

"No, I had everything wrong when I thought you were the woman that I might fall in love with and spend the rest of my life with!"

"I am that woman," she said. The conviction in her voice was so confident it was almost comforting.

"You are not the woman I almost fell in love with," he said, though he regretted that she really was. "You're the woman Ben sent to get close to me. The woman who was supposed to trick me into liking her!"

Shaking her head, she stared at him. "Will you please let me explain?"

"Explain what? How you agreed to drug me so you could look for that fucking envelope?"

She rubbed her eyes with shaking fingers. "Did Bermudez tell you that I was going to drug you? Because that's not true! I would have never drugged you! I would never have done something so sick and vicious like that to you!"

"Bermudez didn't tell me a damn thing!" Sione said. "Ben Chang told me."

"Ben Chang?"

"The guy you met tonight at the Toyota Center," Sione said. "You were supposed to be watching the game with an old friend."

"John, I can explain."

"You mean you can come up with another lie?"

"Why did you follow me?"

"Because I wanted to know the truth, and I didn't think I could trust you to tell me, and I was right."

"The truth about what?"

"About where you were really going tonight."

"So when I told you where I was going, why didn't you believe me?"

"A few days ago, I overheard you talking to your sisters about a burner phone," he said. "Didn't hear the entire conversation, but I heard enough to know you were worried about the burner. Then, as luck would have it, I found the damn phone wedged beneath the pillows. I saw the text messages about you meeting up with someone at the Toyota Center tonight to make some sort of exchange.

Shaking her head, she said, "I can't believe you spied on me!"

"So I spied. You lied." He shrugged. "We don't trust each other."

"No, you don't trust me!" she said. "If you trusted me, you wouldn't have been snooping around, following me!

"If you really trusted me, you would have told me the truth a year ago! You would have been honest with me about your relationship with Ben Chang!"

Glaring at her, he fought the urge to pull her into his arms as he struggled to hold on to the hatred that would give him the courage to tell her to leave. He didn't want her to go. And yet, he knew she couldn't stay.

"John, I need you to understand that I never wanted to lie to you, and I never—"

"You're finally telling the truth," he said. "You're admitting that you lied to me."

"I lied because Ben put me in a position where I didn't have any other choice—"

"So, Ben made you lie to me?" he asked. "He's got that much control over you? You can't make your own decisions? He tells you to run and you ask him how far?"

"I had to do what Ben told me to because…" She looked away.

"Because what?" he demanded.

"I don't know how to tell you!" she screamed, tears streaming down her face. "I'm afraid that if I tell you the truth I'm going to lose you!"

Sione was afraid, too, but not that he would lose her.

He was terrified of giving up a chance at happiness with Spencer because she wasn't perfect. But she was loyal and supportive. She could be kind and compassionate. There were so many moments when she was selfless and generous. She was willing to be vulnerable with him, willing to trust him with the sadness of her childhood.

Still, she'd lied to him about everything.

Sione didn't know if he could get past her lies. How could he forgive her for her part in Ben's scam?

"I'm afraid that I won't be able to make you understand how I feel about you," she said. "Because that's all that matters."

"That's not what matters to me," he said. "I'm not interested in hearing you lie about how much you want to be with me."

"But I do want to be with you!" she said. "Because I love you, John. You know how much I love you!"

I love you…

Those three words filled Sione with a host of conflicting emotions. He felt blindsided, confused, and strangely relieved. He tried to tell himself that her I love you didn't matter, but that was a lie. Those three words mattered more than they should have.

I love you…

Sione couldn't take her words to heart, he wouldn't. She was a liar, not to be trusted, and he couldn't believe a damn thing she said. Spencer was desperate. All her lies had been exposed, and she was grasping at straws, saying what she thought he wanted to hear.

I love you…

Sione loved her too, maybe too much.

15

The Woodlands, Texas
Carlton Woods Gated Community

Heart pounding, Spencer stared up at John, trying to gather her scattered thoughts, trying to think, and trying to breathe.

Their relationship was exploding all around them. Bombs were being dropped, hand grenades were being thrown, and all the feelings between them were going up in smoke. She had to fight for their love. She couldn't let their hopes and dreams disintegrate into a heap of charred ashes surrounding her. She had to find some way to make John understand how much she cared about him and how sorry she was for hurting him and how she hated herself for her stupid mistakes.

Thinking about the baby, the child she was carrying, the miracle created by their love, Spencer knew she could no longer react out of drastic desperation. All her lies would have to be exposed no matter how painful, no matter the risk.

She and John had been shattered by her lies, but now she realized the truth she'd hidden was the only way to fix what was broken between them.

Spencer could only hope that John would believe her.

She had to convince John not to give up on them, and what they had, and what they could have. She had to prove to him that she was worth his love. Yes, she had made some mistakes—horrible, dangerous mistakes—she wouldn't deny that. And she could make amends. She would make it all up to him.

But they had to stay together.

She had a sinking, sick feeling in the pit of her stomach that John was going to tell her to leave. She couldn't let that happen. She had to make him change his mind, had to persuade him not to give up on her. She was afraid he had already lost his faith in her, afraid he no longer believed that the frangipani bloom belonged behind her left ear.

"I should start from the beginning," she said. "I need to tell you the truth."

Shrugging, John sat back down in his leather chair and stared at her, waiting.

Spencer took a deep breath. "When I met Ben, I'd been out of work for almost a year. I had been laid off, and I had a lot of debt, bills that were getting behind. So, things were becoming very desperate for me, financially. I was a month away from being evicted from my apartment when Rae came to me and..."

"And what?"

Wiping away her tears, determined not to look away from his hazel eyes, Spencer took another deep breath and told him everything about the "dating," how she'd met Ben, and how her plan to "date" Ben went so horribly wrong and ruined her life.

As she spoke, John glared at her, his face betraying his

emotions: shock, confusion, anger, and disgust. Eventually, he looked away from her, rubbing his eyes. When she'd finished the sick, twisted, pathetic tale, John was quiet. His silence scared her. Why wouldn't he say anything? She'd expected screaming, yelling, and cursing. The non-reaction was worse.

"John?" she ventured, though she risked igniting his ire or invoking the rage he was struggling to contain.

He remained silent.

Faltering, Spencer stopped to get her nerves together, to push away the panic and mounting fear. "I know you hate me, but—"

"I would have to care about you to hate you," he said. "I don't give a damn about you."

Spencer felt like he'd plunged a knife in her gut. "Yes, I did lie to you, but you're a liar, too. You lied to me and you're lying to yourself."

"Oh, really?"

"You know you love me," she said, forcing herself to go on. "You feel the same way about me as I feel about you."

"Is that right?" John gave her a dubious look as he folded his arms across his chest. His muscles reminded her how wonderful it felt to be wrapped in his protective embrace, a place she would never be again.

"You want me as much as I want you," she said, finding her voice, compelled to tell him what was in her heart even though he might not care—even though it made her feel too much like her mother, made her feel too much like "that wife."

"I do?" John stared at her, an expression in his hazel eyes that she couldn't understand.

"I don't expect you to admit it to me, or to yourself, but you know it's true." She stopped to take a breath, already regretting her impulsive outburst. "No matter how you feel about me, it won't change how I feel about you. I'm going to be miserable without you and hating myself for ruining what we could have had."

"Something tells me you won't be too miserable," he said.

"Something tells me I won't be the only one who's miserable," Spencer said. "You're going to be miserable without me, too."

"I'm already miserable because I made the mistake of getting involved with a woman who made a fool out of me."

"I didn't want to make a fool out of you," she said. "I didn't want to lie to you. I didn't want to steal from you. As soon as I saw you, I just wanted to be with you, and I think you felt the same way about me."

"I thought I did," he said. "But I was wrong."

"No, you weren't wrong," she told him. "That's why you gave me the frangipani flower. You told me you hoped that I would put it behind my left ear, and I did, because I am taken."

"I don't need to hear any more," he said. "My family was right about you. I should have listened to them. You're not the woman I thought you were. You're not the woman I hoped you would be."

"But I *can* be that woman, John!" She looked him in the eye. "I promise, I can. If you just give me a chance, if you let me try!"

"Are you out of your mind? You will never be the woman I thought you were. Even if you died trying, you could not be kind and compassionate and selfless," he said. "All you can be is what you are, a lying bitch."

"You're right, John," she said. "I lied about why I came to Belize, and I lied about my relationship with Ben, but I didn't lie about how I feel about you. I love you so much."

16

The Woodlands, Texas
Carlton Woods Gated Community

"You can't possibly love me," Sione told her. "If you really loved me, you would have told me that Ben wanted you to drug me so you could look for that damn envelope. But you didn't do that. You kept lying to me even when I gave you the chance to tell me the truth. You chose Ben."

"Because I had to," Spencer said. "Ben threatened to show the police that video of me taking the money and the watches from his closet!"

"I wouldn't have let him get away with that," he said. "I told you I would protect you from Ben. I told you that I wouldn't let him hurt you, but you didn't believe me! You didn't trust me!"

"I do trust you," she said. "I love you!"

"Don't say that," he warned. "You're not in love with me. You're a liar and I don't want you in my life."

"That's not true," she told him. "I know you love me. You want to be with me as much as I want to be with you. Please, John, remember why you gave me that flower.!"

Sione thought about the flower. It had looked so perfect behind her ear, where he'd hoped it would be and where he wished it could stay. His memories of the frangipani bloom were distracting, making him think that his decision to tell Spencer to leave was a mistake.

"The flower doesn't matter," he said. "It doesn't mean anything to me."

"Don't say that," she pleaded. "You don't mean that."

"I don't care that you put that flower behind your left ear," he said. "I don't want you."

Gasping, Spencer dropped to her knees before him, clutching her stomach.

"I want you to leave," he told her, while he still could, before he lost his nerve.

Dropping her face into her hands, she burst into tears. Horrible sobs of raw, searing grief tore into him, ripping away all the rage and hate he'd held to so tightly. The rage and hate he'd relied on to tell her to leave. The rage and hate that now disgusted and shamed him.

Sione could hardly stand, knowing he was the cause of Spencer's anguish. Knowing her tears were the result of his fierce stubbornness, his unwillingness to forgive her. More than anything, he couldn't stand knowing that what he wanted most in the world was to pull her into his arms, wipe away her tears, and tell her he loved her and never wanted to let her go.

Slowly, gradually, her sobs subsided to plaintive whimpers, which sounded even worse, as though she were some delicate, wounded animal suffering from the effects of being trampled by something bullish and brutal.

Finally, the whimpering died out, and Sione felt more in control of his emotions, more resolved in his decision.

"Get out," he said, forcing the words past the hot mass in his throat.

"Is that what you really want?" Sniffing, she wiped her face and stood, staring at him. "You want me to leave?"

Gazing at her, at the tears welling in her eyes, he felt empty and forlorn and worried. He didn't want her to go. But she couldn't stay. He couldn't let her get away with all the lies she'd told. He couldn't allow himself to forget she was Ben's Trojan horse.

"You should go," he said, afraid her tears would make him change his mind.

She nodded. "I'll get my things and then I'll go."

"I want you to leave now," he said. "I'll send your stuff to your sister's house."

"Fine..." she said, looking at the floor. "I'll get dressed and—"

"I said I want you gone now," he said, grabbing her arm. "Get out of my house. Forget about getting dressed, just get out!"

"John, wait, please!" she said, imploring, trying to stop him, unable to yank away from him as he forced her out of the home office and into the hallway. Tightening his grip on her arm, he marched her down the long hall, not caring that she could barely keep up with his long strides.

"Don't, John, stop!" She tried to twist away, screaming and crying.

In the foyer, Sione walked her to the double doors. Her cries increased when he opened the right door and shoved her over the threshold. Out on the portico, she stumbled, went down on one knee, and then the other, crying.

Shaking with rage and too many other emotions he didn't want to identify, he rubbed his eyes and tried to silence the voice in his head telling him he'd made a mistake.

"John, wait," she said, rising to her feet and wiping her face. "I have to tell you something, I'm—"

Sick of her lies, he slammed the door in her face, locked it, and turned away.

Moments later, he heard her banging on the door, screaming and yelling.

Panic grabbed him like a hand around his throat, and for a moment, he struggled to catch his breath. The urge to turn around, open the door, and tell her he'd made a mistake and didn't want her to leave was so strong it was almost tangible.

He fought the urge with every conviction he had.

It was a fight he barely won—a fight that left him shaken and desolate.

With a fury he could barely contain, Sione took one step away from the door, and then another, and another, until he was hurrying out of the foyer and then running up the stairs, desperate to escape the sound of Spencer's mournful screams.

17

———————

San Ignacio, Belize
Belizean Banyan Resort – Owner's Office

TWO MONTHS LATER

Sione Tuiali'i stared at the invoices scattered across his desk. He needed to approve them but knew he probably wouldn't.

Not when Spencer was in his head again. She was always in his head. He seemed to always be reliving the night he'd told her to leave, always hearing her heart-wrenching cries, the heaving wails that had scared him and made him want to gather her in his arms and comfort her.

He'd resisted the urge but just barely. Denying her his love and compassion had felt unnatural and vengeful. He hated seeing her in pain. But Spencer had brought the pain on herself when she decided to align with Ben and participate in his scams.

He dragged a hand down the side of his face.

She'd gotten what she deserved that night.

Had Sione gotten what he deserved? Did he deserve to stay up all night, tossing and turning, reaching for a woman who wasn't there? Did he deserve to wake up in a panic when he realized she wasn't in bed next to him, like she should have been, like she would never be again? Did he deserve the forlornness creeping up on him when he remembered she wasn't coming back? Did he deserve to feel so broken and alone? Especially when he'd done the right thing? His lingering doubts and suspicions about Spencer had been confirmed. He couldn't forgive her. She'd had to go. She wasn't the right woman for him, and she never would be.

Still, her absence from his life felt detrimental.

Sione missed her like he was missing something crucial for survival.

The feelings were unusual and unfamiliar.

It made no sense that after two months he still couldn't concentrate and couldn't focus. He had moved back to Belize and was no longer living in Houston where everything reminded him of Spencer, but he couldn't walk into his casita without remembering Spencer had been there. He couldn't sleep in his own bed without thinking about how Spencer used to lie there next to him.

The night she'd left the mansion in The Woodlands, he'd had too much to drink. Close to passing out, he was eager to fall into oblivion for the next ten hours. Approaching the bed in the master suite had been like walking toward a death chamber. Beneath the sheets, the bed had been as barren as the desert, as cold as the grave.

Sione thought he would finally get a good night's sleep once he was back in Belize.

But for some damn reason, in the master bedroom he'd shared with Spencer in the casita, he could sense Spencer's presence. Not just her perfume, but her hair and her skin. She was there, but she wasn't. He was in bed with a ghost. Changing the bed linens hadn't done any good. He'd had to leave his bedroom and sleep in one of the guest rooms. Still, he'd tossed and turned all night, plagued by dreams.

Nightmares of Spencer taunting and teasing him. In the dreams, he'd been chasing her, but she would always manage to slip away from him. She would walk through a door and close it behind her. He would open the door, and the room would be empty. She would rush around a corner, and he would follow and find himself in an empty alleyway. And through it all, he swore he could hear Ben and Richard laughing at him.

Sione had expected the disillusionment and depression to be over by now, but the disappointment was lingering like some viral infection he couldn't shake. Disappointment he brought upon himself, he suspected.

Because he'd been too prideful to forgive Spencer.

His uncle had always told him that pride came before a fall, and that was true. The whole situation had knocked him right on his ass, and he'd be damned if he knew how to get up.

Which didn't make a damn bit of sense.

Telling Spencer to leave had been the right thing to do, he knew that. So why the hell did it feel like he'd made the worst mistake of his life?

A mistake so disastrous he might not recover.

18

Houston, Texas
Torrey Chase Subdivision

A flash of sun peeked up behind the trees towering over the modest two-story brick homes on the left side of the quiet street in the sedate, peaceful north Houston neighborhood. Slowly revealing more and more of its radiance, the sun seemed eager and yet hesitant until, finally, its brilliance was majestically exposed.

Spencer Edwards stared at the cloudless sky, a bright expanse of blue above her as she power walked around the corner, heading back to Shady's house. For the past two months, she'd been staying in one of the extra bedrooms at her sister's place, unofficially helping Rae house-sit while Shady was off on a missionary trip.

A month ago, Spencer had started slipping out of bed just before dawn to walk around the neighborhood, watching the sunrise as she struggled to make sense of her life and the mess she'd made of it.

She greeted each day ruminating on the mistakes, bad choices, and stupid decisions she'd made, imagining what her life might have been like if she had never decided to start "dating." She wanted to believe things would have been better for her and, eventually, she would have found another job and become a productive, contributing member of society.

Those elusive fantasies were always eclipsed by a conclusion she couldn't deny that disturbed her.

If she had never agreed to start "dating," then she never would have met John.

Their encounter could be traced back to her decision to "date" Ben. It was a disastrous mistake Ben had been able to use against her. That fateful choice had led her to Belize where she'd been forced to get close to John.

Taking deep, measured breaths and pumping her arms, Spencer strode past a one-story brick home with a sign that read "For Sale" in the yard. If she hadn't met John, she wouldn't have her precious little one growing within her. For that reason alone, she couldn't bring herself to wish she had never met John.

She was still in love with him. She didn't know how to *not* be in love with him.

Part of her wanted to hate John.

His cruel rejection still sent her emotions spinning out of control. She'd wanted the memories of his hateful words to choke all the love she felt for him from her, but her feelings seemed to have increased. Time wasn't healing her broken heart; if anything, as the days passed, she seemed to love John even more than she did the day before.

Absence was absolutely making her heart grow fonder.

A whisper of a breeze floated across her, lifting her hair from her shoulders.

Being in love with a man was a frightening, unfamiliar situation. A situation Spencer had never experienced; a situation she hadn't planned to be in. She wasn't supposed to have ended up like her mother, desperate and alone and in love with a man who didn't want her.

But she had.

With no references of former heartbreak to draw upon or to use for strength, she wasn't sure how she would get through the pain. There was no comfort to rely on, no belief that everything would eventually be okay.

Being away from John was hell.

Spencer dreamed she would wake up in his arms again. So far, it hadn't happened. After so much time had passed, Spencer believed it never would. At first, she'd foolishly allowed herself to hope John would come back into her life. Maybe he would realize he loved her and wanted to be with her.

Strangely enough, Rae had inspired that wishful thinking. Her older sister had become kinder, if not gentler, for some reason. Contrastingly, Shady had come at her with tough love and routinely reminded her to focus on the most important thing in her life right now—the baby.

The child growing and thriving within her had been her saving grace. As she cradled her little burgeoning "bump" and reveled in the excitement of meeting her little one in seven months, the deep wounds of John's rejection began to hurt a bit less.

She would eventually heal, but she would never forget the pain of losing John and her chance to be with him and to experience the happily ever after they had dreamed about. The scars would remain even when the pain lessened and then faded away.

Cradling her stomach now, hurrying across a boulevard separated by several grassy knolls, Spencer couldn't help but feel forlorn and regretful, knowing John wouldn't be there to share her euphoria and elation when the baby was finally born, when she held her precious little one in her arms for the first time.

Both Shady and Rae—surprisingly—thought she should tell John about the baby, but Spencer couldn't risk it. She had to be selfless and think about what was best for her child. She couldn't let herself get overly stressed.

As she rounded the corner, breathing in the early morning air, picking up a hint of cut St. Augustine grass, a thought she would never share with her sisters made its way into her head.

John didn't deserve to be in the baby's life.

A terrible selfish, shameful thought, but she couldn't ignore it.

Spencer increased her pace, unable to stop herself from thinking about that horrible night, two months ago, when John had been so heartless and cruel.

The next day was even worse. Opening her eyes, Spencer had found herself in a bed she was unfamiliar with and didn't belong in. She had been in one of the guest rooms at Shady's house. Curled into the fetal position, in a lonely bed where John wasn't lying next to her, she felt strange and unnatural, not waking up in his arms.

John's rejection had been heartless and destructive. Her heart broken, Spencer had known she'd lost him forever. She suspected she had never had him. How could a man like John ever belong to a woman like her? At times, she was furious with John. But what the hell had she expected? That he would let her get away with lying to him? That he would forgive her for making a fool of him? Had she expected him to give her a chance to explain?

There was no excuse for what she'd done.

She'd hoped her love would have mattered, would have meant something to him. John had made his feelings painfully clear. He wanted nothing to do with her.

So why the hell would John even care that she was having their baby?

19

Sione stared at the computer on the desk in his office at the resort's administration building.

On the screen was an email with an attachment titled "Transfer of Land-Draft #1." His lawyers had closed the deal with the owners a few days ago. The land Sione wanted for the resort expansion was now his. Following legal formalities and closing, he would meet with the architectural firm he'd hired to design the luxury tree houses.

Sione read a paragraph and realized he'd read that same paragraph twice before. He couldn't concentrate despite two cups of coffee. Exhaling, he leaned back in his chair and rubbed his eyes.

He knew the reason for his lack of focus.

Spencer.

Focusing on the document, Sione tried again to read it but soon found his thoughts drifting.

Every time Sione tried to remind himself of Spencer's deception and her collusion with Ben, another voice in his head would point out she'd only agreed to help Ben because he'd blackmailed her. Ben had told Spencer to drug him and get close to him so she could look for that damn envelope.

Thoughts of the envelope reminded Sione of its fate.

Back in Belize, Sione had directed Truman, his cousin, to take the envelope and put it in a secure place until Sione could decide what the hell to do with it.

Cursing, Sione told himself to focus on the draft of the land transfer. Right now, he had to concentrate on what was important: his expansion plans for the resort. He wanted to break ground on the tree houses as soon as possible. Uncle Siosi's sons had reluctantly approved his ideas, and he was anxious to have them laud his success.

It wasn't going to happen if he didn't get his shit together.

Sione sat forward, frowning at the screen, thinking maybe he should print the document.

A few minutes later, the draft was spread across the desk in front of him. He had to make notes about any questions he had or any modifications he wanted to the contract.

A knock on the door startled him. Sione called out, "Come in."

The door to his office opened, and Marie rushed in, her face tense with worry. "Mr. Tuiali'i, I don't mean to bother you, but..."

"Marie, what's the matter?"

Frowning, his assistant said, "I think we might need to call the police."

"Why?" Sione stood, trying to stay calm. "What's happened?"

"Well, I was getting ready to pay your credit card bills," Marie said, "and I noticed some very suspicious charges on this one card, a platinum Visa, and I think somebody hacked into the account or stole your identity."

Frowning, Sione asked, "What kind of charges? Maybe I gave that card to my mom to use."

Marie pursed her lips and then said, "I don't think so. Somebody charged stuff at Babies "R" Us, BuyBuy Baby, and South Avenue Pharmacy. I called the credit card company, and they told me it was baby clothes, diapers, and prenatal vitamins."

Staring at Marie, Sione felt a strange sensation like something hard dropping into his stomach.

"Probably some little thieving heifer went and got herself pregnant out of wedlock," Marie said, her voice quivering with indignation and judgment. "She can't afford the baby so she steals a credit card to finance her little bundle of joy. That's a damn shame. Whoever she is, she doesn't deserve to raise that baby. I'm so tired of people being so unethical and immoral."

Confused and irritated by Marie's condemning tone, Sione asked, "Do you know who the pregnant girl is?"

Marie looked up at him, as though insulted by his question. "How would I know who she is? According to the statement, you made these charges, but that's not true because you're not pregnant. Unless there's something you haven't told me. The pregnant girl is a thief, that's who she is."

"I want you to find out about these fraudulent charges, okay," Sione said, rubbing his chin. "I want to know about the prenatal vitamins. Find out where that pharmacy is located and—"

"Why do you want me to do that?" Marie asked, frowning at him.

"Marie, just—" Sione exhaled, his heart pounding as strange

thoughts began to form in his head, forcing him toward conclusions that didn't make sense, and yet he couldn't dismiss the thoughts or the bizarre excitement racing through his veins. "Just find out about the charges, okay? And do it as soon as possible, please. Make it your top priority."

20

Houston, Texas
Babies "R" Us Parking Lot

Settling back in the plush leather bucket seat, Spencer crossed her ankles as Rae got behind the wheel, slammed the door of the BMW, and let out a string of frustrated curses.

Spencer marveled at how easy it was to buckle the seatbelt—now. She was only eleven weeks and barely showing, but what would happen when she was eight months? Would she be able to buckle the seatbelt when she was as big as a whale?

"Can you believe that bullshit?" Rae started the car, grabbed the gear stick, and yanked it into reverse. "Damn card was declined."

"Well." Spencer sighed, not sure what to say. "When we get home, you can call the credit card company and find out what's going on."

Moments ago, she and Rae had been in Babies "R" Us, strolling leisurely up and down the aisles, pushing a basket filled to the brim with things for the little one. It was their normal Wednesday afternoon routine, which they'd started a few weeks after the night John had kicked her out of the house in The Woodlands.

"I don't need to call," Rae said, speeding through the parking lot. "I know what happened. We got cut off because we got caught."

"What?" Spencer asked, confused. "We got caught? What do you mean? Wait, please don't tell me you were using Mr. Cephas' credit card to—"

"No, I wasn't using Mr. Cephas' credit card," Rae said, turning out into the traffic on the main thoroughfare. "He did offer the use of his black card, but I turned him down."

Spencer looked at Rae. "Why?" Usually, Rae wouldn't hesitate to take advantage of Mr. Cephas' generosity. Maybe, hopefully, her sister had decided to rethink her relationship with her fence, a man old enough to be her father, and who sometimes did treat Rae like a daughter. Sometimes, however, Mr. Cephas treated Rae like an ex-girlfriend he was still interested in, so their situation wasn't clearly defined.

"Because you're not having Mr. Cephas' baby," Rae said, her tone curt, defensive. "If you were, then yeah, we'd be using his black card. But you're having Sione's baby, so I figured he should pay for his child."

"Rae, what are you talking about?" Spencer asked, feeling her blood pressure spike. "How can John pay for a baby that he doesn't know exists? Oh my God, please tell me you didn't go behind my back and tell him that—"

"Calm down, girl," Rae admonished. "Don't stress the baby out. I didn't call Sione and tell him you're pregnant."

"You think Shady did it?"

"No, Shady didn't tell him," Rae said and then sighed. "Okay, I gotta tell you something."

Worried, Spencer asked, "Do I need to sit down?"

"Girl, you are sitting down," Rae said, shaking her head as she steered the BMW onto the interstate entrance ramp.

"Okay, well, do you need to pull the car over so I can get out and stand up?"

Exhaling, Rae said, "Remember when Sione had your stuff delivered to my place?"

Nodding, her apprehension increasing, Spencer said, "Yeah."

"Well, I unpacked your stuff, remember," Rae said, increasing her speed, steering around slower cars. "And so, in one of your wallets, I found a platinum Visa card with Sione's name on it. But, because it was in your wallet, I figured you must have been an—"

"Authorized user," Spencer whispered, hoping she wouldn't start to hyperventilate. "Oh my God, I remember that card. John gave it to me to use. Rae, please tell me that you have not—"

"Can't tell you that because I have," Rae said. "Or I did. I was using that card to pay for your prenatal vitamins and to buy all the stuff you need for the baby."

Spencer took several deep breaths, but it didn't help. "Why the hell did you do that?"

"I did it because Sione should provide for his child," Rae said.

"He doesn't know I'm pregnant," Spencer practically screamed, struggling to manage her emotions.

"So what?" Rae said. "That doesn't absolve him of his responsibility."

Again, Spencer took several deep breaths. And again, it didn't help to lower her blood pressure or temper her ire. "Desarae, do you know what you've done by using John's credit card?"

"Yes, I have made sure that your baby will have enough diapers and clothes and toys and baby furniture and—"

"No, you have committed fraud," Spencer said through gritted teeth. "I'm sure the first thing John did was remove me as an authorized user from all his cards. By using his card without his permission, you've broken the law. And even worse than that, you went against my wishes. I told you that John couldn't know about the baby. That card didn't go through because he's found out about the charges and had it cancelled. If he saw the diapers and baby clothes, what the hell do you think he's going to think?"

"You don't know that he's gonna think you're pregnant," Rae said.

"But what if he does?" Spencer asked. "And what if he comes to Houston and—"

"Don't get the cart before the horse," Rae said. "He's probably got some accountant who pays his bills, right? That person is probably responsible for resolving any discrepancies or credit issues. Sione ain't got time for that. And, let's just say that he does pay the bills himself. So what? I really don't think he's going to jump to the conclusion that you're pregnant."

21

San Ignacio, Belize

Belizean Banyan Resort – Owner's Office

"You wanted to see me?" Marie poked her head around the corner of the door to Sione's office.

"Come in here." Impatient, Sione beckoned for her. "What have you found out about those fraudulent charges on that platinum Visa?"

Marie blinked, eyes wide, apprehensive. "Well, um…"

"Well, what?" he asked, not in the mood for any pretense. "What did you find out?"

"I found out that all the charges were made in, um…" Marie sighed. "They were made in Houston. The pharmacy was in Houston, too. I wrote down the address. I can get it for you. I guess when you were living there, somebody must have stolen your credit card and—"

"No, that's not what happened." Sione sat, all the nervous

energy draining from his body, leaving behind an emptiness filled with disappointment. He was shocked, confused, and heartbroken. When Marie had told him about the charges to the Visa account, he'd had a strange, sinking suspicion an identity thief hadn't been the culprit. He'd hoped he was wrong. He'd hoped he was just jumping to unfounded, unprovable conclusions, because if he was right, then…

Sione hadn't allowed himself to think about what being right would mean.

Somebody charged stuff at Babies "R" Us, BuyBuy Baby, and South Avenue Pharmacy. I called the credit card company and they told me it was baby clothes, diapers, and prenatal vitamins.

"What do you mean that's not what happened?"

Slightly startled, Sione looked up; he didn't realize Marie was still in his office.

"That particular Visa card was one that had an authorized user." Sione pressed a thumb against the center of his forehead, trying to rub out the numbing ache throbbing beneath his skull, an ache spurred by the anger and sadness growing inside him, emotions he wasn't sure how to process.

"So, you authorized somebody to use that card?"

Slowly sinking into his chair, Sione nodded, his mind in turmoil, thoughts and questions swirling and tumbling.

"Who?"

"Marie, I want you to book me the next flight to Houston," Sione said, his heart slamming, barely able to catch his breath as he pulled out one of his desk drawers, looking for some aspirin.

Marie protested. "Why would you want to go back there?"

Sione stared at her. "Because the authorized user on that Visa card was Spencer."

Marie frowned. "Spencer? Ms. Edwards? You think *she* charged all that baby stuff? Why would she do that?"

"Why the hell do you think, Marie?" Sione jumped up, glaring at his assistant. "Spencer is pregnant. She's having my baby."

22

Somewhere over the Gulf of Mexico

Forty-five minutes into his two-hour flight to Houston, Sione was antsy, fidgety, and anxious to get the hell off the plane. He couldn't figure out if his decision to return to Houston was a good idea or a disaster waiting to blow up in his face.

What would he do when he was face to face with Spencer again after all this time? He couldn't wait, but he wasn't ready. He didn't know what he was going to say to her. What could he say? How could he explain? How could he make her understand? How could he do anything except just beg her to give him a chance to tell her how sorry he was for how stupid and selfish he'd been?

Sitting in first class, Sione took a deep breath. It was impossible to know what he would say to Spencer when he saw her again. He would have to trust his heart to be his guide and hope his sentiment was sincere and would convince her that he loved her and wanted to spend the rest of his life with her. Somehow, he had to make her believe he loved the baby, too, and wanted to be a father to their child.

Smiling to himself, Sione thought of the little elephants in his luggage in the overhead cabin bin. The stuffed toys had been an impromptu purchase. Initially, he'd grabbed the pale pink pachyderm, because he loved the idea of a little girl who would grow up to be just as beautiful as her mother. Secretly, the thought of a son stole his heart, and he picked up a baby blue elephant, as well.

Sione stared at the glass of scotch he'd asked the stewardess for but still hadn't touched. The stuffed elephants had almost given his mother a hissing fit. Yesterday, while he packed for the trip back to Texas, Carmen showed up at the casita with her two cents. Marie had given his mother and his Aunt Perla the news, and of course, Carmen thought flying back to Houston to reunite with Spencer was a dangerous idea. One moment, his mother pleaded and shrieked, begging him not to go, and the next she was eerily calm and methodical, using logic to explain why he shouldn't go.

Carmen didn't think Spencer was pregnant. If she was, then his mother doubted the baby was Sione's. After all, Spencer was a bitchy slut who had probably found some other wealthy businessman to scam after Sione had wised up and kicked her scheming ass to the curb.

"The baby is mine," Sione had said, adamant, pissed his mother would even suggest Spencer could possibly be carrying another man's child.

"You don't know that for sure," his mother said, the calm demeanor fading. "At least get a DNA test first!"

"I don't need a DNA test," Sione said. "The baby is mine. Spencer hasn't been with anybody else since we broke up."

"How do you know that for sure?" Carmen demanded. "Are you

having her followed or something? You got somebody in Houston keeping tabs on her for you?"

"I just know, okay," Sione said, though he wasn't sure how. "It's my baby."

"Sione Dwayne," Carmen said in that passive tone that warned of an impending explosion. "Spencer is a very beautiful girl. Lots of men, I'm sure, are attracted to her. I find it hard to believe that after you dumped her, she sat around crying over you. Do you really think she kept her legs closed in honor of what the two of you supposedly had, which turned out to be nothing."

"What we had was everything," Sione told her. "But I was too stupid to realize that, and now I want it all back."

"Is that right? You want it all back?" Carmen asked, a derisive curiousness in her voice. "Everything? Even the lies? And the scams? Your cousins told me all about her and how she used to drug men and steal from them. That's what you want back? A woman you can't even trust to pour you a drink?"

Sighing, Sione said, "Is she perfect? No. She's made mistakes."

"She's done a lot more than just made a few mistakes," his mother had pointed out, scowling at him. "She's a thief. She's broken the law."

"Mom, please."

"What about Ben Chang?" his mother asked, a challenge in her steely gaze.

"What?"

"You really want to be with another woman who was involved with his crooked ass?" Carmen asked. "You know what happened with that bitch Moana!"

A piercing jolt had passed through him, not surprisingly. Moana's name would probably always paralyze him for a few moments, considering what he'd done to her, even though he wasn't sure if he'd killed her or not. But, he'd meant to, and he'd tried his best to choke her to death.

"What if the baby is Ben's?" Carmen suggested, obviously hoping he might entertain suspicions of Spencer, but Sione hadn't taken the bait. The idea almost brought him to his knees, though. If the baby was Ben's, Sione knew he would be devastated.

"Or what if she plans to use the baby to take you for every dime you have!"

"Mom, listen to me," Sione said, trying to combat his mother's burgeoning hysteria. "I love Spencer. I want to be with her and raise our baby together. And I'm going back to Houston to make my intentions clear. I know that's not what you want to hear, but that's what's going to happen. And there is nothing you can do or say to stop me."

As the plane glided through the clouds, Sione thought about his mother's disappointment. He hadn't wanted to upset Carmen, but if he had listened to her, he would have punished himself by staying away from Spencer. What was the point of trying to prove he could move on without Spencer? He was sick of pretending he didn't want to be with her. He was sick of being miserable without her. He'd tried to resign himself to misery and find some way to live with it, but he'd failed. The constant struggling and wrestling and fighting with his feelings were exhausting.

He didn't want to be with any other woman but her.

He'd finally admitted that to himself. Now it was time to let Spencer know he couldn't live without her. Or their baby.

It was time to let Spencer know he wouldn't live without them.

23

Rae Bedard's gray eyes widened as shock, disbelief, and confusion flashed across her face, but seconds later, the eyes narrowed, darkening to smoky brimstone.

Appropriate, Sione thought, since he was absolutely sure Spencer's sultry, abrasive sister was about to give him hell.

Bracing himself for an onslaught of fury, Sione took a breath and prepared to stand his ground, feet planted firmly on the welcome mat at the front door entry of Shady's modest home, where he'd found out Spencer was staying.

As he'd suspected, Rae's unleashed fury was hellish, but he resolved to endure her caustic insults, judgments, and opinions about the shitty way he'd treated Spencer for no damn good reason; he forced himself to withstand her verbal brutality. He would put up with it, as long as when it was over, she stepped aside and let him in the house so he could see Spencer.

"My sister doesn't need or want you in her life," Rae said. "So, why don't you just go back to wherever you came from. Better yet, go to hell!"

After a few more choice invectives, Rae tried to slam the door in his face. Anticipating her intent, Sione stopped her, pushing the door back and forcing her to retreat backward into the small foyer. An aggressive move. He wasn't proud of his excessive force, but he didn't regret it. He wasn't leaving until he saw Spencer, until he could tell her how sorry he was and how he desperately wanted her to give him a chance to prove his love and devotion to her and the baby.

"I want to see Spencer," he told her. "I'm not leaving until I do."

"What makes you think Spencer is here," Rae sneered.

"DJ told me that Spencer was staying here."

"Spencer doesn't want to see you," Rae said. "And after what you did to her, you don't deserve to see her!"

"I know I hurt Spencer, but—"

"You hurt her? Is that what you think you did?" Rae asked. "You did so much more than hurt her! Hitting her in the face would hurt her. Saying something mean and insulting would hurt her. You destroyed my sister. You put a knife in her heart. You almost killed her. You know, I didn't sleep that night. I couldn't. I stayed up all night watching her, scared to death that she was going to hurt herself!"

Sione looked away, feeling like a heartless bastard. He hated the thought of Spencer broken and abandoned, because of him.

"You shouldn't have come here. You need to leave."

"I'm not going anywhere until I see Spencer."

"She doesn't want to see you," Rae said.

"Then let Spencer tell me she doesn't want to see me," Sione said. "Where is she?"

"What part of she doesn't want to have anything to do with you do you not understand?" Rae glared at him. "You made it very clear that you didn't want her in your life, so why did you come back?"

"I came back to tell her that I love her," he said. "And that I can't live without her. I came back to ask her to forgive me."

"You think you deserve forgiveness?" Rae asked. "After what you did? You kicked her out in the middle of the night, half-naked and barefoot! You better be glad that our sister, Shady, always prays for us, because anything could have happened to Spencer! She could have gotten hit by a car, left to bleed to death in a ditch somewhere."

Rubbing his chin, Sione took a breath and tried not to do something he might regret. Antagonizing Rae wasn't a good idea. A combative, defensive attitude would only hinder his chance to talk to Spencer. Rae's condemning judgment shamed him. He'd been unnecessarily brutal to Spencer that night. He'd wanted to hurt her. He hadn't given one thought to any dire consequences she might have suffered because of his cruelty.

If something bad had happened to Spencer that night, because of him, Sione would never have forgiven himself.

"I think you should go."

Standing his ground, Sione shook his head. "I need to see her."

"I'll tell her you stopped by," Rae said. "And maybe, if she wants to see you, which I doubt she will, then she'll call you."

"I'm not leaving until I talk to her," Sione said, unfazed by the wicked evil eye Rae gave him. "If she's not here, then I'll wait. But, I have to tell her how I feel. She has to know that I still love her. I never stopped loving her, and I never will…"

———

Standing in the hallway around the corner from the living area, Spencer listened, barely able to move, barely able to believe John was here.

With shaking hands, she wiped away tears.

Rae's ranting and raving took her back to the night she'd tried to forget, the worst night of her life. The night John had told her to leave. He'd kicked her out of the house, wearing nothing but a kimono, with no shoes on her feet. Barefoot, she'd managed to walk to the guard house at the front of the gated community. The guard on duty, a young guy she sometimes waved to, recognized her but didn't interrogate her. The tears and disheveled appearance seemed to unnerve him, initially, but he regained his composure. After making sure she wasn't physically hurt and hadn't been assaulted and didn't need him to call the police, he allowed her to use the phone, and she called Rae.

Rae arrived with Mr. Cephas in his dark Bentley. Rae jumped out of the car and ran to Spencer, who collapsed in Rae's arms. Spencer didn't remember much about that night, but she vaguely recalled wanting to die, and maybe she'd said it out loud, but she didn't want John to know that...

She didn't want John to know how weak and helpless she'd been.

She was so ashamed when she thought of how she'd broken down, hadn't been able to keep it together, and had just given in to the desolation and despair, allowing it to drown her, swallow her whole.

Cradling her stomach, drawing strength from the little one, Spencer glanced at the ceiling. She didn't know what to do. Didn't know what to think. She still wasn't convinced that she wasn't dreaming. Moments ago, when she'd heard John's voice, it took her a moment before she'd recognized it. The voice had seemed familiar, but it had been so long since she'd heard the soothing baritone. She'd never thought she would hear it again.

Her emotions were all over the place from rage to elation to fear and back to an anger so intense that the only thing that quelled it was the little one growing within her. The baby kept her from giving in to the psychotic hysteria. The baby she and John had created together…

Spencer sighed and glanced at her barely there bump.

She would have to tell John about the baby, somehow, someway. Two months ago, she would have given anything to have John come back into her life and tell her he was sorry and he still loved her. Now, she wasn't so sure, especially since, in the past week, she'd found peace after arriving at a resolute conclusion. She'd spent the days in thoughtful introspection instead of furtive panic and forlorn sobbing. Seven days had passed and not once had she cycled through the stages of grief. One hundred sixty hours with no desolate hysteria washing over her, propelling her to the brink of insanity and back. Yesterday, while on her morning power walk, she became more and more convinced it was time to give up the silly fantasies about being with John. There was no hope of reconciliation. She loved John, but maybe, love just wasn't enough.

And now, just when she'd given up on John, he was in the living room with Rae, demanding to see her and saying all the things she wanted to hear.

"Where is Spencer?" John was asking. "In one of the bedrooms?"

"Don't worry about where she is," Rae snapped. "You weren't worried about where she was when you kicked her out of the house, so why are you worried about where she is now?"

"Spencer!" John called out.

Gasping, pressing a hand against her mouth, Spencer took a step forward but then immediately retreated two steps back as John called her name again, his voice loud and commanding and yet holding notes of intense longing.

Still frozen, she didn't know what to do. In the next few seconds, he was going to turn down the hallway, and he would see her...unless she ran back to her bedroom and locked the door behind her. Did she want to hide from John? She didn't know.

"Spencer!"

"Leave her alone!" Rae said. "She doesn't want to see you. Don't go back there, or I will call the cops, I swear!"

"Spencer!"

Panicked, Spencer turned and hurried down the hall toward her bedroom. She couldn't see John. Not right now. She wasn't ready. She felt blindsided by his presence. Sucker punched. She needed a moment to think. She needed to—

"Spencer..." John's voice seemed right behind her, low and tender. "Wait a minute...please..."

24

———

Houston, Texas
Torrey Chase Subdivision

Spencer turned and looked up.

John was still as tall, muscular, and handsome as he'd been the day she first saw him.

It would have served him right if, in the months without her, he'd shrank, lost his good looks, and gained four hundred pounds, but she supposed that was too damn much to ask.

At once, memories attacked her.

All the time they'd spent together flashed before her eyes. Vivid images of intimate moments mocked her and told her she should have known John would never love her—that she would never be good enough for him. He'd shown her she wasn't good enough two months ago, on a humid night in October.

She remembered walking down the middle of the street, stumbling, sobbing, and shivering. Instead of the desolation which usually accompanied that memory, Spencer felt a spark of rage. John had shoved her out of the house with derision and disgust, as though he had never loved her, as though they didn't belong together.

Spencer felt her chest tighten and felt the anger intensifying.

The urge to slap him was sudden and strong, but she took a breath and then let it out. She wasn't going to act like a wild, psychotic bitch. She would be civil and polite, the gracious Southern girl her grandmother had taught her to be. And the little one was helping to tame her ire.

"John, what are you doing here?" she asked. "What do you want?"

"I love you and I want you back," he said. "I've been miserable without you, and I hate myself for the way I hurt you. It was cruel and selfish..."

"So, all of a sudden, you love me again," Spencer said, frustrated and tense, desperate not to give in to him, even though he was saying exactly what she wanted to hear, saying everything she'd hoped and dreamed he would say. "After all this time—"

"I never stopped loving you."

"Yes, you did, John," she disputed. "When you kicked me out, you said—"

"I never said I didn't love you," he said.

"But you did say you didn't want me in your life," she reminded him. "You said—"

"I said a lot of stuff that I didn't really mean that night," he said.

"Are you sure you really want to be with me? Can you really forgive me for what I did? Can you even try to understand that I made a stupid, horrible mistake? I know there is nothing I can do to make up for it, and if I could do it all over—"

"If you could do it all over, you would probably make the same bad decisions." He took a step closer to her. "Because you would be in the same damn impossible situation. You made the worst mistake of your life when you stole from Ben. That mistake gave him the power to ruin you. He took advantage of you, making you think that you owed him something. But I didn't come here to talk about past mistakes or Ben Chang. I'm here because I want us to be together. I'm here to fight for us."

Confused, Spencer stared at him, touched and yet terrified by the unabashed devotion in his hazel eyes.

"I tried to tell myself that I would be fine without you," John said. "Tried to convince myself that I was going to move on with my life and—"

"And you probably should," she conceded. "You need to find a woman who can be Mrs. Tuiali'i—a kind, selfless, compassionate woman."

"If I found that woman, it wouldn't matter," he said. "She wouldn't make me forget about you."

"Don't say that," she warned. "Don't tell me…"

"Don't tell you what?" he asked. "The truth? Don't tell you that I love you and I want to spend the rest of my life with you?"

"Don't say things you don't really mean," she told him.

"I mean every word," John said. "I love you. I want—"

"Nobody gives a shit about what you want," Rae said, walking down the hall toward them. "You need to leave. My sister doesn't—"

John faced Rae. "Can you please just let me have a chance to talk to Spencer alone?"

"Spencer doesn't want to talk to you." Slipping around John, Rae stood in front of Spencer, acting as a barrier, though Spencer could still see John, looming over both of them. "You should get the hell out of here. Now."

"Is that what you want?" John asked, staring down at Spencer. "You want me to leave?"

Spencer looked down. She really didn't know what she wanted. She just knew she couldn't talk to John right now. She didn't really know how she felt about him or their situation. She was going to have to deal with him. There was no getting around that. John was back in her life, like it or not, but she wasn't sure if it was a blessing or a curse.

"Spencer?" John prodded.

Glancing at him, Spencer opened her mouth, but words wouldn't come. She didn't know what to say or how to say it. She wanted to explain her feelings, but she didn't understand them herself. With tears threatening, Spencer shook her head, turned, and hurried into the bedroom. John tried to follow her, but Rae blocked him, and Spencer was able to close and lock the door.

Trembling, she walked to the bed and threw herself across it, burying her face in the pillow as she cried.

25

———————

Houston, Texas

Torrey Chase Subdivision

"Maybe you should talk to him," Rae suggested, standing in the doorway of the bedroom Shady had converted into an office.

Spencer glanced away from the computer to frown at her sister and then cut her gaze back to the screen. "I'm busy."

For the past two hours, Spencer had been browsing mommy-to-be blogs, online baby stores, and several "what to expect when expecting" websites. Normally, at nine in the morning, she'd be halfway finished with her morning walk, but she'd suspended that practice last week—because of John.

Sighing, Spencer asked, "Is he outside?"

"Where else would he be except where he'd been every day for the past two weeks?" Rae asked. "Parked across the street. From sunup to sundown. Pathetic asshole. Fucking stalker."

With an irritated exhale, Rae left, grumbling curses.

Spencer sat back in the chair and rubbed her eyes, wondering if Rae was right. Maybe it was time to have a long, serious conversation with John. But would doing so help the situation or make it worse. Ignoring him hadn't worked, that was for sure. Insisting she didn't want to see him again hadn't made him any less adamant about his intentions.

Since his return two weeks ago, John had been determined to prove he wasn't leaving until she changed her mind about being with him. He'd been camped out across the street from Shady's house, watching, waiting for her to leave the house and when she did, he would follow her wherever she went, hoping and praying for a chance to talk to her.

The day John had come back Spencer had thought he'd head back to Belize after Rae kicked him out. But, the next morning, when she'd left the house to do her power walk, she was shocked and irritated, and maybe secretly thrilled, to find him walking next to her.

Trying to walk faster than him was pointless. John was tall, and for every stride he took, she had to take three. As a result, she was forced to listen as he'd begun to tell her everything she wanted to hear. She struggled not to take his words to heart. But then he said something that stopped her in her tracks and yet made her want to run for the hills.

"I want us to have the future that we want and deserve. You, me…and our baby."

Flabbergasted, Spencer had stared up at him, shielding her eyes from the sun. "You know about the baby?"

John nodded and smiled. Spencer had taken a step back and then looked down and bit her bottom lip so she wouldn't smile back at him. She wasn't quite ready to let him see the joy reflected on her face.

"How?" she asked, and when he told her, Spencer hadn't been surprised. It was Rae's damn fault for using John's VISA card.

Spencer said, "So, that's why you came back. Because of the baby."

"I came back because I love you," John insisted. "I never should have let you go."

"You didn't let me go," she scoffed, noticing a U-Haul truck idling in front of a two-story brick house, halfway down the street. "You kicked me out."

His expression pained, John said, "I shouldn't have kicked you out. It was cruel, and I—"

"It doesn't matter," she said, arms crossed, watching the moving van struggle to back into the driveway. "What matters is that we don't belong together."

"Don't say that."

"I have to say it," she said. "Because it's true."

"You don't believe that." He stepped closer to her. "You know we belong together. You, me, and our baby."

"It's not going to be you, me, and the baby," she said, feeling slightly manic, as though she were about to say something she would never be able to take back, something that would make her cringe and kick herself later. "It's never going to be you, me, and the baby, and do you know why? Because you don't deserve to be with me and my baby! Me and my baby will be fine without you! We don't need you!"

"Are you saying that you're not going to let me have anything to do with the baby?" John asked. "You would really try to keep me out of the baby's life?"

"I'm saying that I wish you didn't know about the baby."

John stared at her, and for a minute or two, she thought she might have gotten to him, might have finally convinced him that trying to reunite was a losing battle, one it was pointless to fight. Something flickered in his hazel eyes, darkening the irises to a moss green, reminding her of how his eyes would change colors whenever he made love to her.

The animosity in his gaze began to fade, and in its place, there seemed to be a mix of disillusionment and despair.

Her own spitefulness started to wane, diminishing rapidly, leaving behind regret, frustration, and confusion. And shame. What the hell was her problem? She sounded like some vengeful, overemotional baby mama.

There was anguish in his hazel eyes. It had been too much for her to withstand. As she'd hurried away from him, John hadn't followed her, and she figured she'd accomplished what she'd set out to do—drive John away. Back at the house, she'd sunk to the floor, sobbing and heaving, unable to catch her breath.

She'd been convinced she would never see John again. She tried to convince herself that allowing John to walk away from her and the baby was for the best, but she didn't believe that. All she wanted in the world was to be with John and raise their baby together. But she was wary of giving their love another chance. They'd loved each other when John had broken her heart. Love hadn't been enough to keep them together then. How could love be enough to bring them back together now?

Surprisingly, John had been waiting for her again, the following morning. And he'd brought a present for the baby. Two presents, actually. Two stuffed elephants, one pink and the other blue. As soon as Spencer saw them, her heart started to melt, but she steeled herself.

"Don't know if you're having a boy or girl," John had said. "But either way…"

Despite her reservations, Spencer had accepted the gifts, and to this day, she found she couldn't get to sleep without the elephants. The blue one, especially, she found comforting, and she started to think she might be having a boy.

"So, are you gonna talk to him or not?" Rae cut into her reverie.

"You think I should?" Spencer asked.

"I don't know," Rae said, walking into the home office. "Two weeks ago, I would have told you to tell him to kiss your ass, but now…"

"But now what?"

"But now I think maybe he does really want to be with you and the baby," Rae said. "Maybe he is sorry for being a heartless asshole and he wants to prove his love, or whatever. I don't know."

"You think I should give him a chance?" Spencer asked, hopeful.

Tilting her head, Rae asked, "Do you think you should give him a chance? Or I guess a better question is, do you want to give him a chance?"

———

Her heart beating wildly, Spencer used her index finger to tap on the driver's window of John's SUV. The automatic window descended, and John stared at her, smiling slightly. He hadn't shaved in a few days, and the facial hair gave him a rugged look. Not quite savage, but a bit untamed. Exciting and appealing in a way she wasn't exactly used to.

"Hi," he said.

"Good morning," she said, deciding to keep things formal. "I'm going for a walk."

He nodded, waiting.

Spencer sighed and then said, "You can come with me if you want."

John didn't hesitate to exit the Range Rover, and minutes later, they were strolling down the street at a leisurely pace, not hand in hand, but side by side. Close enough that they accidentally brushed against each other every now and then. Each time, it gave Spencer a jolt, reminding her of just how long it had been since she and John had been together. She missed being in his arms and wanted him to hold her and kiss her and make love to her.

"You been feeling okay?" John asked, after several moments of silence, during which Spencer worried she might be overwhelmed, or overcome, by John's presence. She hadn't forgotten how tall and sexy he was. Not seeing him for two months had done nothing to diminish the effect he had on her.

Spencer nodded. "I've been okay."

"Just wondered because you stopped taking your morning walk."

"Well, that's your fault," she snapped, picking up the pace a bit, swinging her arms. "Every time I opened the door to go out, there you were, parked across the street."

John said nothing. Spencer glanced up at him. His hazel eyes reflected a tempting mix of self-effacing amusement and desire, and she looked away, chiding herself for being enticed.

"Why have you been sitting in your car in front of my sister's house?" she asked, trying to pay attention to her breathing as she struggled to ignore the euphoria of being so close to John again. The giddiness was irritating, and she feared it might make her do something rash and foolish.

"Waiting for this moment we're having right now," he said.

"How long were you going to sit out there?" she asked, determined to ignore her silly emotions and enjoy the warm early morning December sunshine.

"For as long as it took," he said. "I told myself every day from dawn to dusk."

"So, you went back to your hotel at night?"

"Didn't want to," he admitted. "I thought about staying out in front of the house twenty-four hours a day, but I knew I would need to get some sleep, and shower, and maybe get some work done."

"You didn't have to go through all that," she said as they rounded the corner, staying close to the curb.

"Yeah, I did, and I'm glad I did," he said. "Imagine if I hadn't. We wouldn't be having this moment."

"Well, now that we are having this moment," she said and cleared her throat.

John didn't say anything, waiting for her to go on, she supposed.

"I *am* glad you know about the baby," she admitted.

"I'm just happy we created this beautiful life and now we get to raise the baby together."

"About that," Spencer said, trying to steel herself against the effects of his words.

"About what?"

"Raising the baby together," she said. "I don't know if that's a good idea."

"Why not?"

"Because we're not together anymore," Spencer said.

"About that," he said.

Wary, she asked, "About what?"

"Me and you not being together," he said. "I don't think that's a good idea. Meeting you and having you in my life is the best thing that has ever happened to me."

"That can't possibly be true," she disputed. "John, you met me because I came to Belize to trick you. I came to drug you so I could snoop through your casita and find an envelope for Ben Chang. I lied to you, and—"

"Listen to me," he said, stepping in front of her, without warning, forcing her to stop. "When I say you're the best thing that happened to me, I mean that. I wanted to find someone I could fall in love with, someone I could love and who would really love me, and I wanted a family, and you're going to give me the child I always wanted. All that has happened for me because I met you."

"John, why are you saying all these things right now?" she asked, staring at the concrete curb, unable to meet his gaze.

"Because I want you to know how I feel about you."

"How you feel about me doesn't change anything," she said, walking around him, hurrying away.

"Spencer, wait," he called out.

"I know what you're doing," she said, glancing back at him. "You're saying all the right things, trying to make it hard for me to walk away from this relationship, which is what I should do."

"Why do you want to walk away?" he asked. "Why don't you want to try to make this work between us?"

Abruptly, she stopped and spun to face him, not surprised to find him inches away. "Before you decided to just come back into my life without asking me first, I had made a decision about us."

"I made a decision about us, too."

"I decided to give up my fantasies of being with you," she said, "because I knew they weren't going to come true."

"Well, I decided to come back to Houston and tell you that the dreams we had of being together forever are still alive," he said, "and I'm going to do whatever I have to so that all those dreams come true."

Spencer wanted to scream at him. Why the hell was he saying all the right things? And why was he so damn sincere? His conviction made it impossible to dispute his feelings. She couldn't stop herself from believing his promises.

"Spencer?"

She opened her mouth to tell him he was a fool if he really thought their pipe dreams of happily ever after could possibly come true, but the words stuck in her throat. Bursting into tears, she dropped her face in her hands. A moment later, his arms wrapped around her, pulling her close. Unable to pretend she didn't want to be exactly where she was, Spencer gave in, allowing herself the luxury and comfort of his strong protective embrace.

26

Houston, Texas
Torrey Chase Subdivision

"Do you want some tea?" Spencer asked, opening the pantry door, taking a box of Celestial Seasonings from the shelf. "I would offer you coffee, but I can't have it."

"Tea is fine," John said, taking a seat at the table in the breakfast nook at the opposite end of the galley kitchen.

As she removed teacups from an overhead cabinet, Spencer relished the opportunity to concentrate on a mundane task as she struggled to keep it together and regain her composure. Bristling, she got the tea kettle from its spot next to the microwave and tried to ignore the memories of her emotional breakdown. Twenty minutes ago, on a quiet street in a well-kept suburban neighborhood, she'd allowed John's heartfelt promises and tender vows to weaken her resolve to move on without him. Now, back at

Shady's, she hoped to regain her determination to resist his attempts at reconciliation.

At the sink, she filled the kettle, admonishing herself not to give in, no matter what John said or how good it sounded or how much she wanted to hear it.

"Actually, what I want more than a cup of tea is for you to come over here so we can talk."

After taking the kettle to the range and placing it on a back burner, Spencer took a deep breath, hesitating. "What do we need to talk about, John?"

"I don't believe that you don't want us to be together again," he said.

"I don't want to rush into anything," she said, staring at the stovetop. "We need to really think about if we belong together or not."

"I know we belong together," he said. "I don't need to think about it.

"We need to see if we could really make a relationship work," she insisted. "It takes more than love, and lust, and wanting to be with each other, it takes work."

"This is what I know," he said. "I love you and I want to be with you. Can we make a relationship work? I think we have to. We don't have a choice. I have to make this work with you because I can't live without you."

"Me or the baby?" Spencer challenged, facing him. "Because the truth is that you wouldn't have come back if you hadn't found out that I was pregnant."

"The truth is that I never should have left."

"You mean you never should have kicked me out?" she asked, arms folded.

"No, I shouldn't have told you to leave," he said. "That was the worst mistake I've ever made in my life. These past months without you have been absolutely miserable. You told me I would be miserable without you, and you were right."

"No, you were probably better without me."

"Listen, I'm not leaving until I get what I really want."

Spencer stared at him, confused. "And what do you really want?"

"I want you to come home with me, where you belong,"

"I don't know where I belong," she said, turning back to the range.

"You belong with me," he said. "At our house in The Woodlands."

"John, what are you talking about?" She looked over at him. "Our house in The Woodlands? What house in The Woodlands?"

"I bought us a house in The Woodlands," he said. "I know you like that neighborhood."

"I hope you didn't buy that house that you kicked me out of," she said, her blood pressure spiking. "Because I am never going back to that house."

"I didn't buy that house," he said, frowning slightly. "It wasn't for sale, and I wouldn't have bought it if it had been on the market. I don't want to go back to that house, either."

"You shouldn't have done that," she said, watching as steam began to escape the spout of the kettle. "And if you think some giant house in The Woodlands is going to be enough to get me back, then you're wrong."

"Then what do I need to do to get you back?" he asked, standing. "Because I don't want to be without you."

Spencer sighed, worried as he approached her. "Please don't say things you don't mean."

"What makes you think I don't mean it?" he asked. "I'm not going to live without you."

"Even if that would be the best thing for you?" Spencer asked, unable to move as he advanced.

"I've tried to be away from you," he said. "It doesn't work for me. I can't pretend I don't want to be with you."

She looked down, trying not to get her hopes up.

"Look at me," he said, lifting her chin, forcing her to look into his eyes to see the sincerity in his gaze. "You are the only woman I want."

"You want to be with me even though I'm not selfless and compassionate?" she asked. "You want to be with a selfish bitch?"

"That's not what you are."

"You said I was."

"I didn't mean it," he said. "I wanted to hurt you."

"You did a lot more than just hurt me, John," she said. "You pretty much destroyed me that night. I hate saying that out loud. I hate admitting that to you. But, it's true."

"I know I was harsh and cruel and heartless," he said. "And I know I can't take back what I said or expect you to forgive me or even move past it. That night will always be between us, and we'll never forget it, but hopefully we can move on from it."

"I don't know if I can move on," she told him.

"Look, you and I love each other," he said. "That means we owe it to each other to fight for what we have."

"But I don't know if I want to fight for our love," she said. "It's a fight I don't think I would win."

He shook his head. "Don't say that."

"I know you don't want to hear this," she said, "but being in love with you has only made me miserable and sad and terrified."

"I know I broke your heart—"

"John, you broke more than my heart, you broke me," she said. "Now you say we need to fight for our love, but I told you I loved you that night. I begged you to believe in my love for you, and you told me I was a lying bitch and you wanted me out of your life."

"I didn't mean any of those things I said," he told her. "I was hurt so I wanted you to hurt."

"You did hurt me," she said. "But, even more than that, you made me feel stupid and ashamed of myself because I felt like I'd brought all that heartbreak on myself. All that emotional pain and trauma was my own damn fault. It was what I deserved for falling in love with you when I knew better. I knew you were going to hurt me, and you did. And I knew I was going to disappoint you, and I did. So knowing all that, why the hell did I let myself fall for you?"

He sighed and stared at her with a pained expression, something between shame and frustration.

"Knowing all that," she went on, "why would I set myself up to be emotionally decimated again? I don't need any more pain. I have enough already. My heart is still broken. I haven't really gotten over what you did to me that night."

"I'll help you get over what I did to you," he said. "All I want is another chance with you. All I want to know is, do you want to be with me? Do you want to start over? Do you want to try to make this work between us?"

Staring at John, she felt an odd courage, a tenacious boldness rising within her, urging her to see what might happen if she took a chance with John.

A daunting prospect. Very audacious, and probably foolish, but she wanted to try. The truth was, she was too much in love with John to just walk away, especially when he wanted to be with her, too. But loving him terrified her. How the hell was she supposed to be the kind of woman John wanted? He was probably better off without her, she knew. She would be doing him a favor if she walked away from their love.

Spencer looked up at him, and just that quick, she knew the last thing she wanted was to say goodbye to him. She wanted to be with him. She wanted them to raise the little one together, as a family.

"I want to be with you…" She closed her eyes and pressed her cheek against his chest as he held her tighter. "Forever."

27

———————

**The Woodlands, Texas
Carlton Woods Gated Community**

Afternoon sunshine floated through the French doors of the master bedroom of the mansion in The Woodlands, the beautiful Mediterranean showpiece they had returned to last night, the dream house she and John had moved into three weeks ago.

It was hushed and calm in the room. A beautiful golden presence seemed to have fallen over the atmosphere, like a spell.

Lying in John's arms was like being in a sanctuary. Their bodies were so close it was as though they were fused together. Spencer wanted to be even closer. She wanted to seep into John, little by little, until separation was impossible.

Part of her hated those thoughts. They terrified her and confused her. *She wanted to seep into him.* What the hell did that even mean? Was it even remotely possible? Did she really want to totally immerse herself in a man, to bury herself in his soul, in his flesh? Wasn't that something "that wife" would do? And wasn't she supposed to resist and wrestle against foolish thoughts which might trick her into becoming "that wife" to a man?

Spencer wasn't sure if she knew who she was anymore. Her emotions were out of control, unfamiliar. Pregnancy hormones, she'd decided. Sometimes, though, she didn't want to think of John's embrace as a place of solace and comfort. Sometimes, she wondered if she should have given up the fantasies of forever with John. Maybe she should have moved on with her life as a single mother, just her and the baby.

Talk about a crazy, hormonal thought. She didn't want to live her life without John. She couldn't stand being away from him. Two months had been too long, almost like an eternity. How the hell could she survive forever without him? All she wanted to do was fall asleep in John's arms every night and wake up next to him every morning.

Spencer hooked a leg over John's waist and pressed her face against his chest.

"Are you awake?"

Snuggling closer to him, she said, "Yeah, sort of."

"Good," he said.

"Why is it good that I'm awake," she said, anxious for more of John's lovemaking. Two months of abstinence had definitely been too long, but since their reconciliation, they'd been making up for lost time, every day, several times a day.

"Well…" He cleared his throat. "I wanted to ask you about your next doctor's appointment."

"What about it?"

"I wanted to ask if I could come with you."

Elated, and not entirely surprised, Spencer repositioned herself, nestling in the crook of his arm so she could gaze up at him. "You want to come to the doctor with me? Really?"

Nodding, he said, "Really. I do. Actually, I, um, I wish I could have been with you for all the appointments."

"I'm sorry that I didn't tell you about the baby as soon as I knew I was pregnant," Spencer said, looking down.

"Well, you can make it up to me by telling me the story of how you found out you were pregnant," he suggested.

Spencer groaned good-naturedly. "John, I've told you that story a million times."

"I know, but I love that story," he said, holding her closer. "It's the best story in the whole world."

"You're silly," she said, giggling, though she loved the story. She was always happy and excited when John requested a retelling, which was at least once a day, and she never tired of recounting the details, to his delight. Without further prompting, and with much drama, she launched into the tale. Normally, the fifteen-minute story took an hour because John always interjected with questions, but she always managed to cover the major points. After realizing her period was two weeks late, she'd been worried and had confided in Rae, who'd suggested she might be pregnant. Flabbergasted, Spencer had initially disputed her sister's diagnosis. She couldn't possibly be pregnant. Four home pregnancy tests proved her wrong.

"Can't believe you thought I would be mad at you for getting pregnant," he said, when she'd finished the story, about an hour later.

"John, I need to be honest with you about something," she said, glancing away from the worry in his gaze.

"About what?"

Beneath her cheek, his heart raced, but not as fast as hers. "It wasn't that I thought you'd be mad about the baby. I figured you wanted kids someday. I just didn't know if you would want them with me.

"Why wouldn't I want kids with the most beautiful woman in the world who I happen to be crazy in love with?"

"Are you sure you want me to be the mother of your child?" She stared at him, unable to share his levity. "You know I didn't exactly have the best example of motherhood. I probably won't know what the hell I'm doing."

Taking her hand, he pressed his lips against her palm and then asked, "Do you think that because your mother neglected you, I'm going to think you would be a bad mother?"

She pulled her hand away, disturbed by his accurate discernment of her concerns.

"She didn't just neglect me. She abused me. She was crazy and hateful to me. I don't ever remember her being affectionate, or anything, like what a mother was supposed to be," Spencer said. "I remember when I started going to school, my classmates would be picked up after school, and they would run into their mothers' outstretched arms, and their moms would hug them and kiss them and be so happy to see them. It was never like that with me and my mother. She didn't really acknowledge my presence very much.

"I was just this lonely kid, staying quiet and out of her way, so she wouldn't throw something at me. But I never knew what would make her mad. I would try to be good and...but, I didn't really know what she wanted me to be. All I knew was that whatever she wanted, I wasn't it. When I turned six, the physical abuse really escalated. And then, she wasn't the best provider. I was always hungry. And she would leave me alone for weeks at a time. Finally, when I was seven, she left and she didn't come back. I was so terrified, and I knew it was my fault, and—"

"It wasn't your fault."

"Then why did she leave? Why didn't she want me? Why didn't she love me? I don't understand," Spencer said, unable to stop her tears. "Everybody talks about this motherly instinct and how as soon as you see your baby you fall in love, but I don't think my mother had that experience."

"Maybe she didn't," he said. "And that is sad. But she must have been sick. She couldn't have been in her right mind, and that was a tragedy for both of you because she missed out on the experience of being a mother. You didn't get to be loved and taken care of like you should have been, like every child deserves to be."

Touched by his insight and sensitivity, she sobbed a bit harder for a moment, feeling once again like the scared, abandoned seven-year-old.

"I can't go back and change what happened to you," he said. "But I do love you and I always will. And I will take care of you, and I'll do what it takes so that you never feel neglected and abandoned again. I know your mother let you down, but I won't. I promise you. You can trust me."

Wiping her face, she sniffed and said, "But can you trust me? Can you trust that I won't lose my mind or—"

"You won't lose your mind," he said. "You're not your mother."

"You don't know that," she disputed. "And I can't bear the thought that I would do anything to hurt this baby or make him feel like I didn't love him with all my heart because I do."

"The baby knows you love him," he said. "I'm sure he can feel how much—wait, you said *him*? How do you know it's a boy? We haven't—"

"I just know it's a boy," Spencer said. "I can tell."

"How can you tell?"

"I don't know how," she said. "Maybe because of the blue elephant."

"The blue elephant?"

"The stuffed animal you gave me for the baby," she said. "I actually sleep with both of the little elephants, but I get restless if the blue elephant isn't right near my stomach."

"A boy…"

"Did you want a girl?" Worried, Spencer sat up, pulling the bed linens over her bare breasts as she stared at him. "You do know that you determine the sex of the baby, right?"

He smiled, looking contemplative. "Actually, I want both. A boy and a girl."

Spencer gave him a look. "Well, I can't help you because I'm not having twins."

"Maybe not now…" He pulled her into his arms again. "But…"

"But, what?" She moved her head to look at him.

"You might have twins later," he said, smiling. "When you get pregnant again."

"When I get pregnant again?" She sat up to gape at him. "You think I'm going to let you get me pregnant again? Ha! I think we're one and done."

Shaking his head, he gave her a sly, sexy grin. "I think we've just begun."

28

The Woodlands, Texas
Carlton Woods Gated Community

"What are you doing up so early?"

Stepping across the threshold into John's office, Spencer leaned against the doorway.

"Just wanted to get a jump on all the stuff I need to get done today," he said, staring at his computer screen. "What are you doing up so early? You feel okay? The baby okay? You have morning sickness?"

"No, I'm fine and the baby's fine." She walked to the chair in front of his desk. "And no morning sickness, not anymore, thank God. Though, it was more like afternoon sickness, and you should be glad that you weren't around for that..."

"I'm not glad about that." He turned from her, tapping on the keyboard, and then said, "I wish I could have been around to experience everything with you, even afternoon sickness."

Spencer cringed at his not so subtle reminder of how she hadn't told him about the baby and most likely would have kept the child a secret from him if he hadn't accidentally found out himself. It might always be a point of contention between them, one of those issues it was better not to discuss because they would never arrive at a resolution that was satisfactory to either of them.

It would always be something she could never really explain.

Something he wouldn't be able to understand.

"So…" she said. "You have a lot going on today?"

Staring at her, John leaned back in his chair. "Got enough."

"Okay, then, I'll leave you alone and let you get to it," she said and then turned, heading for the door.

"Spencer…"

Pivoting, she faced him.

"Come here."

Excited, anticipating, Spencer hurried to him when he beckoned for her, ignoring the warning in the back of her mind. Eagerly running to a man was something "that wife" would do, but she wasn't "that wife," and she never would be. Still, her jaded inner voice told her John was the kind of man she would always have to put forth effort to please. And maybe the exertion would deplete her, leave her gasping, hardly able to breathe.

Standing next to the large leather chair where he sat, gazing at her, she noticed his erection and immediately felt hot and wet and crazy.

John pulled her down onto his lap, slipping an arm around her waist, holding her close to that enormous bulge in his pants. "I need to tell you something…"

Worried, and yet aroused, she asked, "What?"

"You're very sexy when you're carrying my baby," John told her, moving his hand under the T-shirt she wore. "But I have to admit that I feel a little weird sometimes when we make love."

She opened her legs a bit. "Why do you feel weird?"

"Because the baby is here with us, you know," he said, his hands sliding along her leg, delving between her thighs.

"John, the baby's not born yet."

Slipping his hand inside the crotch of her panties, he said, "I know, but sometimes I feel like we're doing it in front of him."

"I think you have pregnancy brain, now," she said, a gasp escaping as his thumb moved lazily, clockwise around her clit. "We are not making love in front of the baby, don't be silly."

"Oh, speaking of pregnancy brain, I think you're right," he said, staring at her, his hazel eyes darkening to a moss green, reflecting the same desperate, seething desire that had her arching her back and rocking her hips against his hand. "I have found it hard to concentrate. I've been forgetful, too."

"You have any cravings?"

"Only for this..."

The finger inside her pushed deeper, then pulled back a fraction, and then slipped in farther, twirling and thrusting.

Heat pooled inside her, rushing along her hot, slippery walls, and all logical, coherent thoughts faded away until there was nothing left but the incessant, urgent need to have him inside her.

Without much fuss or fanfare, she pulled the T-shirt over her head and flung it behind her. Jumping from his lap, she got rid of her underwear, tossing the damp, lacy thong aside. Naked, she returned to the large, leather chair, and straddled him, then unzipped his pants.

Together, they freed his penis from the confines of his boxers.

Gasping, Spencer stared at it, huge and hard, and the ache between her legs intensified, growing to something she could barely contain. Anxious to impale herself on it, she wrapped both hands around his shaft and rose up on her knees, intent on guiding him inside her, but John grabbed her hips, holding her immobile.

"You got somewhere you need to be?" he asked and leaned forward, taking her right breast in his mouth. Slow and lazy, he licked her breast, his tongue gliding over her skin.

"Why do you ask that?" she asked, closing her eyes as his tongue swirled around the hard nipple.

"You seem kind of in a hurry." He moved his head back to give her a sexy, mischievous smile.

She stared at him as he moved to the other breast, sucking the nipple deep into his mouth. His hard, tantalizing pull on her nipple sent a torrent of something sinful and forbidden rushing through her from the tip of her breast to the core of her, and she moaned, clutching his huge, muscled shoulders. A flurry of bliss danced along the edges of her vagina, and she shuddered in anticipation of the moment when he entered her. She ached to ride him, hard and fast, so much that she thought she might beg for it.

"Well, right now," she said, moaning at the sensations swirling and dancing in and around her, "I really wish you would hurry up because I really have a problem with you not being inside me."

"Don't worry, sexy," he said, gripping her ass, holding her still, and giving her just enough slack to arch. "I'll be in there soon."

Barely able to breathe, she trembled as desire flowed through her.

Her slit hovered just above John's penis, and as he continued the assault on her breasts, he teased her with the large glistening tip. His large, strong hands held her in place, denying her what she wanted, what she needed; the head was close enough to send waves of ecstasy surging forward but not close enough to wash over her and drown her in a rush of pleasure.

"I don't need it soon, I need it now." She panted, trembling from his hot, wet mouth on her breast, tugging at the nipple, gently biting the taut, straining flesh.

"Stop being so impatient."

"Stop playing with me," she told him, quickly losing what little self-control she had left. "These hormones make me crazy horny. So, put it in me right now, or you'll never put it in me again."

"Well, since you put it that way," he said, lowering her a bit and allowing the head to push up inside her. Intense flutters surrounded her clit, and she grabbed his shoulders, sinking her nails into his flesh as raw, searing sweet agony surged through her.

Slow and deliberate, he filled her, and she felt every inch as it moved through her, throbbing and swelling all the way.

And when he was finally sheathed within her, she cried out, her body already convulsing as ripples of sizzling electricity radiated throughout her entire body.

He slid her up and down his long, thick length, over and over, his pace slow at first as she adjusted to him. Moments later, he sped up. Soon, she caught on to his rhythm, matching it with vigor and determination, moaning as she went over the edge.

But it wasn't enough. She wanted more.

Moaning and writhing, she leaned forward and kissed him, swirling her tongue in his mouth.

John stood, and she wrapped her legs around his waist as he walked to the couch and sank down on it, still inside her as she straddled him.

Holding onto his shoulders, she moved up and down on him, wild and maniacal. Each time she rose up, she squeezed him as hard as she could, and when she moved down, she was grinding against him, taking him in all the way. She saw the frown of painful pleasure on his face, and she knew she was affecting him the same way he was affecting her. The way they fit together was perfect, magical, and hypnotic. The way he hid in her and the way she cloaked him was mesmerizing, addictive. It wasn't long before she was thrashing and bucking, and when she came, she was screaming his name.

Collapsing against him, she was vaguely aware of him lifting her up and changing their positions. Soon she felt the warm, distressed leather against her back. Through the fog of lust, she saw him get rid of his shirt and pants.

Seconds later, he returned to her. His jaw set with determination and his eyes even darker, John put one of her legs around his waist and the other on his shoulder and then slid into her.

His pace chaotic and breathtaking, he gave her several, quick, deep thrusts, too many to count, and soon she felt another wave began to crest, and then a ferocious rapture crashed into her, pulling her under, drowning her in mind-numbing bliss.

Several hours later, Spencer sat in John's lap, curled in his arms as he leaned back in the big leather chair behind his desk.

As content as a feline, she was lethargic and ridiculously satisfied after two more sessions of blistering sex, one bent over the desk and another on the floor. She was a bit sore, but if he wanted her again, she would let him have her, even though she felt it was behavior only "that wife" would do.

But she *wasn't* "that wife," she reminded herself. She wasn't going to be "that wife." Still, if sex would always be this spectacular with John, she would be "that wife" all day long; she would never deny him.

"In a few days, I need to go back to Belize for a meeting with the bank," John said, breaking into her reverie. "I was hoping you would come with me."

"Are you sure you want me to go with you?" Spencer asked, wary. "Won't your mom and your family be horribly disappointed to see me?"

"There's something there that I want you to see," he said, caressing her cheek. "Something very important to me. So, please will you come?"

"Well, since you asked me in a way that makes it impossible to refuse you," she said, and then kissed him. "Yes, I'll go back to Belize with you."

29

"Where are you taking me?" Spencer asked as they hiked down a wide path through banyan trees, passing hibiscus, black orchid, bird of paradise, bamboo, and elephant trees as they traveled deeper into the jungle. It had rained early this morning, leaving behind puddles and humidity, but Spencer was used to the damp, cloistered atmosphere and the smell of bark and vegetation with hints of allspice and lush floral notes.

"You'll see," he promised, guiding her between two bushes, pushing aside the wide waxy leaves to expose a large clearing.

Supervising the tree house construction, John had pretty much lived in the rainforest since they'd arrived in San Ignacio two weeks ago. Due to the pregnancy, John was more than overprotective, but Spencer often trailed behind him to the construction site, abandoning the comfort of the casita to be by his side as he directed the vision. John had delegated the day-to-day management operations of the resort to his assistant manager while he devoted all his time and energy to the tree house project. Each day, he gave it his blood, sweat, and tears as he worked side by side with architects and local artisans. There had been stratospheric highs and rock-bottom lows as his ideas and plans came to life.

"Okay, here we are," John announced.

"We are?" Spencer asked. "And where exactly is here? The middle of the jungle?"

"Look up."

She followed his directive; above her, a broad canopy of dense trees obscured her view of the sky; bits of sun managed to sneak through thick, broad leaves, sending down shafts of light, auras glowing and dancing amidst the hanging vines.

"What am I looking at?"

"To the left," he said.

Spencer turned her head, eyes darting as she tried to discern what John wanted her to—

A wooden railing caught her eye, and she followed the stairs as they ascended to what looked like a small house nestled high in the trees.

"Is that what I think it is?" She looked at him. "It's finished?"

"Yeah," he said. "Finally."

She squealed and then clapped her hands. "Oh, can I see it?"

John laughed. "That's why I brought you here."

Laughing, she took off toward the wooden stairs. Jungle vines twined and swirled along the railing as she hurried up the steps, climbing higher and higher into the heart of the rainforest. Behind her, John followed, his pace more measured, yelling at her to be careful, watch her step, and wait for him.

Approaching the last three steps, Spencer slowed to catch her breath and to wait for John.

Together, they took the final steps to the porch, a wide swatch of wooden planks where banana leaves and more jungle vines wrapped around the support beams and meandered onto the porch, giving her the feeling of being ensconced in a living, breathing terrarium.

"These doors are beautiful," Spencer said, stepping closer to examine the carvings of native birds and tropical fauna.

"A local Belizean artist did all the carvings," he explained. "He hand-carved the porch railings, too."

"Were these handmade?" she asked, stepping to a group of rocking chairs flanking the wood double-door entrance.

John nodded. "A friend of my mother's made the rocking chairs."

After fawning over the artistry of the railings and support beams, Spencer said, "Come on, let's go inside."

Moments later, John opened the doors and stepped back to allow her to enter first.

"This is the Honeymoon Tree house," he said. "It's fifteen hundred square feet. It has four rooms. Large bedroom; large bathroom with an oversized claw foot tub and also an outdoor shower."

"This is so beautiful!" she said. "I want to live here! I think you should build us a tree house to live in. Ten thousand square feet spread across the rainforest."

"I don't know about that," he said, chuckling, leading her to the bedroom. "I was thinking about having hibiscus petals on the bed with a welcome note. Nothing too obtrusive. Just a personalized note from me."

"That's a good idea," Spencer said. "Like if they're on their honeymoon, you could say Congratulations, Mr. and Mrs. Whoever, I hope you enjoy your stay, yadda, yadda, yadda. Or, if it's an anniversary trip, you could say Happy Fiftieth Anniversary."

"Yeah, but no matter the reason," he said. "I want to write something personal. I came up with a standard greeting. You read it and tell me what you think."

"I'm sure it's okay," she told him, twirling about the room, giggling and squealing each time her excitement got the best of her, which was every other second.

"I don't want it to sound trite," he said. "Or too hokey."

"What did you write? Welcome to the Honeymoon Tree house! Enjoy your stay!" she said. "That's good enough. What people will appreciate is that it's handwritten. That's the important thing. A handwritten note is a personal touch that shows you really care and—"

"Spencer, will you just read it and tell me what you think, please?"

A bit startled by the tension in his tone, she faced him. "Why is it so important for me to read a welcome note?"

"Because…" John looked away. "I just want you to read it."

"Okay," she said, noting his mood had changed. He seemed jittery and slightly nervous.

Crawling onto the bed, she grabbed the note. "Nice paper."

"Yeah," he said, his tone clipped though not curt. Clearing his throat, he said, "Can you just read it?"

"All right, all right," she said, opening the note, realizing his nervousness was making her nervous. She folded her legs beneath her and then read out loud, "I love you very much, and I want to spend the rest of my life…"

Her heart started to pound, and she read the rest of the words silently in shock and disbelief.

"Keep reading," he said.

She couldn't. She was speechless, and the words were a blur from the tears.

"Spencer…"

Blinking, allowing the tears to fall, she glanced up at him. "John, is this real? Are you serious about this?"

"Will you please keep reading?"

Swallowing, she wiped her cheeks with trembling fingers and made an attempt to continue. "I love you very much, and I want to spend the rest of my life with you and…"

She let the note fall and dropped her face in her hands.

A moment later, he gently removed her hands

On his knees in front of her, he said, "I love you very much, and I want to spend the rest of my life with you, and I want to know if I can be your husband."

"You want to be my husband?" she whispered, flabbergasted as she stared at him, dizzy with confusion. "Are you asking me? What are you asking me?"

"I want to be your husband," he said. "And I want you to be my wife. I'm asking you to marry me."

"You want to marry me?" she asked, still in disbelief, still not sure she'd heard him right. "You want me to marry you?"

Spencer couldn't believe what he was asking her. She could not believe John wanted to marry her. She knew he loved her as much as she loved him. But marriage? She'd never expected he would marry her. They'd never even talked about marriage.

Marriage was a huge leap of faith.

Marriage came with the turmoil of possibly becoming "that wife." She'd promised herself she wouldn't become "that wife," and the only way not to become "that wife" was to not get married. The problem was, she wasn't so sure about that vow against marriage anymore. Maybe she wouldn't end up like her mother. Maybe she would turn out to be a "good wife" instead of "that wife." Maybe John wouldn't force her to devalue and marginalize herself in order to keep him.

Spencer wanted to be with John forever and had planned to do so; she hadn't thought marriage was an option for them, but now that John was proposing, she was really starting to like the idea, really starting to fall in love with the reality of being Mrs. Sione D. Tuiali'i.

"Oh, wait, I forgot something." He stood, dug into one of the pockets on his shorts, pulled out a small box, and opened it.

The flawless brilliance of the emerald-cut diamond nearly blinded her, and she let out a squeak.

"I want to marry you," he said. "I want us to be husband and wife. So, will you marry me?"

"John, I want us to be husband and wife, too," she said, nodding and smiling. "Yes, I will marry you!"

30

—————

Houston, Texas
St. Paul Baptist Church

ONE MONTH LATER

Trembling with barely disguised excitement and anticipation, Spencer stood in the bridal chambers of the church. Moments ago, the room had been filled with a dozen or so people, all of them caught up in the anxious, happy chaos of the impending nuptials as hairstylists and makeup artists made last-minute touch-ups and attendants helped the bridal party into their dresses.

Now it was quiet, hushed and peaceful. Fifteen minutes ago, Shady had herded everyone out to give Spencer a bit of privacy, a chance to reflect on her last moments as a "free woman."

A few feet from the full-length mirror in the corner, Spencer stared at her reflection. This was how John would see her, walking toward him. But, as she did, she was well aware that their guests would have the side view and would probably be secretly searching for telltale signs of her pregnancy. Turning to the left side, then the right side, and then to the left again, she scrutinized herself from various angles. Despite being thirteen weeks, the bump was only barely noticeable, nothing obtrusive or distracting. Not that she was trying not to look pregnant. Even if she'd been twenty-six weeks, she still would have walked—or waddled or whatever—down the aisle, ecstatic that everyone would be able to see the love she and John had beautifully manifested growing within her.

Sighing, Spencer walked closer to the mirror for another hair and makeup check. Satisfied, she turned, walked to the dressing table, and picked up her bouquet. Frangipani, of course. A symbol of her devotion to John. I'm taken. She'd made that promise to him more than a year ago, and despite their devastating breakup and the miserable two months they'd spent apart, the flower represented not only their love but the endurance of their commitment to, and feelings for, each other.

Spencer glanced at the clock above the door.

Shady had promised to be back in thirty minutes. Spencer had fifteen minutes of reflection left, but she didn't need any more introspection. She was ready to become Mrs. Sione D. Tuiali'i. Her heart pounded as she rehearsed the bridal procession. When Shady returned, they would walk downstairs to the vestibule, right outside the main sanctuary of the church, where they'd wait for the cue to enter. Once the bridal entrance music began, an attendant would open the doors, and she would walk down the aisle, escorted by Shady, who would give her away, since their father couldn't be bothered…or found.

Twenty-one steps, Spencer thought, staring at her bouquet of frangipani flowers.

She and John and their wedding party had rehearsed the

ceremony several times. During each rehearsal, she'd counted the steps she took, and each time it had taken twenty-one steps down the center aisle of the church to the altar where John would be waiting.

Twenty-one steps to a life of happiness and love with John.

Nothing from the past could hurt her now. She was protected from her sad childhood marred by neglect and abandonment. Protected from her disastrous mistakes.

And protected from Ben Chang.

John was going to protect her. Life with him wouldn't be perfect or without challenges, but their love would prevail, and more importantly, there was nothing that could potentially tear them apart.

Tears welled, but she blinked them away, worried about ruining her makeup.

She was happy and flabbergasted. Like a pendulum, her emotions swung back and forth between joy and disbelief, hysteria and trepidation, exhilaration and shock.

She was excited and ecstatic to be marrying John because he was the man of her dreams. But her euphoria was tempered and subdued by the realization of her former stance against marriage and her irrational fears of becoming like her mother and turning into "that wife." She'd never wanted marriage to some dream man or soul mate, and yet here she was, moments away from becoming Mrs. Sione D. Tuiali'i.

For so many reasons, she didn't feel she deserved this moment. She wasn't sure she could be Mrs. Sione D. Tuiali'i, wasn't sure if she was the right woman for John—a sentiment shared by most of John's family.

Especially his mother.

Carmen Camareno had made her dislike of Spencer no secret.

Disgruntled and disgusted, Carmen had voiced her displeasure of the upcoming nuptials to anyone who would listen and had found many supporters, naysayers who also believed Spencer was about to trick a good man into a bad marriage.

Spencer didn't care what anyone thought.

She loved John and he loved her.

Only their love mattered.

A knock on the door broke into her thoughts. She jumped as a jolt of nervous energy went through her and was quickly followed by a sense of peace and a giddy joy.

"Come on in," she called out and then dashed to the mirror to make sure her mascara hadn't run. Hearing the door open, she said, "Shady, can you do me a favor and tell the makeup artist—"

"Well, well, well, don't you look gorgeous…"

31

Houston, Texas
St. Paul Baptist Church

Startled by the unfamiliar female voice, Spencer spun around. Confused, she stared at the woman standing in the doorway, a slender, good-looking woman with sun-kissed tan skin and thick, glossy black hair that swirled around her shoulders in cascading waves. Dressed in skintight black—leggings and a sleeveless tank that showcased toned biceps—and combat boots, she smiled and folded her arms.

Was she one of John's Tongan relatives? Maybe, but Spencer didn't think so. None of his Pacific island family members had been able to make the wedding ceremony, which was why they planned to honeymoon on the island where John had spent his late teen years.

"Do I know you?" Spencer asked, her apprehension growing. "Are you—"

"No, I'm not," the woman said, uncrossing her arms, allowing them to fall at her sides as she stepped into the room. "I'm not at all what you're expecting right now."

"What are you talking about?" Spencer took a step back, the apprehension exploding into full-blown fear as two men entered the room wearing black combat fatigues. With grim expressions as dark and deadly as the guns they aimed at Spencer, the men took positions on either side of the woman.

"What are you doing?" Spencer stumbled back again. "What do you want?"

"Don't get hysterical, okay?" the woman instructed as she closed the door and then locked it.

"Do you want money?" Spencer asked, trembling, trying not to scream, terrified one of the men would shoot her. "Just let me—"

"This is not a stick up, black beauty," the woman said, facing Spencer again. "You're about to be taken."

"Taken," Spencer whispered, her heart dropping. "Taken… where? Why? What are you—"

"No time for questions right now," the woman said. "We need to get going before Shady comes back. But, first, you've got to write a note."

Her confusion increasing, Spencer stared at the woman. "A note?"

"Doesn't have to be a heartfelt essay," the woman said. "Just a few words to let Sione know that you've changed your mind about marrying him."

"What? No!" Spencer protested, shaking her head and glancing from the woman, who maintained the carefree smile, to the men and their guns and back to the woman.

"Look, I don't have time to try to forge your handwriting, okay?" the woman said, annoyed. "So, you need to write the note to

Sione, tell him you had a change of heart so he doesn't call the cops, or worse, mount his steed and go charging off to save you."

"I'm not going anywhere with you!" Spencer said, seized by a sudden hysteria. "Leave me alone! Get away from me! Help me! Please! Someone—"

"Shut this bitch up!" the woman commanded.

Immediately, the man on the right lunged at Spencer. Screaming, she tried to sidestep him and run to the door, but an arm snaked around her neck. The other man had grabbed her from behind, she realized with a sickening dread as his hand clamped over her mouth.

Panting, trying to breathe through her nose, she resisted the urge to struggle, as fear for the baby's safety consumed her. She couldn't think of just herself. The little one took priority. She had to protect her baby. Nothing was more important than making sure her baby stayed safe, which meant she could not antagonize these people. She couldn't do anything to make them hurt her, or worse.

If that meant she had to do what these people wanted, even though she didn't know why, or who they were, or where they planned to take her, then she would give in to their demands.

Thoughts and fears battled for her attention, but she forced herself to stay calm. For right now, she would have to do what they told her to do. But she knew she would have to find some way to get away from them. She couldn't let them take her away from the church, from the place where her family and friends were, and where John was, waiting for her to walk down the aisle. She had to get word to someone that these people were trying to take her. If she could just figure out a way to—

"Take her over to the dressing table," the woman ordered.

The man restraining Spencer forced her toward the table. As he dragged her, Spencer stared into the mirror attached to the table, terrified by her wild, hysterical eyes. The man pushed her into the chair and then pressed the barrel of his gun against her temple, igniting fresh terror within her.

"Get the paper and pen," said the woman.

The man standing to the left of the woman, with the mustache, slipped a hand into the pocket of his jacket, removed the requested items and passed them to the woman.

"Okay, black Barbie," said the woman as she walked to the table. She slapped the sheet of paper and the pen down in front of Spencer, who jumped, her heart racing. "Here is what is going to happen, okay? I'm going to dictate, you're going to write, and my friend Gustavo is going to keep his gun pointed at your head so you don't do anything stupid, like scream for help, got it?"

Glaring at the woman, Spencer nodded. Whoever the woman was, she led the vicious trio, exercising and asserting absolute control and authority over the men. Despite their formidable size and bulk, the men were under the complete direction and control of the woman.

"Let's make this quick," the woman said. "Don't have a lot of time. Don't want your sister to come back and catch us, because if she does, I'll have to put a bullet in her, understand?"

Dejected, realizing she would have to pray Shady wouldn't return soon, Spencer picked up the pen with trembling fingers.

"All right, start with *Dear Sione*," said the woman.

Dear Sione? Spencer wrote the words, knowing they weren't right. A letter from her would begin Dear John. She had never called John by his given Tongan name. As the woman continued to dictate lies John would never believe, a spark of hope flared. Dear Sione was actually the best way to start the letter. If these people succeeded in kidnapping her and left the note behind for John to find, he would know she hadn't written the letter of her own free will. As soon as he read Dear Sione, John would know something wasn't right.

"Okay, now sign the letter," said the woman minutes later, once she'd finished the dictation. "And fold the letter in half."

After complying, Spencer stared at the woman. "Listen, you don't have to kidnap me."

"If I want my fee, I do," the woman said, smiling.

"Your fee?" Spencer felt her blood grow cold. Someone was paying the woman to kidnap her. But who? The same man who'd told that bastard Tommy Fong to kidnap her and hold her hostage in that shack in the middle of the jungle? The man who had been referred to as the devil? What was his name?

"Not exactly a boatload of cash," the woman said. "But I need the money."

"Whatever you are being paid," Spencer said, panicked, terrified of being kidnapped again as the nightmare she'd endured in Belize flashed in her mind. "Sione will double it. He'll triple it."

"Get her and let's go."

"No, wait." Spencer struggled as the man with the mustache grabbed her, yanking her to her feet. "You can't do this! You can't—"

Behind her, something cold and hard pressed against her neck, and she sobbed, knowing it was the gun, horrified by thoughts of bullets slamming into her body, killing the—

A painful jolt of something electric and mind-numbing passed through her body in a sizzling wave. Her muscles useless, she felt her body go limp as a suffocating darkness engulfed her.

32

———

Houston, Texas
St. Paul Baptist Church

Sione was anxious, ready to get the show on the road.

He was ready to marry Spencer and get started on the rest of their lives together.

He couldn't imagine what was taking so long.

The flower girls—his second cousins, Keisha, India, and Maggie—had come down the aisle, throwing frangipani petals. And then the bridesmaids—Rae and two of Spencer's cousins—escorted by the groomsmen, four of Sione's cousins.

Everyone was in place.

Except the bride-to-be. Shouldn't Spencer be walking down the aisle right about now? Arm in arm with Shady, who was going to give her away?

Exhaling slowly, Sione told himself not to worry or panic.

He turned his head a bit and sort of side-glanced at his mother. Sitting in the first pew on the groom's side, Carmen looked as though she was at a funeral, but he wasn't surprised. She didn't like Spencer, didn't think Spencer was the right woman for him, thought he was making the biggest mistake of his life.

The same opinions pretty much most of his family held.

He'd tried to convince his family to give Spencer a chance. She was a loving, caring woman, and most importantly, she loved him unconditionally. His family couldn't see past their unwavering opinions of her. In their eyes, she was a scheming woman who had gotten pregnant on purpose and was using the baby to trap him. Eventually, Sione had given up trying to change his family's attitudes and beliefs.

Being with Spencer made him happy. He wasn't backing down from his decision to marry her just because she wasn't the woman his family wanted him to be with. Didn't matter what his family wanted. He wanted Spencer because, even with all her imperfections, she was flawless to him.

Behind his back, his family had predicted his marriage to Spencer would be his biggest mistake. His cousin Micah had confessed that the family had dubbed the upcoming wedding "the disaster," as in "Are you going to the disaster?" The rumor was, according to Truman, there was some betting going on about how long the marriage would last. The odds were basically slim to none —six to seven months, if that long.

Sione had been pissed when he found out, but the anger was just a cover for hurt and sadness.

Bitterness was easier to express than sullen disappointment. He'd been wary of admitting, especially to himself, how shaken he'd been by the way his family felt. Truman had predicted

Spencer's plan was to divorce him and leave him broke. Jared had agreed, though his predictions were more sinister. After divorcing him and taking all his money, Jared believed Spencer would disappear and hook up with the man she really wanted to be with—Ben Chang. Sione couldn't get behind that idea.

Ben had sent Spencer to steal from him, not fall in love with him. There was no way Ben could have known he and Spencer would fall in love. No way Ben could have known Sione would propose and Spencer would accept.

If Ben had known, Sione knew Ben would have done whatever he could to stop it from happening.

As Sione stood, anxious and waiting, a strange apprehension assailed him, almost like a hovering apparition.

As he'd had several times before, Sione had the strangest feeling of gratitude toward Ben. If not for the scheme Ben had set in motion to find the envelope Moana had directed Peter to steal from Ben's place in Jamaica, then Sione would never have met Spencer. In a sick, twisted way, he owed Ben this happiness he felt. He wouldn't be marrying Spencer today, if not for Ben's diabolical machinations.

Sione pushed away the weary, troubling thoughts. This was the happiest day of his life. The most beautiful woman he'd ever seen was about to become his wife. In the next few minutes, they would vow to love and cherish each other until death did them part.

He wasn't going to let anyone or anything ruin this day.

Not his family, with their tears of frustration and fake, half-hearted smiles.

And for damn sure not Ben Chang.

A moment later, the string quartet began a stirring version of Canon in D. The bridal entrance music, Sione remembered from the wedding rehearsals. The guests rose. Smiling, excited to finally see Spencer walking down the aisle toward him, Sione turned and—

His heart almost stopped.

33

———

Houston, Texas
St. Paul Baptist Church

At the end of the aisle, Shady stood in the vestibule, out of sight of the guests, beckoning Sione toward her.

Confused, and trying not to worry, Sione frowned. He couldn't see Shady's features clearly, but the frantic tension in her gestures made his heart pound and his gut twist. What was she trying to tell him? Why did she want him to come to her? What was going on? Where was Spencer? Why wasn't Spencer standing next to Shady?

Wary, Sione glanced at DJ, and then at Rae and Spencer's cousins, looking for reassurance, something rational and calm in their gazes, but the wedding party seemed perplexed and worried, as well.

"What's the matter?" DJ whispered.

"What's going on?" Rae demanded, voice lowered as she sidestepped closer to Sione.

"I'm going to find out," Sione whispered to them.

"So am I," Rae announced.

"Me too," said DJ.

"No, wait." Sione faced them. "Just let me go. Stay here. We don't need the guests worrying, which is what will happen if we all rush out of here."

"The guests already know something is wrong," Rae said as Spencer's cousins crowded closer.

"She's right," DJ told him. "Aunt Carmen and my mom look suspicious."

Ignoring the furtive glances and whispering of confused and anxious guests, Sione headed down the aisle, the wedding party on his heels. In the vestibule, the bridesmaids and groomsman rushed around Sione, leaving him in the rear. Rae and DJ converged upon Shady, shooting questions, terse whispers that made Sione think of suppressed gunfire. The apprehension he'd been trying to contain exploded into a mix of fear and anger. Desperate for answers, he pushed through DJ and Rae.

Shady grabbed Sione's hand, alarm flickering across her features.

"What happened?" Sione demanded. "What's the matter? Where is Spencer?"

"There's something you need to see," Shady said. "Upstairs. In the bride's room."

———

Ascending the stairs, Sione was seized by reluctance and anxiousness, haunted by the need to race ahead and pull back. He didn't want to know what he needed to see, but he had to find out. Each step was a chore, like walking up a steep, slippery slope. Each step took him closer and closer to terror. Anticipation made his legs numb. Anguished, he feared that whatever awaited him was even worse than he could have ever imagined.

At the top of the stairs, Sione hesitated, staring at the wide-open door at the end of the hall. Besieged by terror, he tried to defeat the horror his mind conjured, images of Spencer lying on the floor—

"You want me to go in first?" DJ asked.

Startled, Sione was confused, not sure how to answer his cousin. A dull roar seemed to rush through his head, making it hard to think, or hear, or understand what was happening. He wasn't sure what happened, but he knew that, right now, nothing made sense. Everything was wrong. It was like he was trapped in a nightmare, and he just needed to wake up. If he could wake up, then everything would be okay. Everything would be as it was supposed to be. Once he woke up, he would be standing at the altar, and Spencer would be walking toward him. But first he had to wake up and had to find his way out of this nightmare.

"Spencer," Rae called out, hurrying past Sione as Shady tried to stop the brash, determined maid of honor, but Rae ignored Shady's plea and once again, spurred by Rae's assertiveness, the wedding party hurried down the hall and into the bridal room, leaving Sione behind.

Frustrated, Sione followed and moments later, he was in the room, glancing around, looking for Spencer amongst the lavender silk dresses and tuxedos, heartbroken and furious because he knew she wasn't there. Not anymore.

"Sione..." Shady broke free from the crowd, grabbed his hand, and pulled him to the dressing table.

"Here..." she said and picked up a piece of paper the size of a greeting card, folded in half.

Sione glanced at the folded paper, apprehensive, averse to touching it, not wanting to open it, afraid the words, whatever they were, would confirm that the nightmare was real. And he wasn't going to wake up.

"What is that? What does it say?" The wedding party crowded around him, demanding answers. "Is it from Spencer?"

"Can y'all just give him a moment, please?" Shady implored.

"No, not when our sister is—" Rae stopped, and for a moment, she seemed unable to catch her breath. "What does the damn note say?"

A spark of anger flared within him, realizing they would refuse him the privacy he craved. Sione wanted to read the note alone first, so he could process it, but he could forget about that. He had a frantic audience, demanding information, and maybe they deserved to know. They were worried about Spencer, too. Without further hesitation, Sione unfolded the note. Heart slamming, he stared at the letters, words, and sentences. The note made no sense, but Sione understood exactly what had happened.

"What does it say?" Rae asked with barely contained hysteria.

Shaken, Sione looked up from the note. Staring at the tense, anxious faces of the bridal party, he said, "Call the cops. Somebody took Spencer."

34

———

Location Unknown

Sitting up in the bed, Spencer struggled to think, to remember exchanging vows with John, but her mind was blank. She didn't recall walking down the aisle with Shady or taking her place next to John, holding hands with him as the minister performed the ceremony while hundreds of family and friends looked on.

Rubbing her eyes, slightly sickened by the stickiness in her mouth covering a tongue that seemed too thick and heavy, Spencer fought to clear the fog from her mind.

Did she have too much to drink at the wedding reception? But she didn't remember the reception either. Didn't remember the first dance with her husband or feeding each other cake or any of the corny but sweet toasts from DJ and Rae and Shady. God, why couldn't she remember anything? And where was John?

Spencer called out to him, but her voice was weak and hoarse, a whispery croak.

Maybe he was getting coffee or ordering room service or passed out on the couch in the living room of the hotel suite. Obviously, they had partied very hard. It must have been an epic reception that had lasted all night and into the wee hours of the next day. Maybe, exhausted and half-conscious from their celebration, they'd had to be carried to their suite by the bridal party.

Somehow, that didn't make sense. They had planned to honeymoon in Hawaii for the first week, and then they would enjoy another week of newly wedded bliss on the island where John had spent the latter part of his teenage years. After the reception, they were going to head straight to Hooks Airport and board the private chartered jet that would fly them to paradise.

Invaded by a sudden giddiness, she glanced at her left hand, anxious to gaze at the enduring, unbreakable symbol of the love between her and John.

Her stomach flipped and then seemed to plummet.

Focusing on the third finger, her heart slammed.

There was no wedding ring.

Rolling onto her stomach, Spencer scrambled to her hands and knees in the middle of the bed and then turned in a circle, taking in her surroundings. She was in a large bedroom suite, ornately and luxuriously furnished and appointed. There was a wall of French doors to her left. A chandelier hung from a double-tray ceiling. There was a sitting area with two full-sized couches. A fireplace. Double doors that led to...what? Where the hell was she? Crawling to the foot of the bed, she scooted onto the tufted settee and then stood.

A wave of dizziness assailed her, nauseating her, and she sat back down on the settee, taking a few deep breaths and rubbing her stomach. "It's okay, little one," she said, though she didn't really think so, and she doubted the baby was fooled. After a few more breaths, she attempted to stand again. The swimming in her head dissipated, and she took a tentative, halting step toward the French doors. Beyond them, outside, there was a dense tangle of bushes. The trees were so thick it was hard to see the sun, but there was enough light to tell that it was daytime.

Her mind felt thick and fuzzy. Memories sharpened, then blurred, and then became clearer but seemed to make no sense. Reality seemed to blend into fantasy, and for a few seconds, she wasn't sure if she was dreaming or fully awake.

Spencer tried to open the French doors, but they were all locked. Turning, she walked to the double doors, which she assumed led out of the suite. Once there, she grabbed the right knob, twisted it, and opened the door.

Outside the bedroom suite was a long hallway. She walked to the end, passing several console tables and framed paintings on the wall, and found herself at a crossroads. Another main hall ran perpendicular to the hall she'd just walked down, traversing left and right. Spencer glanced right and saw that the hall ended, and at the end was a console table with a vase of fresh flowers. She looked left. The hall extended about ten or fifteen feet before it gave way to another corridor.

Growing more worried, Spencer cradled her stomach and went left, following the hallway. Determined to figure out where she was and how the hell she'd gotten there, she picked up the pace. Terrified and confused, she looked over her shoulder every now and then as she walked along the seemingly endless hallways.

Questions plagued her, but what she wanted to know most of all was where was John? And why did she have the sickening feeling that he wasn't here with her? Panicked, tears threatening, she walked faster, and after turning another corner, she found herself in a large living area, some sort of den or family room. There were two large couches facing each other, and in the four corners of the room, there were sitting areas, each one with two recliners separated by a small round table.

Spencer inched toward one of the couches, realizing her feet were bare as she moved across the cool hardwood floor. Why was she barefoot? What had happened to her shoes? And her dress? She looked down at herself. She was wearing her slip.

Pulse racing, Spencer sank down onto the couch and then leaned back against the cool, soft leather, trying to think, trying to remember. Where was she? How had she gotten to this place? Whatever this place was. Some kind of house. A large house. But a large house…where?

"Well, well, well…black beauty finally woke up. Did you sleep okay?" The question came from a female voice behind her.

Spencer jumped and then looked over her shoulder.

She knew the woman standing in front of her. No, that wasn't right. She didn't know the woman. She had no idea who the woman was, but she recognized her. She recalled the sultry, sly dark eyes, the long, glossy black hair, and the lips that curved into a smug smirk. She had seen the woman before.

It was the woman who'd been in her bridal chamber.

"Who are you?" Spencer asked. "Where the hell am I?"

"My name doesn't matter," the woman said, walking around to the other couch and sitting across from Spencer. "What you need to know is that you are in a safe place where you won't be terrorized, tortured, teased, or taunted—if you follow the rules. If you break the rules, this safe place will become very sadistic. Now, I understand that this will be the second time that you've been kidnapped, correct?"

"Kidnapped?" Spencer felt faint. The very word *kidnapped* nearly brought her to her knees, and she took another step back, grateful for the couch behind her, sinking down onto the leather cushion.

She had been kidnapped.

Spencer remembered now. Not just the woman with the exotic features but the two men who'd been with the woman. She remembered the men had grabbed her. One had taped her mouth so she couldn't scream. The other had shoved her toward the dressing table and forced her to sit. Then the woman had slapped a sheet of paper and a pen in front of her and forced her to write words that she didn't mean…

Dear Sione…

"Having experienced this hellish loss of freedom before," the woman said. "I'm sure you have a high level of fear and uncertainty of the moment, but I will attempt to put your mind at ease."

Spencer stared at the woman, unsure of what to think or say or do, tempted to jump up and run away but terrified that the woman would immediately be on her heels, chasing her down, overtaking her, and then punishing her for trying to get away.

"I'm sure that you've noticed something around your neck?"

Apprehensive, Spencer touched her neck and gasped when she felt something hard.

"It's a shock collar with an embedded GPS chip," the woman said. "It functions thusly: if you get out of line, or try to escape, or try to call for help, etcetera, I will pull out a remote control, push one of the three buttons, and you will be shocked. Depending on which button I push, the voltage will be from moderate to severe. Now, should you happen to escape, the collar has GPS, as I said, so I will know exactly where you are. The collar can only be removed by a specific key, which is in my possession, and if you try to remove the collar by any other way except the key, it will automatically shock you."

"A shock collar?" Spencer was horrified and livid. "That's what you use to train a dog."

"That's right." The woman smiled and then said, "Bitch."

Propelled by anger, Spencer jumped up and lunged at the woman. She hadn't taken three steps before a sizzling jolt of electricity passed through her, leaving her stunned and shaking as she dropped to her knees.

"I know it stings a little..." the woman said. "But the pain will fade, I promise."

Panting and gasping, Spencer clutched her abdomen, trying to breathe and trying to get to her feet.

"Listen, I don't want to hurt you, don't want this to be a difficult situation for you," the woman told her. "This doesn't have to be combative or confrontational, okay? Your stay here can be pleasant or difficult, it's up to you. Stay in line and things will go easy for you until you are returned to Sione."

Spencer took deep breaths, still trembling, still unable to move.

"Now, you try to make yourself comfortable," the woman said. "Victor will take you back to your room, and I'll see about getting you some lunch."

Spencer glanced up at the woman and saw one of the guards angling toward them.

"You probably thought I was going to starve you, black Barbie," the woman said. "But don't count on it. I need to keep you alive."

The guard grabbed Spencer and pulled her to her feet. Still dizzy and disoriented, Spencer was forced to lean against him and allow him to drag her as she tried to put one foot in front of the other.

"Oh, and another thing," the woman said as the guard walked Spencer toward the wide arched opening leading out of the den. "You will be allowed to shower once a day and relieve yourself as needed."

Back in the bedroom suite, the guard took Spencer to the bed and pushed her on top of it. Muscles twitching, Spencer managed to roll over onto her side and draw her knees close to her chest. When the doors closed behind her, she heard locks tumbling. Her hopes faded, crashing to the ground. She prayed for the strength to get up and run to the doors, grab the knobs, and twist them. But, she knew the double doors wouldn't open. The guard—Victor? Wasn't that what the woman had called him?—had locked the doors, had locked her in. Again, she was a hostage. The accommodations were much better, opulent, in fact, but still, she was a prisoner. She'd been kidnapped and was trapped in a gilded cage.

35

———————

Location Unknown

The double doors opened.

Unprepared, Spencer jumped and almost screamed when a man dressed in black fatigues walked in, carrying a tray.

She wasn't surprised to see the guard, but she wasn't really ready, wasn't prepared for him, not the way she hoped to be. She'd spent all night trying to come up with a plan of escape, one that would involve convincing one of the men to help her, but her thoughts were scattered, all over the place. It was hard to focus, hard to keep the frustration from derailing her efforts. It was hard to stop thinking about John, wondering and worrying about him and what he was thinking. In the end, she gave up, cradled her stomach, and sang lullabies to the little one until she fell asleep.

Now, faced with her first chance to escape, she resolved to ignore the desperate panic racing through her veins. She had to be rational and methodical, using her wits and manipulation to escape.

When she'd opened her eyes, she'd seen a sliver of bright sunshine slanting across the small terrace outside the French doors and had known it was morning. Her first night as a hostage had come and gone. The thought of being kept captive a second night, despite the grand surroundings, ignited a hysteria within her. Pacing around the room, desperate to come up with an escape plan, she realized she was in no position to overpower one of the tall, bulky guards. Her only hope was to talk her way out of the room.

The guards seemed like ex-military types. Men who'd spent their lives in various types of special forces. Once their assignments had ended, for whatever reason, they had been unable to reintegrate successfully into society and had become mercenaries of some sort. Of course, she was engaging in generalizations. How the hell could she really know what their backstories were? Still, she had to at least imagine what kind of men they could be. Disloyal. Selfish. Willing to follow the orders of the highest bidder. She had to hope she could convince one of them to help her. One of the guards had to be willing to go against the woman, hopefully.

The guard put the tray on the low coffee table in the sitting area. Food on a paper towel. A Styrofoam cup and a sandwich. No utensils. Nothing she could use as a weapon.

Vaguely, she recalled the woman promising to feed her, and though she wasn't hungry, she had to eat for the baby's sake. Her own appetite didn't matter. The idea of her baby suffering any type of malnutrition terrified her. She was thankful for the food even if she would probably have to force herself to chew and swallow.

Eating was the last thing on her mind. Escaping this house, wherever it was, continued to dominate her thoughts. Yesterday, after being deposited on the bed and left to recover from the punishing jolt of electricity, Spencer had eventually drifted into a fitful sleep. Even her dreams had been about escape. Though vague and fuzzy now, she recalled running down corridors and walking through a wide, never-ending passageway, twisting the knobs on all the doors she encountered, desperate to find a door that was unlocked.

Hesitant, she walked toward the sitting area, keeping a wide birth, watching the guard. Spencer didn't recognize the man, didn't remember him as one of the men who'd helped the woman kidnap her, but like the other men, his face was passive and yet grim, menacing.

"Breakfast," the guard grunted. "You have one hour to eat, and then someone will return to get the tray. Any food you do not finish will be trashed, so I advise you to clean your plate."

Glaring at him, irritated by his so-called advice, Spencer asked, "What's your name?"

The guard frowned. "What?"

"Your name? What is it?" she asked, hoping to establish a rapport with the man and arouse his sympathy. "You have one, don't you?"

"Why do you want to know my name?"

"Because..." Spencer faltered and felt panic rising. "If you're going to be bringing me breakfast every day, then I would like to thank you, and—"

The guard turned and walked toward the doors.

"Wait a minute," Spencer called out, frantic. "Who is the woman who took me? Why did she kidnap me? Who told her to kidnap me? Where am I? Can you at least tell me where I am? Am I still in Houston? In Texas? In the United States? Look, whatever she's paying you, I'll double it. My fiancé..."

The word *fiancé* caught in her throat. She had to catch herself so she wouldn't break down, but she wasn't quick enough. *Fiancé.* John was supposed to be her husband. She was supposed to have walked down the aisle to him. *Twenty-one steps* to happily ever after. But that hadn't happened because—

The door slammed, breaking her solemn reverie. Startled, Spencer ran to the closed doors. Yanking the knob with her right hand and beating against the door with her left fist, she screamed and yelled.

"Let me out of here!" she demanded. "Open the door! Let me out! You can't keep me here!"

Moments later, her hand throbbing and her stomach growling painfully, she backed away from the door. Sobbing and heaving, she turned toward the sitting area, staring at the food. She only had an hour to eat. *Any food you do not finish will be trashed.* She had to clean her plate.

Exhaling, she wiped the tears away and lurched to the sitting area. Collapsing on one of the couches, she fought the urge to give in to despair and hopelessness. Her first attempt to escape hadn't gone exactly as she'd wished. Didn't matter. She would just have to try again. Right now, she had to eat. Spencer took a bite of the sandwich. Ham, a fried egg, and cheese on toast. Not bad, actually. The food would provide nourishment for her and the baby and hopefully help her think a bit more clearly, help her to come up with a definite plan.

The woman had promised her two meals and a shower. She was having the first meal now, so she would see the guard again for her second meal and then the shower. Although, the same guard might not deliver the second meal. Didn't matter. If another guard showed up, she would offer him the same deal she'd offered the first guard. If the same guard returned, she'd double down on the offer.

———

"My fiancé will triple whatever you're being paid," Spencer said. "He's very wealthy. We can call him. He'll help you get away. I won't tell the police you were involved."

The guard—a different man from the one who'd brought her breakfast, and the one who'd returned for the breakfast tray, and the one who'd brought her towels and soap so she could shower— ignored her. The other guards had ignored her, too, but she wasn't going to give up.

"What day is it? How many days have I been here?" she asked.

"Dinner," the guard said, pointing to the tray. "Someone will return for the tray in an hour."

"The woman told you to tell me that?" Spencer asked, deciding on a different tactic. "She tells you everything to do? And you just blindly follow her orders? What, are you her bitch or something?"

Glaring at her, the guard growled, "Watch your mouth."

Wondering if she might have hit a nerve, one that might help her to convince the man to turn traitor, Spencer rose from the bed and walked toward the couch. "You sure you can trust her? Are you sure that she's not going to put a bullet in your head when all this is over?"

"Worry about your own life," the guard said and headed toward the double doors.

This attempt at escape hadn't gone as bad as her earlier attempts, but still, she hadn't cracked any of the woman's guards. Maybe the guards were her bitches. *A group of pussies,* she thought, taking a bite of the roast beef sandwich. Or maybe they were afraid of whoever had paid them to kidnap her.

Spencer hadn't thought much about the person who'd paid the woman to hold her hostage. But did it matter who had ordered the kidnapping? Would it be a waste of precious time, trying to figure out who'd wanted her smuggled from the church moments before she was set to walk down the aisle? *Twenty-one steps,* she couldn't help but think, though it was pointless to ruminate over her doomed nuptials. Just as stupid to tax her brain, trying to determine who was behind her kidnapping. She had to focus on escape. Every thought, every speculation, and each contemplation had to be about how the hell she could get out of the house without ending up with a bullet in her back.

After she finished the sandwich, Spencer went to the bed and lay down. Staring at the ceiling, she thought about her escape plan. Her offer to triple the amount of money being paid to the guards hadn't enticed any of the men she'd encountered thus far. But why? What did she need to do to convince one of the guards to flip? What did she need to change? What did she need to say? Being friendly hadn't worked. Neither had being a bitch. A wave of hopelessness threatened to overtake her, but she managed to stop it from pulling her under. Praying for strength and guidance, she placed both hands over her abdomen. Humming a lullaby under her breath, she closed her eyes and allowed herself a moment to imagine the little one in her arms walking and then talking, growing healthy and strong, and loved unconditionally.

———

"Wake up."

Startled, her lids fluttering, Spencer opened her eyes. At the foot of the bed stood a grim-faced man with a scruffy, unkempt beard and cold, hard eyes as black as obsidian. Gasping, Spencer sat up and scooted back against the headboard. Another guard, she realized, desperate to clear the fuzziness from her head. A different man. Groggy and, again, unprepared, she wasn't sure what to say.

"Time for you to bathe," he said, dropping a large towel and a small bar of soap on the bed.

Worried, she stared at him. "I'll take a shower later."

"You'll take the shower now," he said, his tone inviting no protest or argument. "You have fifteen minutes."

"Can I close the bathroom door?" she asked, afraid he would demand to watch her, terrified he might try to rape her.

Arms crossed, he shook his head. "Leave it open."

Her heart kicked. "But—"

"Relax," he said, dismissive. "I don't intend to watch."

He was lying, she was sure, but she was wary of what he would do if she refused to shower with the door open. Most likely, he would drag her into the bathroom, strip her, and force her beneath the stream of water. Shuddering at the possibility of that indignity, Spencer grabbed the soap and towel.

In the bathroom, she scanned the area. It was small, like an apartment bathroom, with a toilet, a pedestal sink, and a combination shower and tub. After removing her slip and underwear, she turned the water on. It was a healthy stream, and she didn't hesitate to step into the shallow tub, having decided to get the shower over within five minutes or less. Surprisingly, the water was warmer than she'd thought it would be. The soap seemed to be a sample size, something found in a motel room, but it lathered sufficiently. After soaping herself thoroughly and quickly, she rinsed her body, turned the water off, and grabbed the towel. It was thin but large, and once dried, she wrapped it around her body.

Staring at the slip and underwear, she wondered if they would be laundered and returned to her. Should she ask? Forlorn, she couldn't stop herself from thinking that John should have removed the slip and underwear. Spencer pushed the maudlin thoughts away. Instead of remorse, she thought of offering herself for her freedom. Why not? Her original offers had been rebuffed. Maybe the guard would give in for the opportunity to make love to her. The baby bump had grown but still wasn't overly obvious. She hadn't really gained much weight and still possessed the curvaceous figure most men found sexy and irresistible.

Maybe she should walk out of the bathroom, stark naked, and proposition the guard. Maybe he would become aroused by the sight of her. If she could lure him to the bed, she might be able to knee him in the groin. While he clutched his injured balls, she could grab his gun, whack him in the head, and then…what? Shoot her way out of the house?

Frustrated, Spencer walked into the bedroom, the towel still wrapped firmly around her.

The guard was gone, but there were several items on the bed that hadn't been there when she'd left to take the shower—a pair of gabardine pants with an elastic waist, a long-sleeved T-shirt, and a pair of white cotton Granny panties.

The guard must have left the room while she was showering to get the clothes, left them behind, and then left again. Something to remember, to possibly take advantage of, maybe. When the guard left to get clothes for her, she might be able to listen for the moment when he left the room so she could be waiting for his return. As soon as he walked back through the door, she could kick him. A good kick to the shin might stun him enough so she could—

Stun. Enraged and disgusted, Spencer remembered the shock collar. Her hand flew to her throat. Disappointed, she sank onto the bed. The collar, which seemed to be made from some outdoor, all-weather fabric, still graced her neck, hindering her chance to escape. Even if she did manage to get the best of one of her guards, she wouldn't get far before several jolts of electricity brought her down.

36

Location Unknown

The next morning, her mind still flooded with bittersweet remnants of dreams about John and the baby and their life together, Spencer got out of bed, determined to find a weapon.

Though still groggy and disoriented, she was desperate to escape. She couldn't wait around to be released. What if they didn't let her go? What if the woman had lied to her? Spencer had to assume she hadn't been told the truth. She'd read news articles about kidnapping victims who'd been killed even when ransom demands were paid.

She had to find her way back to John even as he was finding his way to her.

John was searching for her, Spencer knew that. But that didn't mean she couldn't help him out somehow. Once, back when they were first getting to know each other, John had accused her of not wanting a hero. Back then, that had been true, somewhat. It wasn't that she hadn't wanted a hero. She just didn't know if she could count on a man to keep his promises. Her father had been largely absent from her life, and her stepfathers had been like Jekyll and Hyde.

As time passed, her fear and panic escalated. She would not make it out of the house alive if she didn't find some way to escape. There were so many reasons for the woman to kill her. Spencer had seen the woman's face. She could identify her kidnappers. Whatever the woman's demands were, once John met them, Spencer knew the woman would put a bullet in her head.

Standing in the middle of the room, she took a cold, critical, calculating look around. At first glance, she saw nothing she could weaponize in the bedroom. A more thorough investigation of the bed revealed it to be three mattresses stacked on top of each other. There was no box spring with wooden slats and wire coils she might use to poke out an eye. None of the furniture had sharp edges. There was no art on the walls. Nothing on the accent tables, and the drawer seemed to be glued shut.

In the bathroom, there were no shower curtain or shower rods. No mirror hung above the pedestal sink. No potential weapons, she thought, not surprised. There were no towels. No soap. No toiletries. There was a roll of toilet paper on top of the tank, but when Spencer tried to remove it, the thing wouldn't budge and seemed to be cemented in place.

Back in the bedroom, she took deep breaths and paced, determined not to get upset or discouraged. She might have given in to hysteria if not for thoughts of the baby. And John. Though, thoughts on John reminded her of the ruined wedding.

Spencer sat on the edge of the bed. What was John doing right now? Was he missing her? Crazed with worry? Was he out looking for her? Desperate to find her? Determined to rescue her? He had to be, Spencer told herself. Because if he wasn't out looking for her, that meant... She didn't want to think about what it would mean. *Dear Sione.* No, John couldn't have believed the note was real. But what if he had?

Crying, she dropped her face in her hands. What if, right now, he was somewhere thanking God he'd dodged a bullet and hadn't married a diabolical bitch like her? What if his family had convinced him the note was real?

A loud, familiar click jolted her. Someone was opening the door. Spencer wiped her eyes and stood, forcing herself to focus on escape. Each time a guard entered the room was an opportunity to find some way to flee. She couldn't let her emotions get the best of her.

The left door opened wide, and the woman walked into the room.

"Surprised to see me, black Barbie?" The woman carried the breakfast tray to the coffee table. "Well, I'm sick of you trying to get my guys to mutiny. Offering them double and triple to go against me. That's not going to happen, okay?"

"How can you be so sure?" Spencer challenged, scrutinizing the woman. She wasn't much taller than Spencer, but she was slim with an athletic build. The sleeveless black tank she wore showcased lean muscles. Spencer was quite sure the woman would kick her ass, but she was equally sure that she would put up a damn good fight.

"I'm sure because I know these men," the woman said. "They can be bought but not at the expense of their lives. They help you, and all they'll get for their heroic efforts is a bullet to the head."

Frustrated, Spencer rolled her eyes though she realized the

woman had, perhaps inadvertently, given her some insight into what the guard's thought about her offer.

"Now that we've got that settled," the woman said, turning from Spencer. "Enjoy your breakfast. I'll be back in an hour."

"Wait," Spencer called to her.

At the door, the woman pivoted, facing her. "What is it?"

"Who told you to kidnap me?" Spencer asked. "Why did they want Sione to think I left him at the altar?"

"I told you," the woman said. "I don't question my orders. My guess is that if Sione calls the cops and reports you missing, it might complicate the situation."

"What is the situation?" Spencer asked. "Why was I kidnapped?"

"I didn't ask because I don't really care," the woman said. "But, again, my guess is that the person who had you kidnapped wants something from Sione."

"What does this person want?"

The woman shrugged. "Something that this person thinks Sione will give him in exchange for your safe return."

"Has this person given Sione a ransom demand?"

"I'm not sure about that," the woman said. "But you better hope that Sione gives this person what they want because if he doesn't, unfortunately, I'll have to kill you."

The woman turned to leave.

"Wait a minute," Spencer called out. "Please, wait."

Facing Spencer, the woman frowned. "What now?"

"If you let me go," Spencer said. "Sione will give you double what this person is paying you, and he'll make sure you won't go to jail for what you've done."

The woman's laugh was short and scornful. "Thanks, but no thanks."

"You don't want to make twice as much money?" Spencer asked. "You don't want to stay out of prison?"

"Let me tell you something about Sione," the woman said. "He hates me, okay? And if he knew that I had kidnapped you, he would kill me."

37

Location Unknown

"By the way, there are cameras everywhere." The woman placed the dinner tray on the coffee table, hours later, after Spencer had showered. "The entire house has interior surveillance, so stop trying to come up with ways to escape, okay?"

Sitting on the couch, arms folded, Spencer said nothing. She listened intently, though, fighting discouragement. She should have figured there were cameras all over the house. *Interior surveillance.* Reminded Spencer of Ben's townhouse. Her whole life had gone to hell because of interior surveillance. Cameras in Ben's closet had caught her stealing from him and had given him the evidence he needed to blackmail her in to going to Belize to search for that damn envelope.

"Now, before you dig in," said the woman. "I need a favor."

Spencer remained quiet, but she was curious, worried. The word favor made her think of Ben, the last person she wanted haunting her thoughts.

"It's been a few days since you left Sione at the altar," the woman said.

"Since I left him at the altar?" Spencer glared at the woman. "Are you out of your mind? I would never have left him at the altar if you hadn't kidnapped me."

The woman shrugged. "Anyway, I'm sure he's worried about you, so I think you should call him."

"You want me to call him?" Spencer's heart raced, thinking of what it would mean to hear John's voice again. It seemed as though an eternity since she'd spoken to him, the last time being at the day before they were supposed to be married. He'd told her how much he loved her and the baby and how he couldn't wait for them to be married and—

Quickly, she pushed the memories away before she burst into tears. She couldn't cry, couldn't give in to hysteria. She had to focus, to think of how to take advantage of the conversation she would have with John. Somehow, she would have to give him some clue as to who had taken her and where she was, even though she had no idea who the woman was or where the house was located.

"My sources confirm that Sione is out at the moment," the woman said. "We have someone watching him, and apparently, he's out looking for you."

"I told you he wouldn't believe that note you made me write," Spencer said, allowing herself a moment to feel smug. "He knows how much I love him and want to marry him and—"

"So, I've prepared a statement for you to read," the woman said, pulling a piece of paper from the back pocket of her jeans. "It's going to be a voice message."

"A voice message?" Spencer echoed, disappointed. She'd been

looking forward to hearing John's voice, and knowing she wouldn't, she wasn't sure how to manage the remorse washing over her.

The woman sat next to her on the couch. "Here." She held out a small burner phone and the slip of paper on which the prepared statement was written.

After a slight hesitation, Spencer snatched the phone and the paper.

"Say it like you mean it," the woman instructed.

Spencer scanned the paper and then made the call.

"Good job, black Barbie," the woman said after Spencer did her bidding. "Hopefully he'll have a change of heart."

"Don't count on it."

"Don't be surprised if he does," the woman warned. "Sione is fickle."

"Fickle?" Spencer asked, remembering what the woman had said about John hating her. How did the woman know John? Her lazy familiarity suggested more than just a casual acquaintance.

"Sione bends over backward to get you," the woman said. "He makes all these promises, professing his undying love and devotion, and then when you fall for him—and you will fall for him, trust me —he decides that he's no longer interested, and he moves on to the next dumb bitch eager to believe his lies."

Trust me, the woman had said, intimating some personal knowledge of the way John treated women.

"How do you know that?" Spencer asked. "Do you know Sione?"

"As a matter of fact, I know Sione very well," she said, emphasizing the word know, using it in the Biblical sense, Spencer thought. Was the woman trying to imply she had been involved with John? Intimately? Romantically? Sexually?

Smirking, the woman said, "Sione is my ex-fiancé."

"Your ex-fiancé?" Spencer struggled to recover from the bomb the woman had just dropped.

"You're not the first woman he asked to marry him," the woman said. "Once upon a time, Sione proposed to me, too. And I said yes."

"But you didn't get married," Spencer noted. "You said ex-fiancé. Not ex-husband."

"No, we didn't make it down the aisle," she said. "Didn't even set a date."

"Why not?"

"Things just didn't work out for us." The woman stood. "Guess it wasn't meant to be. Although sometimes, I wish it could have been."

Spencer stayed quiet, waiting for the woman to fill the silence, wondering if the woman would get caught up in the past, reminiscing and regretting, maybe let her guard down and then Spencer could attack her.

"Sione was the first guy I ever really fell in love with," the woman said. "The only guy I fell in love with. There was no one before or after him."

"How did you and Sione get together?"

"A'arotanga. A little tiny dot in the Pacific," the woman said. "Nobody has ever heard of it, but I'm glad because it's a special place, you know? Unspoiled beauty. You just know that it looks the same way it did when our ancestors arrived. I would be so pissed if it turned into Honolulu."

"Sounds lovely," Spencer said, praying she would have the chance to see the island where John had spent the latter part of his teenage years. She and John would be on the island right now if not for this wicked bitch—his ex-fiancée.

"It was lovely when I lived there. So was Sione. He was the most beautiful boy I ever saw. As soon as he looked at me with those hazel eyes, I had to have him, and I did." The woman looked wistful. "All summer. Nothing but blue skies, sunshine, white sand beaches. And sex. Lots and lots of sex. It was so magical I never wanted it to end. But it did. I went back to Oahu to finish my senior year. Then I went to the University of Hawaii, and Sione went back to Belize two years later, but we never broke up."

"Until…"

"What?" The woman scowled.

"You're his ex," Spencer pointed out. "You said it didn't work out, so you must have broken up."

"It was my fault," the woman said. "Made some bad choices. Stupid decisions. I cheated on him with his best friend. I realize how crazy that was, now. But, at the time, the guy who came between us, he was very sexy, very manipulative. Dangerous. He made me feel like Eve in the Garden of Eden. I fell for his lies."

Spencer stared at the woman, still unable to believe John had asked her to marry him. The woman was beautiful, yes, but she was mercenary. And insane. How the hell could she have cheated on a man like John? Spencer couldn't imagine any man being enticing enough to lure her away from John.

The woman said, "You know him, actually."

"What?"

"The guy I cheated with," she said. "You know him."

Apprehensive, Spencer said nothing.

"He's the same guy who came between you and Sione," the woman said, smirking. "Ben Chang."

38

The Woodlands, Texas
Carlton Woods Gated Community

"Sione, it's Spencer. Hopefully, by now, you've gotten my letter, and I hope you take it to heart. Move on with your life. Your family is probably very happy about this turn of events, and I know your mother is probably not surprised. In time, you'll realize this was best for the both of us because we probably wouldn't have lasted a year, anyway."

Sione took another sip of scotch and then listened to the voicemail again, closing his eyes. What he hoped to hear was some sort of clue as to where Spencer had been taken. A subtle, almost imperceptible, sound to lead him in the right direction.

He'd first heard the message a week ago, when Spencer had been taken from him. Spencer's voice, loud and clear in the suppressed silence of the home office, provided a grim narration of the day he couldn't get out of his head, the day he'd been reliving for the past week, the day Spencer should have become his wife.

Standing at the altar, he'd been nervous and worried as Shady had beckoned him, her expression grave. Upstairs in the bride's waiting room, he'd read the note Spencer had supposedly written.

Dear Sione,

This is going to be very painful and difficult for you so I won't drag it out. I have been thinking a lot about us and our relationship and realize that I just do not love you and I can't marry you. Please don't look for me. Just move on with your life, Sione, and find a woman who is truly worthy of you, a woman worthy of your love and a woman worthy to bear your children. Take care of yourself, Sione.

Goodbye, Spencer

Immediately suspicious and distrustful, Sione had disputed the words, refusing to believe Spencer had written them even though it was her handwriting.

"Spencer never calls me Sione," he'd told the wedding party. "She didn't write this damn letter."

Spencer had been kidnapped.

Sione was convinced she hadn't left him of her own volition, and it wasn't just the wishful thinking of a heartbroken, stunned groom. The police had been called—to pacify him, Sione figured, but he hadn't cared. The cops suggested Spencer might be a runaway bride, particularly because there were no signs of foul play. Still, Sione had insisted on filing a missing person report though he doubted the police would make any effort to find Spencer.

After searching the church grounds and surrounding area and every other place her family could think to search, practically all over Houston, the wedding party returned to The Woodlands mansion. In the kitchen, the entire wedding party plus his mother, Carmen, and his aunt Perla and his cousin Peter circled the large center island.

Everybody seemed to be talking at once, determined to share their own opinions about what the hell should be done, but Sione was only half-listening. He couldn't concentrate. Couldn't stop thinking that Spencer had been taken from him, again. He didn't care that there was no sign of foul play. He didn't give a damn about that Dear John letter they'd found, the kiss-off she had supposedly written.

A knock on the door shook him.

Irritated by the interruption, Sione pressed the stop button on the answering machine. He wasn't really in the mood to deal with another friend or family member, stopping by to provide more insight about their unsolicited advice, two cents, or whatever the hell they felt compelled to share with him about the situation.

He'd already heard pretty much everything everybody had to say. The consensus was that he'd been left at the altar. Spencer had changed her mind about marrying him. She was a runaway bride. Sione didn't believe that; he couldn't. It didn't make sense.

He knew in his heart, soul, and everywhere else it mattered that her feelings hadn't changed. More than anything, he knew Spencer hadn't left him because she was carrying his child. She wasn't going to go off somewhere and be a single mother. They were committed to, and ecstatic about, raising the baby together.

Spencer was gone because she'd been taken from him. Again. But he would get her back, just like he had a year ago. No matter what, no matter who the hell had to die.

The knocking became more insistent.

"Yeah," Sione called out, looking toward the door. "Come in."

When his mother walked in, Sione was relieved it wasn't Rae, telling him to back off and give her sister some space and time to figure out what she wanted to do. Or DJ, telling him that if Spencer had been kidnapped it was probably because of something related to her past, when she'd made the mistake of drugging old men and stealing from them. Or Shady, wanting to pray again. Or Truman, trying to convince him that he'd dodged a bullet—especially, as Truman had pulled him aside to say, since Sione hadn't forced Spencer to sign a prenuptial agreement.

Still, Sione braced himself. So far, Carmen had resisted giving any motherly advice, opting instead to provide comfort and support in the form of prayers, hugs, and reassuring smiles at just the right moment. The day Spencer had been taken, when the bridal party had convened in the spacious kitchen, Rae and DJ, with their dominant, overbearing alpha tendencies, had each taken on strategic roles, determining and assigning tasks in the search efforts.

Sione, standing on the fringes, despite being the focus of the nightmare, felt useless and incompetent. The situation seemed to be out of control. He didn't know what to do or think. There were moments when he felt like the rug was being pulled from beneath him, and the sensation of falling nearly gave him vertigo. But then he would glance up and see his mother's calm, compassionate gaze. Their eyes would meet, and the chaos would recede, and he knew, somehow, that he would not fall completely apart.

After another comforting embrace and more encouraging words, Carmen kissed the top of his head and then took a seat in the chair on the opposite side of his desk. "Well, your aunt Perla wants to go back to San Ignacio," his mother said, a bit haltingly. "And I'm thinking I might go with her."

"Yeah, you should," Sione said. "There's no need for you to stay here. There's really nothing you can do."

"I can be here for you," Carmen said. "You need someone on your side. Someone who believes in you."

"Except you really don't, Mom," Sione pointed out. "Just like the rest of the family, you think Spencer left me at the altar."

"Son, think about it from the family's point of view," Carmen said, her expression pained. "It does appear that Spencer changed her mind about marrying you."

"She didn't, though," Sione insisted, irritated and weary, not inclined to try to persuade his mother. "She was taken. Kidnapped."

"I know that's what you believe," Carmen said, as though choosing her words carefully, maybe so as not to offend him or incite him to anger. "And maybe it would be easier for the family to believe she had been kidnapped if not for the letter she left you and the voicemail."

"Yeah, Mom, I know," Sione said, his frustration mounting. "Everybody would believe Spencer had been kidnapped if that note had been from the kidnapper, demanding money from me in exchange for her safe return. Or if she had sounded scared on that voicemail. Or if there had been a broken window in the bridal room or some signs of a struggle."

Sighing, his mother said, "Sweetheart, believe it or not, but I actually do think it's strange that she left you at the altar. You know that I think she got pregnant so she could trick you into marrying her. So, why wouldn't she go through with the marriage, if that was her intention all along? But, still, I can't ignore the facts."

"That's the problem, Mom," Sione said. "You and the family and Spencer's sisters and cousins, you keep saying you can't ignore the facts. But the facts don't tell the whole story. The facts don't tell the truth. The facts are that Spencer didn't marry me and there was a note, written in her handwriting, left behind in the bridal room. The truth is that Spencer was kidnapped and whoever took her forced her to write that note and leave that voicemail. Whoever took her doesn't want it to look like she was kidnapped."

"Then why kidnap her?" Carmen shook her head. "That doesn't make sense. Why is there no ransom demand?"

"I think whoever took her didn't want the cops involved," Sione said. "If the police are looking for her, they might find her, and they might figure out who took her. Whoever took her can't risk getting caught, so this person decided to make it look like a crime hadn't been committed. This person made it look like Spencer got cold feet."

Frowning, Carmen asked, "Do you have any idea who took her?"

"I know who took her," Sione said. "It was Ben Chang."

"Ben took Spencer?" Carmen stared at him. "Are you sure?"

Sione was beyond sure. That bastard had arranged for Spencer to be kidnapped, and because of their previous relationship, the son of a bitch had been able to convince Spencer that it was in her best interest to go along with his "runaway bride" scenario.

"I know Ben took her, Mom," Sione said. "I just can't prove it."

"I don't understand," Carmen said. "Why would Ben kidnap her? Does he want something from you? Something he thinks you'll give him in exchange for Spencer?"

"I'm not going to assume that I know his motives," Sione decided to say, not willing to reveal the truth to his mother. He knew exactly what Ben wanted. Any day now, Sione suspected the bastard would make a formal demand. "I'm guessing he's pissed at me for some reason. But I'm not going to wait around for him to contact me. I'm going to figure out where he's keeping Spencer. I'm going to find her and bring her home."

After several moments of silence, during which his mother wrung her hands and appeared to be wrestling with some internal debate, Carmen cleared her throat and said, "I think you should call your father."

"What?"

"Richard will know how to deal with Ben."

Staring at his mother, Sione tried not to be offended. "You think I don't know how to deal with him?"

"Ben needs the discipline of a father," Carmen said. "Not the scolding of a brother."

"I plan to do more than scold him," Sione said. "Trust me."

"That's what I'm afraid of," his mother said. "I don't want you to get hurt. Ben will not fight fair."

"Neither will I," Sione said.

"I don't want you to fight," Carmen said. "This is not your battle, but you're caught in the middle. Why should you get blood on your hands? That's not what Siosi Tuiali'i wanted for you."

"Maybe Uncle Siosi expected too much," Sione said, slouching in the leather chair. "Maybe he looked at me and saw what he wanted to see, what he thought I could be, and not what I really was—what I really am."

"He saw who you really are," Carmen said, "not what Richard tried to make you think you should be."

Sione shrugged. "Don't know about that."

"Richard started this war with Ben," his mother said. "He should finish it."

"I don't want Dad involved," Sione said. "If I give him an inch, he'll take more than a mile. He'll think I owe him. He'll want to be in my life, and that's not happening, especially now that I'm going to be a father. I have to protect my child."

"I have to protect my child, too," his mother said, her gaze as fierce as her determined voice.

"Mom, please, let me handle it, okay?"

Carmen didn't look convinced of his capabilities, but Sione refused to feel inadequate.

"When was the last time you ate?" his mother asked.

"I don't know," Sione leaned forward and put his elbows on the desk. "I'm not hungry."

"You have to eat," Carmen told him and stood. "I'll go fix you a sandwich."

After his mother left, Sione thought about her suggestion to call Richard and shook his head. He knew his mother was concerned, meant well, and only wanted the best for him, but he was pissed that she didn't think he could handle Ben. How could she think he would willingly rely on Richard to solve his problems? Did she think he didn't have the guts to go against Ben and beat him at his own twisted games?

Sione sighed. Involving Richard in this beef with Ben was the worst damn thing he could do. It was bad enough that, once again, Spencer had been caught in the middle of Ben's bullshit. For the same damn reason, too. The envelope Ben had sent Spencer to Belize to find. The envelope Spencer had delivered to him three months ago at the Toyota Center, on a Thursday night in October. The envelope Sione had taken after he'd left Ben unconscious on the kitchen floor at the house in Third Ward.

Ben wanted the envelope back.

And he had kidnapped Spencer to get it.

39

The Woodlands, Texas
Carlton Woods Gated Community

Standing in the middle of the kitchen, Sione stared at the rust-brown splotch staining the ceramic tile. A few feet away, an overturned chair, a length of frayed rope, and several metal parts of a broken toaster littered the floor.

Sione rubbed his jaw. He didn't want to be where he was right now, in Third Ward, at the old dilapidated Colonial where he'd found Ben Chang two months ago. Driving through the neighborhood, Sione tried to ignore his surroundings, but the revitalization juxtaposed with the urban blight worried him. The blur of streets, houses, traffic lights, stop signs, and manicured lawns whispered *"We know what you did."* Behind the windows of the neglected Colonial mansions, eyes watched and remembered what he'd done.

He'd been summoned to the place where he had intended to kill a man.

The summons had arrived earlier this afternoon via courier. Sione had known exactly who'd sent it and why. He wasn't about to risk Spencer's, or the baby's, life by hesitating or posturing, pretending he didn't understand the demand, typewritten on a three-by-five index card: *Your presence is required tonight at the place where you left me to die.*

Glancing around the kitchen, shame assaulted him, forcing him to admit painful truths about himself. Compelled by rage, he'd made disastrous decisions, arriving at a point where he'd been willing to kill a man, allowing himself to rely on the lessons his father had taught him.

"It's nice to see you, old friend."

The voice, somewhere behind him, was deep and raspy with just a hint of an island lilt, conjuring up memories, filling him to the brim with rage and bewilderment.

Sione couldn't move for a moment, holding himself rigid. He didn't want to turn around. He didn't want to face what he knew was behind him, waiting to drag him back to some dark corner of hell.

Slow, reluctant, Sione turned. Avoidance wasn't an option. He had to deal with the monster.

Ben stood near the back door, pointing a gun at Sione.

"Where is Spencer!" Sione took a step toward Ben. "What the hell have you done with her?"

"Spencer is fine." Ben held his hands up, the gun pointing toward the ceiling. "She's resting."

"Where is she?" Sione took another step, dropping his gaze to the gun, still in Chang's hand but hanging at his side now, pointing at the floor. "Where did you take her?"

"Someplace safe." Ben leaned back on the edge of the stove and crossed one ankle over the other, casual, almost relaxed, obviously thinking he had the upper hand, had the situation under control. "Don't worry, old—"

Sione went for the gun, closing his hand around the barrel as he slammed a fist into Chang's gut, putting him on his knees, coughing and gagging.

"Where is Spencer?" Sione asked, trying to ignore the flare of self-condemnation. He didn't want to rely on violence, didn't want to go too far, but if he had to go farther than he wanted to get Spencer back, he would. And hopefully, he wouldn't go so far that he was unable to find his way back.

"Help me up, old friend." On his hands and knees, Ben looked up at him, laughing. "I'll show you that she is alive and doing well."

"I'm not your old friend," Sione said, walking to the table. "Help yourself up."

Grunting and wincing, Ben made it to his feet, wobbling like a drunk, and yet his dark glare was pure, raw hate. Joining Sione at the round breakfast table, Ben took a seat and then pulled out a smartphone, quickly swiping across the screen several times.

"Look here," Ben instructed, holding the smartphone up, screen facing Sione. Heart pounding, Sione glared at Ben. "What am I supposed to be looking at?"

"You wanted to know that Spencer is safe," Ben said, pushing the phone across the table toward Sione. "See for yourself. You'll be looking at a live video feed of Spencer, at her present location, which must remain undisclosed, of course."

Worried and wary, Sione grabbed the phone, and after a moment's hesitation, he looked at the screen. Spencer sat in the middle of a bed with her legs tucked beneath her, her hand on her abdomen, moving back and forth. Sione recognized the calming gesture. Spencer always rubbed her stomach to relax herself.

Sione swallowed, steeling himself against an onslaught of emotions. The video feed of Spencer was a cruel reminder of her absence. It did nothing to comfort Sione and only made him long to have her in his arms again. Since their reconciliation, they had developed a habit of sleeping in a position where they were both able to cradle her stomach as they drifted off. Often, he would wake before she did, and during those pre-dawn moments, he would talk to the baby, sharing hopes and dreams with their unborn child.

"Why did you kidnap Spencer?" Sione asked, slamming the smartphone on the table, screen down so he wouldn't be distracted. "You knew I had the envelope. Why not just take me? Force me to give it to you."

"If you want to bring a man to his knees or force him to return something he stole from you," Ben said, "then you find out what that man cannot live without and take it away from him. I know that Spencer is important to you and you'll do anything to get her back."

"And by anything, you mean, I'll give you that envelope."

"You shouldn't have taken it. A stupid thing you did. But even more stupid is that you actually thought I wouldn't do whatever was necessary to get my envelope back," Ben said. "You must have known that the only way to make sure I wouldn't come back would have been to kill me, and you know you weren't capable of that. So, you should not have taken my envelope. If you hadn't, you and Spencer would be man and wife, enjoying your honeymoon."

Ben was right. Spencer's kidnapping was his fault. He'd brought this misery on himself, and for what? Why had he stolen the envelope? What had taking the envelope accomplished? What had he expected to do with it?

"If you want Spencer back," Ben said, "then you need to return the envelope."

"Might be difficult."

"Difficult? Why?" Ben asked.

"I don't have the envelope in my possession, and it won't be easy to get it."

"What do you mean?" Ben demanded. "What did you do with that envelope? Where is it?"

"It's in a safe deposit box at a bank in A'arotanga," Sione said.

"A'arotanga? Are you serious?" Ben exhaled, rubbing his eyes. "My envelope is in some bank on an island no one has fucking heard of on the back side of the fucking world?"

Sione nodded. "In order to get it, I have to go to A'arotanga, get the key, go to the bank—"

Ben exploded, cursing in patois, stalking back and forth across the kitchen.

"I told you it wasn't going to be easy to get," Sione said.

Ben glared at him. "If I didn't need that envelope, I would kill you."

"But you do need that envelope," Sione taunted, enjoying the upper hand, though he doubted it would last long. "So you're not going to kill me, and you won't hurt Spencer either."

"You think I don't have plans for that treacherous bitch? I intend to snap her neck like a twig. She will be punished for her betrayal, but if you think you'll be able to protect her, think again," Ben said. "You will know neither the time nor the place, but one day, you will have the opportunity to cradle her dead, lifeless body in your arms."

Raging inside, Sione fought the urge to lunge at Chang and rip his throat out. He could do it, but Ben would expect it and would have an answer, a counter. Richard had taught them to fight to the death, if necessary, but Sione didn't want to die today.

He didn't want to kill anyone either, not even Ben, who deserved something worse than death for kidnapping Spencer. He wouldn't be baited into the violent reaction Ben wanted. He wouldn't give in to the need to exact revenge. His rage didn't matter. Revenge didn't matter. Nothing mattered except getting Spencer back.

"The fact remains," Sione said, "that if you want that envelope then I have to go to A'arotanga."

"We," Ben said, eyes shrewd, smile sly.

"We?"

"Here's how it's going to work, old friend," Ben said. "You and I will fly to A'arotanga tomorrow. I'll arrange all the flights. Once on the island, you'll go to the bank and get the envelope. When the envelope is in my possession, I will authorize Spencer's release."

Sione shook his head. "You're not getting the envelope until Spencer is back with me, safe and unharmed."

Ben sighed. "That will be difficult since you and I will be on the other side of the world. What, do you expect me to fly her to A'arotanga, too?"

"What I expect is for Spencer to be returned to me, safe and unharmed," Sione repeated, glaring at Ben, refusing to back down. "Or you can expect to forget about getting that damn envelope. How you get her back to me is your problem. But the only way it's going to work, old friend, is that I will exchange the envelope for Spencer's safe return to me."

"Well, old friend," Ben said, "you do appear to have me by the balls."

"Remember that," Sione said. "Because if you try to fuck me over, I will cut them off."

"There will be no need for that," Ben said, his easy, indifferent tone a contrast with the ire in his gaze. "We'll do it your way, and we'll both get what we want. The envelope for me, and that evil, treacherous bitch for you."

40

Location Unknown

In the shower, Spencer washed quickly, soaping beneath her arms, while thoughts of escape consumed her. She had to make some sort of a break for it.

All night, she'd tossed and turned, thinking the woman wasn't going to kill her. The woman needed her alive. If the woman killed her, there was no chance the woman would get what she wanted, whatever it was. The end game of any kidnapping was getting the ransom paid. But had there been a ransom demand? John would have paid it as soon as he'd received it ... so, what the hell was going on? Who had hired the woman to take her? What did that person want? Surely by now the person would have communicated the demands to John.

Spencer turned, allowing the water to rain down on her back as her thoughts drifted to John, the ex-fiancée and Ben. The dynamics of the situation were hard to fathom. She didn't know how to begin to wrap her mind around the circumstances. There was no way to ignore, however, the bizarre parallels to her relationships with John and Ben.

John and Ben.

The woman's most startling revelation was a confirmation of Spencer's secretly held suspicions and conclusions. John knew Ben. They had some sort of contentious, fractured relationship. How long had they known each other? Why had John lied about knowing Ben? It had always been clear that Ben knew John, but John had never acknowledged the relationship. Why? Because Ben had slept with John's then fiancée?

John's disdainful feelings about Ben made more sense now. Obviously, John hated Ben. And yet, Spencer wondered if John's anger toward Ben was for some other reason besides the betrayal of a fiancée and a best friend. Maybe it was something to do with Ben's crazy claims that he and John were more alike than different, though she doubted it. Unless Ben had been slyly referring to their interest in the same women.

Spencer wrapped the towel around her, walked out of the bathroom, and gasped.

The woman stood near the foot of the bed, giving her a slight smirk. "Clean as a whistle?"

Rolling her eyes, Spencer grabbed the clothes, folded neatly on the corner of the bed, and returned to the bathroom to put them on. Minutes later, back in the bedroom, the woman was still there. Trying to ignore the woman, Spencer went to the couch and sat.

"Okay, black beauty," The woman tossed a burner phone toward Spencer. "Time to call Prince Charming."

"I already called him," Spencer snapped, not bothering to pick up the phone when it landed on the couch, a few inches from where she sat, near the far-right side.

"Well, you need to call him again," the woman said. "And this time, you need to make sure he understands that you want nothing to do with him because, apparently, last time you called, he wasn't convinced."

"How do you know that?"

"Prince Charming filed a missing person report with the police," the woman said. "Which means he thinks you were kidnapped, and not a runaway bride, which is what we need him to think."

"Why do you want him to think I left him at the altar?" Spencer asked. "He will never believe that."

"And why is that?" the woman asked, giving her a smug sneer. "Because you love him with all the breadth and depth and height of your soul or whatever the hell? Because your love will never fail? Because you two were planning to be together forever until the end of time?"

"Because he knows how much I love him," Spencer said. "He knows how much I wanted to marry him and how much I wanted to be his wife and how I wanted him to be my husband. He will never believe that I would turn my back on him, on our love."

Taking a seat on the opposite couch, the woman said, "We can't have Prince Charming running to your rescue. Now get on the phone and convince Sione that you want nothing to do with him."

"And if I don't?" Spencer asked. "If I can't?"

Rolling her eyes, the woman said, "You know, I heard that you're a pretty good liar."

Spencer glared at the bitch. "You don't know anything about me."

"I know that you stole Ben's money and Rolex watches," she said. "And then you put a knife in his gut. You pretended that you cared about Ben. Pretended that you loved him. How difficult can it be to pretend that you never loved Sione?"

Spencer said nothing.

"You lied to Sione, too," the woman said. "You lied to him about why you really went to his resort. You didn't tell him Ben sent you there to look for that envelope. So, don't act like you can't lie to Sione, okay?"

"How do you know Ben wanted me to look for that envelope?" Spencer asked.

"Ben told me why he sent you to Belize," the woman said. "Turns out you were successful. In more ways than one. You got the envelope for Ben, which meant he wouldn't call the cops on you. And you snagged the rich, good-looking resort owner. I'd say it was a pretty good trip."

"A good trip?" Spencer scoffed. "It was hell."

"You think so?"

"Ben forced me to lie to Sione. He wanted me to drug Sione," Spencer said, not sure why she was conversing with the woman. "But that wasn't even the worst part."

"What was the worst part?"

Folding her arms, Spencer crossed her right leg over her left. "Trust me, you don't want to know."

"Trust me," the woman said and then leaned forward, resting her elbows on her knees, her dark eyes alight with some strange, primal excitement, "I do want to know. The worst part is always the most interesting."

"There is nothing interesting about three women being murdered," Spencer said, disgusted by the woman's sick fascination. "They were shot in the head, and they had their left hand chopped off."

"You're talking about the three women who Ben told you to deliver money and fake passports to, right?"

Spencer nodded, not surprised the woman knew the whole sordid tale.

"So, who killed the three women?" the woman asked, her eyes shrewd as she sat back. "Did the cops ever find out?"

"As far as I know, the murders are still unsolved," Spencer said.

"You think Ben killed them?"

"I don't know, maybe," Spencer said, shrugging. "Or had them killed. But that doesn't make sense. Why give them money and passports and then kill them?"

"Ben is diabolical," the woman said. "He might have wanted to lull the women into a false sense of security before he got rid of them. If the women thought they could trust Ben, and that he was going to help them, it would be easier to get rid of them because he would know exactly where they were."

"I guess," Spencer said, troubled by the theory. "But…"

"But what?" The woman sat back. "You can't imagine Ben being so heartless."

"I know exactly how heartless Ben can be," Spencer said.

"He's crazy about you," the woman said.

Spencer stared at her. "What?"

"Ben is in love with you," the woman said.

41

Location Unknown

"Ben is not in love with me," Spencer said and stood. "If Ben was in love with me—"

One of the guards in black fatigues, the guy with the scar, lurched into the room, panting and sweating. Eyes wild, he clutched his chest, blood seeping between his fingers.

"Gustavo, what the hell happened?" the woman demanded, but her voice was shrill, laced with panic. "What…"

Gustavo lumbered toward them, unable to speak, and held up his left arm.

"Oh my God," Spencer whispered, stumbling back, staring at the guard's bloody wrist. The man's left hand had been hacked off. Coughing blood, Gustavo dropped to his knees.

The woman spun toward Spencer. "We have to get out of here. Stay behind me!"

Spencer took another step back, wary of the fierce terror in the woman's dark eyes. "What's going on?"

"No questions right now, okay?" The woman took a knee next to Gustavo's foot. Lifting the hem of Gustavo's pant leg, the woman removed a large gun from an ankle holster.

Spencer stared at the guard's left arm, missing its hand, and winced. Memories assailed her, forcing her into the past, when Ben had forced her to do favors for him in Belize, one of which had brought her into direct contact with a bloody, dismembered hand.

Spencer couldn't help but wonder if the guard's missing hand was somehow connected to the missing hand she'd found in Belize, but there was no time for speculation or conjecture. There was no time for anything except doing whatever it took to stay alive, to make sure her baby was safe.

On her feet again, the woman grabbed Spencer's wrist and pulled her, rushing toward the wall of French doors. "We are under attack and if we don't get out of here—"

"Under attack?" Spencer stumbled along, trying to keep up with the woman's frantic strides as they crossed the bedroom suite. "What are you talking about? Who—"

Abruptly, the woman stopped and Spencer nearly collided with her. "What is it?"

The woman cursed and then turned, forcing Spencer to mimic her moves. Seconds later, Spencer glanced over her shoulder and realized why the woman had done a dizzying about face. Two men stood outside the French doors. Dressed in what appeared to be custom-tailored business suits and wearing dark sunglasses, the men were armed with assault rifles.

"Hurry! Let's go!" the woman demanded, yanking Spencer as she ran toward the double doors leading out of the bedroom suite. "Move your ass!"

"What's happening?" Spencer asked. "Who are those men?"

"Mercenary bastards," the woman said. "I don't know how the hell—"

Glass shattered and burst under a barrage of rapid gunfire. Spencer screamed and tried to drop to the floor, but the woman forced Spencer to stay on her feet.

"Keep your head down, but don't stop moving!" the woman commanded.

Bullets followed them out of the bedroom suite, slamming into the walls and the door frame. They dashed down the wide hallway and at the end, they went left. Halfway down the hall, another man in a business suit rounded the corner. As he walked toward them, raising his gun, Spencer screamed and tried to flatten herself against the wall. The woman raised the weapon she'd taken from the dead guard and fired several shots. One of the bullets caught the man below the right eye. He dropped to the floor.

"Here, take this." The woman shoved the gun at her. "I might need you to cover me!"

Spencer shook her head. "I don't know how to use a gun!"

"Just point and squeeze the trigger!" The woman hurried to the well-dressed mercenary, grabbed his rifle, and turned, cursing. Spencer glanced right. The two men they'd seen outside the French doors stood where the main hall and the hall leading to the master suite formed a T. The men started shooting, and the woman returned fire.

Screaming and covering her ears, Spencer dropped the gun the woman had given her and sank to her knees, crouching next to an accent table against the wall. Despite the terror of the gunfire, Spencer couldn't help but wonder if, instead of cowering behind a table, she should be trying to get away. The woman was engaged in warfare. Wouldn't this be the best time to crawl to the end of the hall, using the distraction of the shootout as a cover? But what if she made it around the corner and came face to face with another attacker? She would be a sitting damn duck, shot on sight. Maybe, maybe not. Was it possible that one of the attackers might help her?

The rapid discharge of fire continued, and Spencer closed her eyes, thinking that she was going insane. She had to be out of her damn mind, thinking she could get a mercenary to listen to her story and convince him to help her get away and get back to John.

For now, it was best to stay with the woman.

John's ex-fiancée had been paid to kidnap her and keep her alive until demands were met. Eventually, the woman would release her. Who the hell knew what these men had planned? Why had they attacked?

Covering her head, Spencer prayed she wouldn't be shot as a volley of bullets burst through the air above her, filling the hallway with smoke and the smell of gunpowder.

"Come on!" the woman ordered when the gunfire ceased.

Shell-shocked, Spencer glanced up. The woman reached for her, but Spencer resisted, shrinking back.

"I held them off, but we have to go now!" The woman yanked Spencer to her feet. "Come on!"

As she ran behind the woman, Spencer glanced back. The men were gone. Spencer guessed they had retreated back around the corner, maybe to reload, maybe because they'd been wounded. Didn't matter. The woman was right. They had to go. Hesitation and reluctance would guarantee her a bullet to the back of the head.

After heading around the man the woman had shot in the face, they followed the hall as it turned to the right and then opened to the large den with its oversized couches and recliners. In the den, the woman angled left, toward an opening to a hallway that led to the dining room and kitchen. Spencer detected movement to her right and glanced that way. Two men ran into the den from the opening on the right and immediately began shooting.

As bullets flew, Spencer hit the floor, following the woman's lead. Crawling across the hardwood floor, they headed between two recliners and then around to the back of the couch.

The woman got to her knees, peeked above the back of the couch, and fired a hail of rounds. Quickly, she crouched down again when a hail of bullets came back, many of them slamming into the wall across from them, ripping holes into framed art, the crown molding, and the wainscoting.

"Crawl to the hallway and then get to the kitchen," the woman said when the bullets stopped for a moment. "I'll cover you, but stay on the floor and go as fast as you can. When you get to the kitchen, wait for me."

Trembling, near hysteria, Spencer managed to nod.

"But don't get any ideas about trying to escape, black Barbie," the woman warned. "You've still got that collar around your neck."

Anger and annoyance flared when Spencer touched her neck and felt the collar. With World War III going on around her, she'd forgotten about the shock device.

"Go!" the woman ordered as she rose above the back of the couch and began firing again.

Spencer flattened her body and half-crawled, half-shimmied across the floor. In the hallway, she stood and took off, heading for the kitchen. Once there, Spencer paced around the island, contemplating making a run for it. But she couldn't forget about the collar. If she wasn't in the kitchen when the woman came looking for her, she would make her pay for trying to escape. Spencer didn't want to be shocked again. It was painful, and she was terrified of the effects it might have on the baby.

What if the woman never made it to the kitchen? The gunfire was intermittent but hadn't completely ceased yet. What if the woman was shot and killed? If the woman was dead, then Spencer would have no choice, she would have to—

The woman ran into the kitchen, holding her shoulder, sweating and wincing.

"Oh my God," Spencer said, staring at the bloody, mangled flesh just beneath the woman's left shoulder. "They shot you!"

"I'll live," the woman said. "We gotta go."

"What happened to the gun?" Spencer asked, noticing that the woman didn't have the rifle.

"Ran out of bullets," she said, heading to the kitchen door. "But those bastards are reloading so we need to leave!"

Spencer followed the woman outside. The sky was overcast, but despite the lack of sun and the low cloud deck, Spencer blinked as her eyes adjusted to the natural light. It was humid, and the breeze carried a familiar tropical scent that, along with the smell of bark and foliage, gave her a feeling of déjà vu.

She and the woman ran around the side of the house, following a wide stone path. Behind the three-car garage, on a pea gravel plaza surrounded by hibiscus bushes, two golf carts were parked near a banyan tree. The woman jumped into one of the golf carts and started it as Spencer climbed in next to her.

Shifting the cart into gear, the woman reversed the cart to back it away from the tree, and then she sped off, steering the cart in a wide arc, heading toward the front of the garage.

Several feet from the courtyard in front of the house, Spencer heard an engine motor behind them and looked back.

Two of the mercenaries were in the second golf cart, speeding behind them, quickly gaining ground. The woman looked back and cursed. Spencer tried to get her bearings and tried to think. Her thoughts were scrambled, her emotions chaotic. She entertained ideas of jumping out of the cart and leaving the woman to deal with the men. She wondered if the best thing would be just to give up. Raising the white flag would most likely mean certain death. Jumping from the cart would be even worse, especially for the baby.

"Sonofabitch!" The woman swerved the cart right, then left, and then right again, careening over puddles and sending Spencer across the bench seat and almost out of the cart.

Her heart beating wildly, Spencer looked back again. The men stayed on the woman's tail as she headed away from the house, speeding down what seemed to be a private road, wide enough for two vehicles, bordered by thick jungle.

Belize, Spencer realized, as a gust of wind swept past her face. She was in Belize. Somehow, someway, the woman had taken her to Belize. Questions crowded her mind, but Spencer ignored them. She had to focus on staying alive and making sure she didn't fall out of the golf cart.

The woman made a wide arc to the right, and the man driving followed, and then abruptly, the woman switched back left. The man, still heading right, almost clipped the back of the woman's cart. Spencer clutched the side support bar, praying the woman wouldn't crash or tip the cart over, praying for her baby, and praying that God would save her life so the baby could be carried to full term and then delivered and placed in her arms. Mimicking the woman's move, the man overcorrected as his cart's tires lost traction for a moment, but he managed to stay with the woman as she sped toward the end of the road.

Gunshots cut through the sound of roaring engines. A bullet hit the hood of the golf cart, the force of it sending the cart left, toward the jungle. Spencer screamed.

Grunting, the woman yanked the wheel right—

Another shot.

The bullet hit the bench seat, inches from Spencer's leg.

"Damn!" The woman pulled the wheel hard, sending the cart skidding and spinning in a dizzying circle before she was able to get control again and steer straight. "Take the wheel!"

"What are you doing?" Spencer screamed, horrified as the woman took her hands from the wheel to remove something from beneath the seat—a gun.

"Grab the wheel!" the woman shouted as she turned and maneuvered onto her knees on the seat, facing the back of the cart. Grabbing the seat rest for support, the woman aimed and fired the weapon.

Spencer grabbed the wheel and yanked it hard, trying to keep the cart from careening into the trees, but her actions caused the woman to pitch forward, and she dropped the gun. A shot went off. The woman yelled out a curse and then scrambled back to a sitting position, resuming control of the cart as it skidded off the shoulder and crashed.

42

Jarred from the slam into the queen palm tree, Spencer looked to her right, stunned and confused. Next to her, the woman moaned, her body twisted at an odd angle, trapped between the golf cart's front brush guard and the palm tree. Somewhere in her mind, it registered that the woman must have been thrown forward out of the cart, but she wasn't sure.

The mercenaries steered the golf cart toward her, stopped a few feet away, and got out. Though she felt shattered and bruised, Spencer stumbled out of the woman's cart. Crying and praying they wouldn't kill her, she staggered toward the trees, desperate to escape.

"Not so fast..." a voice behind her ordered. Spencer froze, panic and fear slicing through her like a knife, and yet there was something gentle in the man's command that confused her. "Are you hurt?"

Bewildered, Spencer turned and looked up at the man.

"It's okay," said the man, taking a cautious step toward her. "You're going to be okay."

Spencer shook her head, shivering despite the balmy atmosphere. "What? How?"

"Come on." The man slipped an arm around her and guided her away from the cart where his partner was dealing with the woman, who, despite being banged up, was cursing and struggling to free herself from the choke hold he'd trapped her in.

As the mercenary walked Spencer to the other golf cart, three large black SUVs with black tinted windows sped down the road toward them, tires spraying gravel, and then parked in a row on the opposite shoulder. From the first SUV, three men emerged, each man dressed in a custom-tailored suit. The doors of the last SUV opened, and two men got out, dressed impeccably. One of the men from the first car walked to the second SUV and opened the passenger door.

Spencer saw a black boot descending beneath the door and then jumped when the boot slammed down against the gravel. The mercenaries stood at attention, waiting. Something strange and electric swirled in the air, something magnetic and reverent that unnerved and fascinated her. Whoever the man was, Spencer had a feeling that he was the boss. These mercenaries in their expensive suits were under his command, control, and direction. Whoever he was, he seemed to demand respect and deference.

Moments later, the man from the second SUV exited, and one of the mercenaries rushed to close the door behind him. Just like his team of assassins, the man was dressed in a tailored suit and wore dark sunglasses, but there was something slightly more sophisticated and elegant about him. He seemed more powerful, and more diabolical, like some sort of island dictator, Spencer thought, watching him stride across the road.

"No! No!" the woman screamed and struggled more violently as the mercenary boss stopped in the middle of the road and then nodded his head. It must have been some sort of signal, Spencer realized, because the man restraining the woman began to drag her, kicking and screaming, toward the mercenary boss.

Apprehensive, Spencer watched as the man restraining the woman stopped about a foot away from the boss. He removed his arm from around her neck but then held the woman's arms behind her back so she couldn't get away. No longer struggling, the woman whimpered and cried, her tone pleading. She was begging, imploring, but she was speaking a language Spencer couldn't understand. It wasn't European, Asian, or Middle Eastern. It sounded tribal.

The mercenary boss spoke to the woman in the strange language, and Spencer wondered if they knew each other. Or maybe they had heard of each other. The woman was, obviously, the kind of woman who dealt with criminals. Maybe the mercenary boss had a fearsome reputation in the criminal world, and the woman was well aware of it.

As the conversation between the woman and the mercenary boss continued, Spencer stared at the man, noting something familiar in his stature and commanding presence.

After another mournful scream, the woman began speaking more rapidly, her tone desperate.

The mercenary boss nodded again, and the man holding the woman released her and stepped back. The mercenary boss gave the woman a backhanded slap that sounded like a gunshot. Reverberating, the report made Spencer jump and leaves rustled as birds took flight.

Groaning, the woman dropped to the ground. The mercenary boss kicked her. Spencer gasped, horrified, as the woman flopped over onto her side. A silent protest rose within Spencer, but it stuck in her throat, and she realized, with sickening terror, that something awful and heinous was about to happen, something she would never be able to forget, something she might never recover from. Something…evil.

The mercenary boss spat words at the woman, reached into his custom-tailored jacket, and pulled out a gun. Crying, the woman writhed in the gravel, struggling to roll over. Something roared in Spencer's head, rushing through her body, propelling her to move, to do something, to stop something.

"Easy," said the man with his arm still around her, and from the pressure of his hold, Spencer knew he was not about to let her break free. There was nothing she could do to prevent what was about to happen, and the thought was both infuriating and irritating. Part of her didn't want anything bad to happen to the woman, and yet another part wasn't sure how to feel. The woman had kidnapped her and put a shock collar around her neck. She should hate the woman for destroying her wedding day. But the woman hadn't really mistreated her. And when the mercenaries had attacked, the woman had protected her.

A gunshot burst through the still atmosphere. Spencer looked away and closed her eyes, jumping when another bullet was fired. The third shot startled her, and so did the fourth. But, the fifth shot was mind-numbing, and the sixth one didn't seem to register with her. The final shot, the seventh bullet, was almost anticlimactic, or maybe she was too shocked to be hysterical and horrified anymore.

"Make sure this wicked whore of Babylon is really dead," said the mercenary boss. One of the mercenary minions checked, taking a knee in the gravel next to the woman's bullet-ridden lifeless body. He nodded at the boss and then stood.

"Now make sure no one finds her," said the boss, speaking to no particular minion, and yet each one harkened to his words, nodding and paying close attention. "Make it as though she never existed. Understand? Because it would have been better if she had never been conceived."

As the minions gathered around the woman, like vultures, talking among themselves in low tones, the mercenary boss walked toward Spencer. Worried, she glanced at the minion who'd helped her from the golf cart, but he was removing his arm from around her, and as the boss came closer, the minion walked away.

"How are you, dear?" the boss asked, his voice deep, his tone concerned. "I pray you were not violated, mistreated, or degraded by that evil bitch."

Wary, Spencer stared at him.

He'd just put seven bullets into a woman, and he wanted to know how she was? She didn't know how to answer. How was she? Somewhere between repulsed and relieved. She was terrified, and yet something about him comforted her, made her feel protected despite his brutality. It was a tender savagery, and for some reason, she knew he was not going to hurt her. She wouldn't end up sprawled in the dirt, bleeding, dead from several bullets to the face.

"I am sorry you had to witness that, but evil must not be allowed to flourish or prosper. It must be eradicated."

Spencer just stared, not sure what to do or say.

"One of my men will get that ridiculous thing off your neck," said the boss, giving her a reassuring smile. "And then we can get going."

"Where are you taking me?" Involuntarily, Spencer touched the collar. In all the chaos and confusion, she'd forgotten it was there. "Where are we going?

"We're going to reunite you with my son," he said. "Then the two of you can realize your dreams of becoming husband and wife."

"Your son?" Spencer asked, struggling to catch her breath. "What are you talking about? Who is your son?"

"My son is your fiancé," said the mercenary boss. "Sione Tuiali'i."

"Sione is your…son?"

Nodding, the mercenary boss removed his dark glasses and stared at her.

Spencer almost collapsed. She was shocked by how much the mercenary boss looked like John. He was an older version of John— John in ten, maybe fifteen, years. They shared the same height, muscular build, and handsome features. And the same eyes, Spencer noticed. The mercenary boss and John had the same hazel eyes.

"Will you take me to…Sione?" Spencer asked, tears spilling down her cheeks. "Please, will you take me back to him?"

43

———————

Somewhere over the Pacific Ocean

The plane glided through billowy clouds at cruising altitude.

Sione took a deep breath and tried to relax, but he was anxious and fidgety, knowing he'd have to endure ten more hours before the aircraft arrived in A'arotanga. Ten hours was too long and not long enough. Too much time to think of the worst, to worry about everything that could go wrong when the plane landed.

He was exhausted but couldn't sleep. The last twenty hours had been a hellish blur, disconcerting and disorganized, hard to believe, hard to wrap his mind around. One minute, he'd been at the house in Third Ward, and the next morning, he'd arrived at Hooks Airport at seven a.m. to board the Gulfstream Ben had chartered for their transoceanic trip. Eight hours later, they touched down in Oahu at eleven a.m. for a fuel stop and some breakfast. Six hours later, wheels up at five p.m., and now they were back in the air.

Yesterday, during the first leg of the trip, the spacious, luxurious cabin had been silent except for the gentle hum of the jet engines. Both he and Ben had been distracted by respective internal musings. The peaceful atmosphere had lulled Sione into a strange sense of security, where he allowed himself to doze every now and then. The silence provided opportunities to think about Spencer and the baby. He found himself creating fantasy scenarios of what their life would be like. He imagined the moment when he would hold his child in his arms for the first time.

His little boy. The sonogram had confirmed what Spencer had surmised from the blue elephant. They were having a boy. Sione had been overjoyed when viewing the ultrasound image. Hearing the fetal heartbeat had been his undoing. It had been pure unspeakable, indescribable joy, knowing his son was alive and thriving. And in five months, he would meet his precious little boy. He imagined rocking his son to sleep, bathing him, changing his diapers, and soothing him with lullabies when he cried. He envisioned first steps and first words.

Today, he was worried, tense, apprehensive, and anxious. He couldn't stop worrying about Spencer. What if she was already dead? He couldn't trust Ben to tell him the truth. The video Ben had showed him could have been faked—filmed when Spencer was alive. Spencer couldn't be dead. If Spencer was dead, then the baby…no, he wouldn't think it, he couldn't. If anything bad happened to the baby, Sione wouldn't want to live anymore. What would be the point? How could he exist in a world where Spencer and the baby were gone?

Sione took a few deep breaths, trying to remain calm. He had to think logically. Spencer wasn't dead. Ben wanted the envelope, and the bastard knew he wouldn't get it if anything happened to Spencer. Still, Sione couldn't shake his apprehension. He had a feeling Ben was plotting some type of double cross, devising a scheme to get the envelope and get back at Spencer. *She will be punished for her betrayal.* Sione couldn't take Ben's threats lightly, couldn't dismiss them. Ben was dedicated when it came to revenge. He had plans to make Spencer pay, and he wouldn't be satisfied with ruining Spencer's life. Ben wanted to kill her.

"Where is Spencer?" Sione asked, though he didn't really expect Ben to tell him—not yet, anyway. If he could get the bastard talking about the kidnapping, maybe Ben would let some crucial detail slip, some clue as to where he was keeping Spencer. A long shot, Sione knew, but he had to try. Ben had promised to do things Sione's way, but that was bullshit. Ben's word meant nothing. Sione had to figure out where Spencer was before the plane landed. Once on the island, he would find a way to contact his cousin Roy, a local detective, and pass the information to him.

"Somewhere safe," Ben said, reclined in his seat across the aisle.

"How do I know that for sure?"

"You saw the live feed," Ben said.

"I saw what you said was a live feed, but how do I know you were telling the truth?"

"You have to trust me, old friend."

"Trust you?" Sione glared at him. "Are you out of your mind?"

Ben said nothing.

"Where the hell is somewhere safe? Who is she with?"

"She's with someone who has been told to take good care of her," Ben said. "Someone who has been told to make sure that she is fed and—"

"Who is it?" Sione asked. "One of your triad friends?"

"Actually," Ben said. "It is an old mutual friend of ours."

"We don't have any mutual friends," Sione said.

"Forgive me, I should have said, a woman we were both involved with at one time."

"What the hell are you talking about?" Sione stared at Ben, his heart racing. Besides Spencer, there was only one other woman they had a relationship with, but it couldn't possibly be the woman he was thinking about because that woman was dead.

"Correction, a woman we were involved with at the same time," Ben said. "Moana."

Sione closed his eyes as a painful dizziness rendered him speechless, unable to think or move.

"You know, old friend," Ben said, chuckling softly. "The next time you kill someone, make sure they're really dead."

"I don't understand," Sione whispered, finding his voice.

"Makes perfect sense to me," Ben said. "As I've told you before, time and again, you don't have the guts to take a life. You never have and you never will. You're probably relieved to find out that you didn't kill her, aren't you?"

"How did you..." Sione took a quick breath, trying to focus. "How did she..."

"It's an interesting story," Ben said. "And since we have some time..."

44

An island off the coast of Belize

The large SUV rumbled over the gravel road.

Jostled side to side from potholes and rough terrain, Spencer clutched the seatbelt across her body. Confused, still unable to believe the horrible things that had happened moments ago, she stared out of the window, focused on the blur of trees, trying to reorient herself. How the hell was she supposed to recover from what she'd experienced? An attack on the house where she'd been held captive had ended with the brutal murder of the woman who had taken her hostage. How could she ever get past the calm savagery of the man sitting next to her on the plush leather bench seat, separated by an armrest?

"Sione's mother tells me that congratulations are in order," said the mercenary boss.

Startled, Spencer glanced at him. "Congratulations?

"You and my son are expecting, is that right?"

Wary of confirming the news, Spencer hesitated. The thought of this man as her little boy's grandfather was strange and terrifying. Her baby's grandfather was a murderer. A cold-blooded killer with an army of well-dressed mercenaries at his disposal, eager to do his diabolical bidding.

Eventually, when she realized he was waiting for a response, she nodded and said, "Yes, Sione and I are having a baby."

"What a wonderful blessing," he said, beaming. "Do you know if it will be a boy or a girl?"

Again, she was reluctant to share any details about the baby but said, "We're having a boy."

"My son is going to have a son," he said. "My grandson."

Spencer tried to smile but couldn't force the corners of her mouth to lift.

"Have you and my son thought of any names?"

"Actually, not really," Spencer said. "It was something we planned to do after the wedding, while we were on our honeymoon, but..."

He reached across the armrest and took her hand. Spencer cautioned herself not to flinch. The strong fingers wrapped around hers had squeezed the trigger of a gun, putting seven bullets into the woman who had kidnapped her.

"What do you think about calling him Richard?"

"Richard?" Spencer snatched her hand away. "I would never name my baby Richard."

"You have a problem with the name Richard?"

"I have more than a problem with that name," Spencer spat. "A man named Richard..."

"What, dear? A man named Richard did what?"

"He made my life hell," Spencer said.

"How did he do that?"

"I was kidnapped before," Spencer said.

"That's terrible."

"The person who had me kidnapped was a man named Richard, a man I don't even know," she said. "Richard told a man named Tommy Fong to hold me hostage in a shack in the jungle. It was so horrible, it was the worst...I thought I was going to die there, and no one would ever know what had happened to me."

"I am sorry about that," he said. "But, before we go on, I must tell you something."

"What is it?"

"My name is Richard Tuiali'i," he said. "I'm the man who told Tommy Fong to kidnap you."

45

———————

Somewhere over the Pacific Ocean

"After you failed to strangle Moana last year," Ben said. "She found her way back to me, and I nursed her back to health. She was regretful and apologetic for trusting Richard, and she begged me to let her back into my good graces. After you failed to kill me two months ago, I woke up and escaped my restraints, which you hadn't tied as tight as you could have, and I discovered you had stolen my envelope. Of course, I had to get it back."

"You told Moana to kidnap Spencer?"

"She wanted to make up for going against me," Ben said. "It was the perfect opportunity for Moana to make amends."

"You sure you can trust Moana?"

Ben said nothing.

"You think Spencer is treacherous?" Sione asked. "Moana is worse than that. You think she won't stab you in the back?"

"She knows better than that."

"You think?" Sione goaded. "Moana has betrayed you before. She had your envelope stolen and hidden in my casita."

"But the envelope was found, remember?" Ben said. "Spencer was the perfect Trojan horse."

"Yeah, and Spencer was the perfect delivery girl, too," Sione said. "Passing money and fake passports to those three women you tried to protect. Except you didn't. Despite your best efforts to keep them alive, they were all killed. Moana murdered those women because Richard told her to. Moana was working for my father, against you."

"She apologized for that mistake," Ben said. "And I forgave her."

"If she went against you once, she'll do it again," Sione said. "Moana will do whatever is in her best interests, and if it means working with my father to take you down, she'll do it."

"Trying to make me doubt Moana is not going to work, old friend," Ben said. "You think I trust that bitch? You think I haven't always known, from the moment I first met her, that she's a backstabbing whore. You were the one who was fooled by her. You thought you saw something good in her, something that made you get down on one knee and propose. All I ever tried to do was show you what a crazy bitch she was, but you didn't realize it at the time."

"What are you talking about?"

"When you caught us together," Ben said. "Wasn't what you thought. Wasn't some passionate love affair going on behind your back. I was trying to show you that she wasn't the right woman for you, but you didn't want to see that. You got pissed off when you should have thanked me."

"I should have thanked you for screwing my fiancée?"

"I did you a favor," Ben insisted. "Moana wasn't the right woman for you. And neither is Spencer. That bitch made a living drugging men and stealing from them. She stole from me and then stabbed me in the gut and left me to die."

"Too bad you didn't."

"Think about that, old friend," Ben said. "If I had died, you never would have met Spencer. Although, that may have been for the best. You actually have me to thank for that sick, sadistic relationship the two of you have."

Ignoring Ben's insults, Sione said, "If Moana hurts Spencer—"

"Moana has orders to treat Spencer with dignity, as if she were a guest in her home," Ben said. "Certainly, Moana is treating Spencer better than your father told Tommy Fong to treat her. At least, I'm not having her kept in some filthy shack on a dirty mattress."

"Where is Spencer being kept?" Sione asked.

"Don't concern yourself with that," Ben advised. "She's someplace safe."

46

———

An Island off the Coast of Belize

"You're...Richard?" Spencer gaped at him, her heart racing as memories assaulted her mind. "You're the bastard who had me kidnapped in Belize?"

"Let me explain my actions," Richard said. "I believe you have been given some misinformation about me, and I would like the opportunity to help you understand why it was necessary for me to do what I did."

"Nobody gave me any misinformation about you," Spencer said. "They told me that you're the devil, and I believe it after what you did to me! Tommy Fong tied me up like an animal in that filthy shack!"

"Relax, dear," he advised. "Calm yourself."

"Calm myself?" She stared at him, wondering if he was insane. "How the hell am I supposed to calm myself when I'm sitting next to the man who—"

"Getting upset is not good for the baby."

"Go to hell," Spencer said, yanking on the inside door handle. "Stay away from me! Let me out of here!"

"I do regret that you had to suffer that experience," said Richard. "But it was unavoidable."

"Unavoidable?" Spencer scoffed. "You couldn't avoid having me kidnapped?"

"Despite the deplorable conditions in which you were kept," Richard said. "You were never in any danger of being hurt. It was always my intention to release you."

She bristled at the self-justification in his tone. "So, since you were eventually going to let me go, that makes what you did okay?"

"Having you kidnapped was not one of my finer moments," Richard conceded. "But let's not pretend that you were some innocent victim."

"What the hell does that mean?"

"It means you never would have been forced to go to Belize if you hadn't stolen from Ben."

Spencer stared at him, feeling condemned.

"Sione's mother informed me of your past after she concluded her lamentations about the consequences of your pregnancy on our son's life," Richard confessed. "I know what kind of woman you used to be. You have a history of drugging men and taking off with their valuables, which, in my estimation, would disqualify you from throwing stones."

"I know I've made terrible mistakes," Spencer said. "And bad decisions."

"Admittance is only the first step," said Richard. "After that, there should be some responsibility and restitution for your actions. Some repentance for your sins."

Spencer looked away, knowing what he meant.

She'd never confessed her crimes. The things she'd stolen would never be returned to their rightful owners. Responsibility and restitution would have to be avoided if her hopes and wishes for a life with John and the baby were to come true. Maybe the right and honorable and moral thing to do would be to turn herself in. Maybe a part of her wanted to do just that, but she lacked the willingness and the courage. It was selfish, she knew, but she didn't want to go to jail. She wanted what she didn't really deserve—the chance to be with John and raise their baby together.

"There is a saying that goes something along the lines of you cannot be fooled without your own participation," Richard said. "So, it could be perceived that the men you targeted should not have been fooling around with a woman young enough to be their granddaughter in the first place. Dirty old men shouldn't be surprised when they get scammed. After all, if something is too good to be true—for example, a beautiful young woman interested in an octogenarian—then it probably is."

Spencer remained silent.

"How about we not pick at each other's faults and flaws?" Richard suggested. "We've both done things we regret, things we've gotten away with that we should be behind bars for."

"The things I did were not directed at you," Spencer pointed out. "You were never one of my targets. I never did anything to you, but still you forced me into the middle of this beef you have with Ben so you could teach him a lesson."

"The problem with Ben is that he will never learn."

"What exactly was kidnapping me supposed to teach him?" Spencer asked. "Tommy Fong said you were trying to make Ben obey your orders, but I would like to hear from you what you think Ben will never learn."

"Ben will never learn that he should not go against me, because he won't prevail," said Richard, rubbing his eyes. "I told him that we needed to get rid of those traitorous bitches, Karen, Carla, and Maxine, but he was of a different opinion. A misguided, foolish opinion that compelled him to envision himself as some sort of protector of those women, providing them with money and new identities so they might be able to escape the consequences they deserved."

"Oh my God," Spencer whispered, realization dawning. "You killed those women."

"I did no such thing," Richard said, slightly indignant. "You will never find their blood on my hands."

"Maybe you didn't pull the trigger," Spencer said, "but you gave the order to have those bullets fired and their hands chopped off."

"I had to protect my interests," said Richard. "I would think you would understand that. Your little mission trip to Belize wasn't done out of the goodness of your heart or because you wanted to help Ben out. You didn't want to go to jail."

"You seem to think that we have something in common, but I am nothing like you," Spencer said. "Yeah, I used to be a thief, but you're a cold-blooded murderer. You shot a woman seven times."

"Again, I was protecting my interests," he said. "It was a judgment that had to be carried out. That woman was a two-faced bitch, trying to play both sides from the middle."

"What do you mean?"

"She used to work for me," he said. "I sent her to Belize to protect my interests."

"You hired her to kill those women, you mean?" Spencer said, horrified but not terrified.

"She was able to provide the level of protection I required," said Richard. "But then there was an attack on her life, which was almost successful. Instead of coming to me, she went to Ben, crawled back into bed with him."

"Crawled back in bed with Ben?"

"Moana's orders to kidnap you came from Ben," Richard said.

"I don't believe you," Spencer said. "Why would Ben want to kidnap me? That doesn't make sense."

"Obviously, he wanted something from you in exchange for your release."

"I already gave him what he wanted from me."

"That envelope he sent you to Belize to look for," Richard said, nodding. "Apparently, he lost possession of it. The envelope was stolen from him after you delivered it to him."

"So, it's my fault that Ben was careless and let somebody steal the envelope?" Spencer shook her head. "That's Ben's problem, not mine."

"I'm afraid it became your problem when Sione stole the envelope from Ben."

"Why would Sione steal Ben's envelope? Spencer shook her head, confused. "How could he have…"

Spencer sighed and closed her eyes for a moment. She knew how John could have stolen the envelope. The night they'd broken up, John had confessed to following her to the Toyota Center, where he'd seen her talking with Ben. Later, he'd confronted Ben. During the confrontation, he might have taken the envelope. But why?

"Ben had you kidnapped to get the envelope back," Richard said. "That bitch Moana helped him."

"Moana?"

"Moana is the woman who kidnapped you," Richard said.

"The woman you shot seven times," Spencer said, images of the murder flooding her mind.

"She was a backstabbing whore," Richard said. "My son never

should have gotten involved with her. She broke his heart, betrayed him in the worst way."

"She told me about that," Spencer said. "She was engaged to Sione when she cheated on him with Ben."

"She was the genesis of the feud that exists between Sione and Ben to this day," Richard said. "She burned the bridge between them, and I don't think it can ever be rebuilt."

47

Somewhere over the Pacific Ocean

"Why didn't you kill me? Or let me die?" Ben asked a few hours later, after their last conversation, which had left Sione with a sour taste in his mouth. Even the malted scotch the flight attendant had poured for him couldn't get rid of the bitterness.

"You should have killed me," Ben went on. "If you had, we wouldn't be on this plane right now, flying halfway around the world."

"We're on this plane because you kidnapped Spencer."

"I kidnapped Spencer because you stole my envelope," Ben said. "This fool's errand is all your fault. Completely unnecessary. If you had killed me, you would be married now, enjoying your honeymoon, if you hadn't been so cowardly."

Ben was right. Sione had planned to kill him, had known death was the only option, the only way to be rid of Ben for good. Why the hell hadn't he killed Ben when he'd had the chance? It was a question he couldn't answer, a question he didn't want to answer. The truth was disturbing, unfathomable.

"I wouldn't have killed you either," Ben said. "I could have the night you showed up at the house in Third Ward. I had a loaded gun in the desk drawer. I could have pulled it out, shot you stone cold dead."

"Why didn't you?"

Ben laughed. "Maybe because I didn't want to be running from Richard for the rest of my life. Or maybe because we are brothers. Not like Cain and Abel, but Jacob and Esau. We have had our differences, but one day they will be settled."

"Nothing will ever be settled between us."

"You and I were not raised to hate each other," Ben said. "And yet, we are constantly at each other's throats."

Sione didn't want to think about how they had been raised.

"We were brought up as brothers," Ben reminded him.

"We were trained to be monsters," Sione corrected. "My father wanted us to be in his league of gentlemen assassins, but that's not what I wanted for my life. I never wanted that. You, on the other hand, didn't seem to have a problem killing and destroying people's lives."

"So that's why you hate me?" Ben asked. "Because I joined Richard's crew?"

"I thought you felt the same way I did about it," Sione said, disturbed by the conversation, wishing he weren't in the middle of it. "I thought you wanted something better for your life. I thought you wanted to be a better person. When you chose Richard, it made me realize that I didn't really know you."

"When you chose to go halfway around the world and live with your uncle, I realized I didn't really know you," Ben countered. "You left me behind. What the hell was I supposed to do? I had no choice but to follow Richard. I had no other family. My mother and father were both dead. I didn't have a lot of options. And it wasn't like you were extending me an invitation to come with you to live in paradise and become a better man."

"I only went because my uncle insisted and my mother wanted me to go," Sione said, wondering why he felt the need to explain his actions, the fateful decision which had caused so much division between them.

"You went because you're a coward," Ben said. "You didn't have the guts to stand up to your father and tell him that you couldn't be what he expected of you."

"I didn't want to be what he wanted."

"No, you couldn't. You were not able," Ben said. "You didn't want your father to know that you weren't capable. When one lacks ability, one feigns disinterest in the skill."

"What's that?" Sione scoffed. "One of your triad proverbs?"

"If you could have been the man your father wanted you to be, you would have," Ben said. "But, once you realized you could not meet his expectations, you fled."

"I didn't want to meet Richard's expectations," Sione insisted. "I didn't want to take a life. That's why you're still alive."

"You know why you're still alive, old friend?" Ben asked, his smile grim. "Because of that promise Richard forced us to make to each other. You remember? He told us that there may come a day when we would fight, but it could never be to the death."

Sione remembered his father's words, the promise Richard had forced them to make. *Swear you'll never kill each other*, Richard had demanded, eyes wild, slightly feral. It was hard to look at his father, to see an older reflection of himself, a fierce, crazed version of himself, bizarre and terrifying, a version he prayed he would never become. His father could never know that, Sione recalled, bombarded by memories of his fifteen-year-old thoughts.

Swear you'll never kill each other.

At the time, Sione thought Richard was being weird, paranoid, in the throes of mania, having a moment, as his mother referred to those times when Richard seemed to be losing it. Why would he and Ben ever want to kill each other? How would they even get to the point where one of them one would want to see the other dead? Didn't make sense. Ben was his best friend, the brother he'd always wanted.

Little had Sione known. Richard hadn't been crazy. Somehow, his father had sensed the rivalry and acrimony between them, lying dormant, simmering beneath the surface.

Swear you'll never kill each other.

It was a promise Sione realized he had to keep, but not out of obedience to Richard or loyalty to Ben. He would keep the promise in honor of his uncle and out of respect for what his uncle had taught him. His little boy was another reason not to give in to murderous intent. He wanted to be the kind of loving compassionate caring father his son could rely on to be rational, thoughtful. He wanted to protect his son from men like Richard and Ben.

"And what were the results of your tropical sabbatical?" Ben asked. "Are you a better man?"

"Better than you."

"Hardly." Ben laughed, but soon his mirth faded as the flight attendant hurried down the aisle toward him. The slight furrow between her arched brows made Sione's heart slam.

The flight attendant crouched next to Ben's seat, speaking to him in rapid, whispered Chinese. Sione kicked himself for never learning the language. Ben had offered to teach him the basics, when they were younger, but Sione hadn't had the patience or the interest. The flight attendant stood and hurried to the back of the plane, disappearing behind a curtain.

"What's the matter?" Sione demanded when Ben stood. "What's going on?"

"Relax."

"Tell me what's happening," Sione said, angered by Ben's dismissive tone. "Is it the plane?

"Never knew you to be a nervous flyer, old friend." Ben smiled but it seemed forced. "Stay calm. I just need to speak with the pilot."

Ben made his way to the cockpit door, opened it, entered the cockpit, and slammed the door shut.

Sione gripped the armrest. Despite his efforts to stay calm, he couldn't stop himself from dwelling on the dozen or so disastrous scenarios in his head. The plane was going down. What the hell else could it be? Some kind of mechanical issue? Or maybe they were out of fuel? Desperate, he fought to stay calm, rational. There was nothing wrong with the plane. It was not about to crash. The aircraft seemed stable, steady. They weren't rapidly losing altitude, in some steep, nosediving descent. The plane could not crash. He had to see Spencer again. They had to get married. More than anything, he had to welcome his son into the world. Tears pricked his eyes. He couldn't die without seeing his son, without holding him.

The cockpit door opened. Ben walked out. Sione's heart shot into his throat as he focused on Ben's right hand. The son of a bitch was holding a gun, pointing it at him.

"What's the gun for?" Sione asked, struggling to deal with his confusion and anger, trying to plan his next move and think his way out of a situation he didn't quite understand.

"Insurance," said Ben.

"Insurance?"

"It seems the devil has been busy," Ben said.

"What the hell does that mean?" Sione asked, heart pounding, eyes trained on the barrel as his mind raced, trying to come up with a plan to get the gun away from Ben.

"Apparently, your father has come to the rescue of that deceitful bitch you plan to marry," Ben said. "As we speak, your father and Spencer are on a private plane headed to A'arotanga. They're following us. And when Richard gets to the island, I have no doubt he plans to kill me."

"Richard rescued Spencer? How? When?" Sione asked, his emotions conflicted. How had Richard known Spencer had been kidnapped? Had his mother called Richard? Why the hell would she do that? Sione had made it clear he didn't want Richard involved. Carmen's interference could ruin the deal Sione had made with Ben.

"What a hypocrite you are," Ben said. "You make all these grand pronouncements about how you don't want anything to do with Richard because he's the gentleman assassin, but who do you call for help when—"

"I didn't call my father," Sione said. "I don't know how he found out that you kidnapped Spencer. And if I knew where you were keeping her, I would have gone there to get her myself!"

"Why take that risk when you could have the gentleman assassin and his merry band of mercenaries do the extraction for you?" Ben asked. "Your plan worked. Richard sent his team of wet workers to the island where Moana was keeping Spencer. There was a bloody battle. Moana was killed. For real, this time."

Shaken by Ben's casual admission of Moana's death, Sione suppressed his conflicting emotions. "Ben, listen to me—"

"Shut up," Ben said, tapping the barrel against his jaw.

"If you kill me," Sione said, itching to lunge at the son of a bitch, "then you'll never get the envelope." He entertained ideas of wrestling the gun away and beating him unconscious with it, but he knew it wouldn't be that easy and he didn't want to get shot.

"Don't worry, old friend," said Ben, his smile grim. "I will get my envelope back. You're going to help me."

"You don't need my help," Sione said. "You need me to go to the bank and get the envelope from my safe deposit box and give it to you."

Ben laughed, and then said, "You really think I'm stupid enough to believe that you'll uphold your end of that fool's bargain I made with you?"

"I gave you my word."

"Your word means nothing to me!" Ben roared, aiming the gun at him again. "Richard rescued Spencer. So you know what that means? I have no leverage over you anymore. You have no reason to give me my envelope now."

"That's where you're wrong," Sione said. "The reason I'm going to give you that damn envelope is because I want you to leave me and Spencer alone. I want you out of our lives for good."

"You think I believe that?"

Trying to fight frustration, Sione rubbed his jaw. "So what are you going to do? You said it yourself, you have no leverage."

"Now, that's where you are wrong, old friend," Ben said, aiming the gun at him. "You are my leverage."

"What the hell—"

Sione jerked, and then slumped forward, realizing too late, as blackness closed around him, that Ben had shot him.

48

____

A'arotanga, South Pacific
Royal A'arotangan Inn

"Welcome to paradise," said Richard, as the private jet taxied along the runway.

After almost twenty hours in the air, they were finally in A'arotanga. The trip had taken them from Belize to Houston to Hawaii and then on to the Pacific island where John had spent the last of his teenage years. Anxious, and yet apprehensive, Spencer unbuckled her seatbelt. Moments later, they disembarked and headed across the tarmac. Vaguely, Spencer was aware of sunshine, palm trees, vibrant hibiscus, and a salty ocean breeze, but she experienced paradise in her periphery.

The lush surroundings were a cruel reminder that she wasn't on her honeymoon with John, as she should have been, as she would have been if she and John had been married, if she hadn't been kidnapped. Cruelest of all ironies was that she and John were both on the island, but for reasons she still didn't fully understand. For reasons Richard seemed hesitant to reveal or explain, John had traveled to A'arotanga without her. She hated being on the island without John and refused herself the luxury of basking in the gorgeous scenery. John was supposed to have introduced her to the beauty and the splendor of the island.

Following a quick, uneventful trip through the small, thatched-roof airport, they cleared customs. Richard led them out of the building to a car waiting at the curb. Once settled in the back seat, they were driven to a sprawling, luxurious beachfront resort where Richard booked separate bungalows for the two of them.

"Is Sione at this hotel?" Spencer asked as she and Richard took a winding palm-lined path from the front desk to the bungalows. "Are we going to see him now?"

"Soon," promised Richard, but his tone was distracted and a bit too pacifying. Spencer had the feeling he was keeping something from her, and she tried not to jump to the worst conclusions, but it was hard to keep the hysteria under control. She couldn't stop herself from wondering if coming to this island with her future father-in-law had been a mistake. Or some sort of trap. Maybe Richard wasn't as altruistic and sympathetic to her plight as he claimed to be. Several people had referred to him as a devil, and she couldn't forget that. Couldn't forget he'd murdered John's ex-fiancée, Moana. For all Spencer knew, Richard might have given Moana the orders to kidnap her before the wedding. He'd had her kidnapped before. What the hell was to stop him from doing it again?

Spencer and Richard reached her bungalow. He opened the door for her, escorted her inside, and then asked her if she needed anything.

"It was a long flight," Richard said. "You must be hungry."

"I really don't have much of an appetite," Spencer said, wringing her hands. "I just want to see Sione. Where is he?"

"I really think you should rest for a while," Richard suggested condescendingly. "In an hour or so, I'll have room service bring you something to eat."

Spencer nodded though she was reluctant to let him leave, desperate for answers about John's whereabouts. After Richard left, Spencer wandered through the suite and out onto the terrace. Surrounded by beauty she couldn't enjoy or appreciate, Spencer tried not to think the worst, but she had a bad feeling that something terrible had happened to John.

Returning to the living area of the suite, Spencer paced around for a while, cradling her abdomen for comfort. On pins and needles, she decided to sit for a moment and soon found herself drowsy. Most of her time on the plane, she'd spent dozing, her thoughts consumed by daydreams about the baby and nightmares of never seeing John again. Despite being tense and nervous, she gave in to residual exhaustion and stretched out on the couch, closing her eyes.

An insistent knocking startled her awake. Disoriented, she opened her eyes and sat up. The room was awash in a cozy, coppery glow. She stood, still fuzzy, trying to focus, walked to the door, and opened it.

"Richard would like to see you," said the mercenary minion standing in front of her.

"What?" Spencer's heart thudded. "Why? Is Sione with him?"

"Come with me, please," the minion said and then grabbed her arm, gently but firmly guiding her away from the bungalow.

49

"Where is Sione?" Spencer demanded, jumping up from the couch where she'd been instructed to wait for Richard after she'd been escorted to his bungalow, a bigger and grander model than the glorified hut she'd been given. As John's father walked down the cantilevered staircase connecting the upper and lower levels of the bungalow, Spencer was jarred by the uncanny resemblance between father and son.

"Where he is, at the moment, doesn't matter," Richard said, stopping in front of her and taking her hand.

"The hell it doesn't." Spencer snatched her hand from his possessive grasp. "You don't know where he is, do you? Or...oh my God, did something bad happen?"

"Calm yourself," Richard admonished, guiding her back to the sofa. "You must think of the health and well-being of my unborn grandson."

"Please just tell me if something bad happened to John," Spencer pleaded. "I promise I won't get upset."

"John?" A smiled played at Richard's mouth.

Frustrated, she shook her head. "I meant Sione, I—"

"You meant John," Richard said. "His mother did mention that you refer to him by the English translation of his name."

"You don't know where John is, do you?"

Richard exhaled. "No, but I—"

"Then why did you bring me here?" Spencer snapped, standing and glaring at Richard.

"Please, don't—"

"Is John dead?" She stared at him, shocked she had even been able to ask the question.

Richard shook his head. Relief made her knees buckle, and she wobbled, unsteady. In an instant, Richard was at her side, snaking an arm around her and helping her back to the couch.

"Tell me what happened to John."

"You and my son suffered the same fate," said Richard. "And at the hands of the same ungrateful son of a bitch."

"The same fate?"

"Sione was taken against his will," Richard said. "He is on the island. His specific location is unknown, at the moment, but my men are searching for him, and they have orders to find him. What you and I have to do is make sure that you and my son are reunited."

"How do we make sure that happens?"

"I'm glad you asked, sweet girl."

Spencer went hot, then cold, and then blazing, burning with rage. She jumped up from the couch and turned. Ben walked toward her, coming from a room behind the staircase, his sly smile igniting her fury.

"You evil hateful sonofabitch!" Screaming her fury and anguish, Spencer lunged at Ben. "You told me you would let me have a chance with John! You said you wouldn't stand in the way! You lying asshole!"

"What the hell are you talking about?" Ben asked. "Who the hell is John?"

"You lied to me!" she screamed, slamming her fists against his chest. "You don't want me to be happy!"

Ben grabbed her, but Spencer jerked away from him, stumbling back.

"Get your hands off of her! Don't you hurt her!" Richard thundered, glaring at Ben before he turned to the group of four minions, rushing toward him from their designated corners, where they'd been stationed, like sentries waiting for orders. "One of you take my son's fiancée back to her room and stay with her until I call you."

Spencer charged at Ben again, intent on clawing at his face in a frenzy, letting all the animosity and anguish have its way, but two of the minions took her by the arm.

"Where is John? Where are you keeping him? Why did you take him from me when you said that if I wanted to be with him, then you wouldn't stand in my way!" she shouted at Ben, shaking with rage as Richard's lackeys guided her toward the door. "You evil bastard! I hate you! I hate you!"

50

A'arotanga, South Pacific
Royal A'arotangan Inn

"Here, drink this."

Spencer looked up at Richard, walking toward her and holding a mug of steaming liquid. Sitting up on the couch, where she'd been reclining for the past hour, she asked, "What is it?"

"Warm milk," Richard said, extending the mug toward her.

Wary, she took the mug from him, glancing down into the frothy white brew.

Richard sat on the couch next to her. "How are you?"

She blew away a wisp of steam and then took a sip. "I would like to say that I'm fine, but I can't. I won't be fine until John is okay, until we're back together and moving on with our lives."

"Well, fortunately, we may be one step closer to that reality," Richard said. "After your episode, Ben and I came to a rapprochement, if you will, and we agreed on the details of our dénouement. Though, détente is probably a better word."

"What does that mean?" Spencer asked.

"Détente?"

"What you said about agreeing on the details," she clarified. "What does that mean? What are the details you agreed on?"

After a resigned sigh, Richard outlined the results of his negotiations with Ben.

Spencer said nothing as she took a few more sips, wary of what Richard and Ben had decided, what had to happen in order for John's safe return. A man she loathed and a man she didn't trust had come to resolutions she didn't really agree with. Normally, a settlement required promises from the negotiating parties, but neither Richard nor Ben would be expected to do anything except, of course, force her to do their bidding.

Once again, she was in the position of being compelled to perform tasks or else. This time, she wasn't taking risks for her own freedom, but for her future with John and their little one. She'd done favors for Ben selfishly, to save her own ass and stay out of jail. But Richard's and Ben's dénouement was for the sake of John's life, and no matter the risks, she would take them.

"So, if I agree to do what you and Ben want me to do, then—"

"There is no if you agree, dear," Richard said. "The terms of the deal have been negotiated."

"Funny how I wasn't allowed to participate in the negotiations, but I'm the one who has to fulfill the obligations of these terms you and Ben agreed to," she said, standing, walking to the glass pocket doors which opened to the lanai.

"The negotiations were to save my son's life," Richard said. "I made a deal to secure his safe release, which I assumed was what you wanted as well."

"You know that's what I want," she said, pissed at his insinuation, as though she didn't have John's interests at heart. "I just wish…"

"You just wish what?" he asked, a sinister edge to his voice. "That there was some other way to save my son's life that didn't involve you having to be selfless or thinking of the well-being of someone other than yourself?"

"I don't have a problem with what you want me to do," Spencer insisted, facing him.

"I don't care if you have a problem with it or not," Richard said. "Your wishes don't mean shit. You will do what is necessary to make sure that Ben releases my son, do you understand me?"

"I never said I wouldn't," Spencer said, wary of his brusque tone. "I will do anything to make sure John is returned to me safe and sound. But I just wish we didn't have to trust Ben to keep his word because I don't think he will."

Richard exhaled and then said, "I don't trust Ben either. I love him like a son, but he may try to betray me."

"And if he does, then what?" Spencer asked, though she had a feeling she knew the answer. "Will you kill him?"

"I sincerely hope it doesn't come to that," Richard said. "I hope Ben wants that envelope more than he wants to stab me in the back."

"What's so damn important about that envelope, anyway?" Spencer returned to the couch and sat. "Is it really worth Ben having me kidnapped and then taking John hostage?"

"Have you ever looked inside the envelope?" Richard asked, eyes shrewd.

"Once," Spencer admitted. "But I didn't understand what it was. All I saw was a small piece of paper with drawings of animals all lined on a row. A dog and a rooster and a pig, I think. There was a snake, a tiger, a rat."

"Those animals represent signs of the Chinese zodiac," Richard explained. "The year you were born determines whether you are a snake or a rat or a goat. Each animal has certain traits that give insight to personality. For example, the dragon is said to be confident and charismatic and yet also jealous, vindictive, and deceitful. The tiger seeks true love and is loyal and protective but can also be impulsive and stubborn."

"So the envelope is some horoscope or something?"

"Those animals on that piece of paper have nothing to do with horoscopes," Richard said. "It's a code. Each animal, for Ben's business purposes, represents a number. You look at the paper and see a row of animals. Ben looks at it and sees a row of numbers."

"Numbers for what?"

"Numbers to access some numbered bank account somewhere," Richard said, sounding slightly perturbed. "It's the passcode, and there's one hundred million dollars in the account."

51

———

A'arotanga, South Pacific
Location Unknown

Outside the wall of French doors, the sun began its steady ascent, rising above the natural barrier of tropical vegetation.

Sione turned from the A'arotangan sunrise, questions crowding his mind. Why hadn't Ben tied him up? Why had he just thrown him on the bed, leaving his hands and feet unbound? Maybe because it didn't matter. Except for the mattress he'd been lying on when he woke up, the room was bare. Nothing could be used as a weapon. There was no other furniture in the room. No closet. No bathroom. A locked door led out of the room, and the locked French doors had thick, triple pane glass.

Touching his shoulder, Sione winced. It was still sore from the needle of the dart piercing his skin, delivering a dose of some sort of anesthesia. He had no idea how much time had passed since Ben had shot him. Damn tranquilizer gun had knocked him out for too damn long, but he was awake now, although still not fully alert. The strange thickness no longer swam in his head. When he'd regained consciousness, he'd been disoriented, staring at the blades of a ceiling fan, swirling lazily. Things were becoming clearer, and priorities were shifting.

He took a deep breath, fighting desperation and anger. Giving into dangerous emotions would hinder his ability to think logically, dashing any hopes of figuring out a way to escape his current confinement. Restless, he scanned the room again, searching for some way to breach the impenetrable security.

Sione knew why Ben was holding him captive. *You are my leverage.* Ben had drugged him and locked him in an empty room because Richard had ruined his plans. *Your father has come to the rescue of that deceitful bitch you plan to marry.* Ben was probably hoping Richard would find some way to get that damn envelope for him in exchange for Sione's release. Talk about a fool's bargain. Ben had to know he would end up on the business end of any deal he tried to make with Richard.

When Richard gets to the island, I have no doubt he plans to kill me. It would end that way, Sione was sure. Richard would betray Ben and then kill him. Not that Ben's death mattered to Sione, because it didn't.

He couldn't be distracted from what was most important—escaping and finding Spencer. Any and all mental activity had to be centered around those specific tasks.

Sione rubbed his eyes. It was hard to focus on a seemingly impossible goal when success required the ability to outthink a murdering psychopath hell-bent on getting revenge. He had to get out of the room, somehow. Brute force was not the way out, he'd quickly learned. He'd already tried kicking the doors down and using his left shoulder as a battering ram, all to no avail. Pacing the room, he took deep breaths, trying to keep it together, trying to—

He heard a soft click and then metal moving against metal. Sione turned toward the door, saw the knob twisting, counterclockwise. His heart pounded.

Someone was opening the door...

52

A'arotanga, South Pacific

In the back of the cab, Spencer stared at the third finger on her left hand.

She struggled to fight the sullen sadness threatening to overtake her. There should have been a ring on her finger, and there wasn't. So many things which should have been weren't. She should have been a married woman. Should have been on her honeymoon with John, exploring the island with him as her unofficial tour guide.

As the cab sped along a winding two-lane road cut between lush scenery, Spencer tried to focus on her upcoming task, but her thoughts wandered as she gazed at sun-splashed palm trees passing by the window. When she and John had talked about honeymooning in A'arotanga, he'd promised to show her the beauty of the island, the hidden gems and lovely surprises only the locals knew and held dear, sacred, private places their ancestors had discovered centuries ago. She'd been looking forward to basking in the warm sun with him, hiking through the rainforest, and making love in the ocean.

She sighed, scolding herself. There was no time for reminiscing or feeling sorry for herself. She and John could still have their beautiful, magical honeymoon. And they would but only if she got herself together and played her part. Clutching her blue Birkin, Spencer recalled Richard's instructions, based on the negotiations with Ben.

"At nine in the morning, you'll take a car to the First National Bank of A'arotanga," Richard had said. "At the bank, you will ask to speak to the bank's vice president, Mr. Afoa. He is an associate of mine and will assist us in this endeavor, making sure things go smoothly. Mr. Afoa will escort you to the vault, where the safe deposit boxes are kept. He will be able to open the safe deposit box my son has there."

"But safe deposit boxes need two keys to open them," Spencer pointed out. "We don't have John's key."

"Mr. Afoa will be able to open the box, trust me," Richard said. "He will remove the contents and give them to you."

"The contents?" Spencer stared at him. "You mean Ben's envelope."

Richard nodded. "After you get the envelope, you'll take a car back to the hotel. Two men will be waiting to escort you to my suite. One of the men works for Ben, and the other works for me. This is necessary to ensure that you don't do something stupid, like run off with the envelope."

"Why would I do that?" Spencer snapped. "The envelope is the key to John's freedom."

"Yes, well, Ben thinks that I might try to convince you to go against the agreement and bring the envelope to me," said Richard. "Naturally, I think that Ben might entice you into giving the envelope to him before he releases my son. So, we decided to each have one of our men shepherd you back to my suite."

Spencer closed her eyes for a moment and pressed a hand against her abdomen. Her stomach had been in knots since yesterday, and last night, she hadn't been able to sleep. So much was at stake, and there were so many risks, for her, John, and the baby. Their lives and their happiness, their happily ever after, together forever, depended on her now, and she couldn't blow it.

Last night, as she'd tossed and turned, praying for courage and strength, she'd entertained fantasies of stabbing both Ben and Richard in the back. Betrayal was the least those murderous, vengeful bastards deserved. More than anything, she wanted to destroy the envelope and make sure both men ended up in jail. Or better yet, dead. There had to be a way to make them turn on each other and destroy one another while she and John rode off into the sunset.

She wasn't stupid though.

She didn't want to be doused with gasoline and set on fire or shot seven times. Ben and Richard were not to be messed with. She would not risk their collective wrath in some misguided attempt at revenge. She couldn't give in to anger and frustration. She had to concentrate on John and the baby and the life they would be free to lead once Ben had his damn envelope and John was released.

"Don't worry, little one," Spencer whispered, staring at the growing bump. "Mama is not going to mess up. You, me, and daddy will be together again soon. I promise."

53

A'arotanga, South Pacific
Location Unknown

Staring at the twisting door knob, several options flashed through Sione's mind. One, press himself against the wall next to the door, and when whoever the hell came into the room, he could grab the son of a bitch from behind, wrestle him to the ground, grapple, and then disarm. Or two, go back to the bed and pretend he was still knocked out. Let the person get close and then attack. With a stealth quickness, Sione returned to the mattress, lay down on his back and closed his eyes just before the door opened.

He forced himself to go limp and stay still. Ignoring his pounding heart, he fought the instinct to jump up and fight and cautioned himself to wait, to determine if he could find out more about the situation, before he made his move. If nothing else, he needed to determine if more than one person had entered the room. His entire plan of attack would have to change if two or three people had been assigned to watch him.

Footsteps shuffled across the hardwood floor, light and quick. A small, thin opponent, maybe.

Something hard and smooth pressed against his cheek and then his chin a few times. Seconds later, he felt three quick taps against his jaw followed by a slight pressure on his left eyelid before it was forced open. An Asian man peered at him, black eyes intense. He had a heavily lined, leathery, weather-beaten face.

The man was trying to determine if he was conscious, Sione realized, attempting not to stare back at the man, still unsure of his next move and yet knowing he had to attack. There was no other option. He would have to fight his way out of the room, and once out of the room, he'd have to fight to get out of the house.

He had to be prepared, smart, and cunning to make sure he survived the battle before he could wage war. He couldn't hesitate and ruin what might be his only chance to escape. Neither could he be too hasty and make the wrong move at the wrong time. The last thing he wanted was to end up chained to the bed with a concussion.

Grunting, the man released Sione's eyelid and stood. Before Sione allowed the lid to lower, he saw the man turn from him. His heart kicked, knowing it was time to act. "Chen Shu…" said the man, voice loud and raspy, launching into Chinese.

Sione opened his eyes and raised his head from the mattress a fraction. The man had his back to Sione with a cellphone pressed to his ear. Thin and wiry, the guy reminded Sione of Tommy Fong. Probably a disgraced Triad enforcer on Ben's payroll. Most likely proficient in martial arts, subtle and quick, and able to get the best of an opponent twice his size.

Not today, Sione thought, and then rolled onto his side as he pushed himself toward the bottom of the mattress. With his right leg leading, he slammed his foot into the man's ankle. The man cried out, a mix of pain and shock, as he fell to his knees, dropping the cell phone.

In an instant, Sione scrambled to his feet and lunged at the man, slipping an arm around the man's neck, trapping him in a rear choke hold. "You speak English?" Sione demanded, giving the bastard just enough slack to speak. "Where is Ben?"

Sputtering, the man cowered, feeble in his pointless attempts to free himself.

Cursing, frustrated, Sione tightened his hold. *Squeeze until there is no more life left within the enemy.* His father's voice, deep and sinister, was strangely soothing. Letting those decade-old instructions guide him, Sione squeezed harder as the man gasped and gurgled, hands desperately trying to remove Sione's arm, but it was no use. The man stopped fighting and went limp. Sione removed his arm, letting the man drop to the floor.

Breathing heavily, Sione took a knee next to the unmoving form and checked for a pulse. The man was still alive. He wouldn't be unconscious for long, though. Quickly, Sione patted the guy down, looking for a weapon, hoping to find—

A shocked exhale followed by several Chinese phrases made Sione look up. Another Chinese man stood in the doorway, tall and wiry, dressed in black fatigues. The man lunged, throwing a right punch. Sione stepped toward the man, blocking the blow with his left forearm, and hit the man in the throat. After picking the man up and slamming him to the ground, Sione searched him for a weapon. Finding a gun, he pressed the barrel under the man's chin.

"Where is Ben Chang?" Sione asked. "Where am I? What the hell is going on?"

Cowering and sweating, the man trembled, whispering Chinese.

Sione jerked the man to a sitting position and slammed the pistol across his face. Blood spurted from the man's nose as he cried out in shock and pain.

"I know you can speak English," Sione said. "Where is Ben? What is going on?"

"Do not kill me," the man pleaded, his dark eyes wary. "Please."

"You want to live?" Sione pressed the barrel against the man's cheek. "You tell me what I want to know."

"I will tell you." The man nodded. "Please do not kill me. I will tell you."

54

_____

A'arotanga, South Pacific

Seconds after she got into the cab, Spencer reached into the blue Birkin bag for her cell phone.

Her fingers brushed the envelope, and she flinched, snatching her hand away. Opening the purse wider, Spencer stared at Ben's envelope, nestled between a compact mirror and her iPhone. She was shocked by how smoothly everything had happened with Mr. Afoa, a slight, dour man who'd been expecting her. As he led her into the vault, he barely spoke two words, and after he'd opened John's safe deposit box and handed her the envelope, he simply bowed his head and wished her a pleasant day.

Her next instructions, according to the negotiations between Ben and Richard, were to call both men, a three-way conversation, and tell them she had the envelope.

Spencer's thumb hovered over the key pad on the screen, trying to remember the phone numbers to the burner phones both Ben and Richard would be using to take her call. Trembling, she took a deep breath. This was no time for pregnancy brain. What was the number Richard had given her? Panicked, she tried to force the chaotic thoughts and fears from her mind. Ben had given her his number, as well. No, wait. The numbers had been programmed into her phone, hadn't they? Her heart thudding, she checked the phone's stored contacts, looking for—

The driver's door sprang open. The driver gave a short, strangled cry as someone yanked him from the cab. Heart slamming, Spencer leaned between the front seats. What the hell was happening? She sat back and scooted to the passenger's door, panicked and desperate, staring out of the window. The thud of flesh smacking into flesh combined with a blur of an arm swinging sent terror racing through her body. She had to get out of the car. She didn't know what was happening, or why, but this wasn't part of the plan Richard and Ben had agreed upon. Something was wrong. Fighting hysteria, Spencer grabbed the inside door handle.

A body slammed against the back door. Spencer screamed and scooted away from the door, paralyzed, not sure what to do. Feeling trapped, realizing the car was slowly inching forward, she struggled to decide if she should climb into the front seat and drive away or—

Someone jumped into the driver's seat and slammed the door, and the car shot forward. Holding on to the headrest for dear life, Spencer glanced over her shoulder. Through the back window, she saw the cab driver sprawled in the middle of the road. Fresh panic exploded within her.

The cab veered toward the shoulder and then shuddered to a halting stop.

"Spencer…"

Panic gave way to dizzying confusion and then elation and then disbelief. She had to be dreaming. Hallucinating. Shaking, fearing her mind was playing tricks on her, Spencer turned her head.

Gasping, she stared at the hazel eyes gazing back at her. "John?" she whispered, leaning forward and inching her hand toward his face, desperately wanting to believe he was really there. As he twisted in the seat to face her, his hand closed around her fingers, and he pulled her hand to his mouth, kissing her palm. Crying, she angled her body between the two front seats, placed her free hand against the stubble on his cheek, and kissed him. John released her hand and wrapped his arm around her as she wound her arms around his neck, reluctant to let him go.

"John, oh my God! I don't understand...what happened?" she whispered against his mouth. "I thought...how did you get away from Ben? How did you know—"

"Sweetheart, are you okay?" he asked, pulling away and cradling her face in his hands. "Is the baby okay?"

"John, I'm fine. The baby is fine," she said as John kissed away her tears. "What about you? Are you okay? Why did Ben kidnap you?"

"The same reason he took you," John said, rubbing his eyes. "Because of that damn envelope. After you gave Ben the envelope, I stole it from him."

"I don't understand," Spencer said. "Why would you do that?"

"I still don't know." He exhaled, shaking his head. "Or maybe I do. I was kind of out of my mind that night..."

"Because that was the night you found out the truth about me," Spencer said. "You found out that I had lied to you about everything."

"Not everything," John disputed. "You didn't lie about how you felt about me. You told the truth about loving me, and maybe if I had believed you, none of this would have happened."

"You can't blame yourself," Spencer said. "If anyone is to blame, it's me. I should have told you the truth from the beginning, when I first met you. I should have trusted that you would protect me from Ben."

"But you were kidnapped because I took that stupid envelope," John said. "If I hadn't done that, we'd be married right now. We'd be on this island for our honeymoon, not because I made a deal with Ben to get you back."

"You were supposed to give him the envelope, and he would let me go," Spencer said.

"That didn't happen," John said. "Everything went to hell. Ben found out Richard had rescued you, so he drugged me and locked me in a room at some beach house on the west side of the island. When I woke up, one of the guys Ben had guarding me came into the room. I forced the guy to tell me what the hell was going on. That's how I found out about the deal between Ben and Richard for my freedom. But Ben was going to betray Richard. He never planned on letting you go."

"I knew it!" Spencer said. "He was going to betray both of us. He was going to keep us apart. He was never going to leave us alone and let us be together!"

John faced the steering wheel. "I'd never let Ben keep us apart. He will never come between us again. I'm going to make sure that bastard pays for what he did to you. You have a phone?"

"I have my cell," Spencer said, reaching for her purse as John started the car and steered back on the road.

"We need to call my cousin Roy," John said, shifting gears. "He's a cop. We need to call him, let him know—"

The cab hit a bump and the iPhone slipped from her hand. Spencer cursed.

"Sorry," John said.

"It's okay. I'm fine." Spencer bent over and reached toward the floorboard, running hesitant fingers over the dusty plastic mat. "The phone fell on the floor."

"Do you see it?" John asked.

"Yeah, I see it, but…" The car rocked slightly. Spencer felt something thin and hard tumble across the back of her hand. The iPhone. Spencer grabbed the phone and then lost it as the car hit another pothole. Cursing again, she scooted across the backseat until she was behind John. She leaned down across the seat, looking toward the floorboard.

The car bounced, and the cell phone slid across the mat, but she was able to grab it.

A deafening pop, like something bursting open, sent her heart into her throat, choking her scream. An explosion of glass shattered around her, razor-sharp chunks and shards tumbling down and hitting the plastic mat.

John cried out, a grunt of shock and pain, and the cab jerked violently.

Somewhere in the chaos and confusion of her mind, Spencer realized what she'd heard. Gunshots. With the realization came fear and paralyzing panic. Spencer rolled off the seat. Gasping and confused, trying to breathe and think, she scrambled to get back up onto the back seat.

What the hell was happening?

"John!"

The cab hit several bumps, jostling her, and then swerved again.

Another explosive pop burst through the air. Spencer screamed. The car skidded, tires shrieking in protest as the car smashed broadside against a cluster of bushes and squat Sego palms, the impact rocking the chassis.

"John!" Gasping and coughing, Spencer made her way onto the back seat. "What happened? What—"

Slumped over the wheel, John was unconscious, a thin trail of blood streaming down the side of his face.

"John! Oh my God," Spencer cried, struggling to maneuver into the front seat. "John!"

The rear passenger side door opened. A hand reached in and clamped around her ankle. "No!" she cried, struggling to get away as she was dragged along the cracked leather. Kicking and screaming, she fought, confused and desperate, trying to understand what was happening. An arm snaked around her waist, and seconds later, she was yanked out of the cab.

Heat surrounded her as a floral breeze blew tendrils of hair across her face. Struggling to get her footing, she stumbled. A hand clamped around the back of her arm, pulling her away from the car. "No!" she screamed, desperate to get away. "No! Get away from me! Leave me—"

"So, we meet again, sweet girl."

The menacing island lilt froze her, sending a jolt through her entire body, making her knees buckle. Dizzy and stunned, Spencer looked up into the face of Ben Chang.

55

"Where is my envelope?" Ben said, pointing a large, black gun toward her face.

Trembling, Spencer whispered, "It's in my purse.

"Get it," Ben ordered, releasing her arm. "And don't try anything stupid, or I will put a bullet in Sione's head."

Nodding, too terrified to think of anything stupid to try, Spencer climbed back into the car. She grabbed the blue Birkin and then glanced at John, still unconscious, and willed herself not to cry or scream or do anything stupid, as Ben had warned her. There was no need to test Ben. All he wanted was the envelope. All she had to do was give it to him, and then he would go and leave them alone. Once Ben was gone, she would call an ambulance for John and then call the police. No, John's cousin. She was supposed to call John's cousin. What was his name?

Spencer reached into the purse, pulled out the envelope, and thrust it toward Ben. "Here's your damn precious envelope."

After checking the contents, Ben smiled. "Okay, come on."

"What?" Spencer shrank back from him.

"You're coming with me."

"What are you talking about?" Spencer stared at him. "I gave you the envelope. The deal you made with John was if he gave you the envelope, then you would let me go."

"Change of plans," he said, dropping the Birkin to grab her wrist. "You can thank your future father-in-law for that. He should not have gotten involved. Sione and I did have a deal. We were going to make an even exchange. You for my envelope. I planned to hold up my end of our bargain, and I thought Sione would, too. But he lied to me. Betrayed me."

Spencer said, "John didn't betray you."

"The hell he didn't," Ben said. "Sione called his daddy. Now I got that psychotic bastard on my ass and I'm in Richard's territory. He runs this fucking island like it's his personal fiefdom. He plans to make sure I don't make it out of paradise alive. That's why I need you."

"You need me for what?"

"You, sweet girl," Ben said, "are my ticket off this island."

"I'm not going anywhere with you," Spencer said, taking another step back, panicked, her head whipping left and then right. She prayed she'd see another car or maybe someone walking down the street, hoping to see someone who could help her, but there was no one. The street was deserted, a strip of asphalt marred by cracks in the foundation and potholes. On either side of the road, dense tropical jungle bordered the graveled shoulder.

Ben slipped the envelope into the back pocket of his pants and then grabbed her again.

"Let me go!" Spencer said, struggling to get away from him as he forced her across the road, toward the opposite shoulder. "Leave me alone!"

"Shut up!" Ben growled when her frantic yells became screeching screams for help. "Scream again and I go back and shoot Sione. I will kill him. Is that what you want to happen? You want your baby to grow up without his father?"

56

A'arotanga, South Pacific

Pain throbbed near his right ear.

Lifting his head from the steering wheel, Sione touched the spot just beneath his hairline and winced. Breathing shallow, he glanced at his fingers. Slick blood, bright and red. His heart slamming, he glanced in the rear-view mirror, turning his head to examine the wound. The bullet had grazed him, searing his skin. It felt worse than it looked, but it was more terrifying than painful. An inch or a nod or a tilt back just so and he might be dead. Or brain damaged. A lifeless shell. Alive, but unable to really live. Unable to be a father to the baby. Or a husband to Spencer.

Sione stared at the blood on his fingers, trying to ignore the macabre thoughts. He wasn't dead. The bullet hadn't hit its target. Rage dominated his thoughts and his emotions even though he tried to be grateful for each breath he took. The bullet that missed should never have been fired. The bullet wouldn't have left the chamber, Sione knew, if he hadn't stolen the envelope. Ben could have killed him, and it would have been his own damn fault. He'd accused Ben of unleashing hell, but he was giving the bastard too much credit. Spencer and the baby had been put through hell because of his dangerous mistakes.

Grimacing, Sione tried to get his bearings, struggling to orient himself. The car had skidded off the road, onto the shoulder, and into a shallow ditch. The driver's door was pinned against the branches and leaves of several sea grape trees.

Sione massaged the back of his neck, trying to determine if he'd suffered whiplash or—

Spencer. His heart slammed. Where was Spencer? What had happened?

"Spencer..." His voice a whispered croak, he cleared his throat.

Had Spencer been shot? He looked over his shoulder. The back seat was empty. There was no blood, thank God. But where was Spencer? Had she gotten out of the car? The rear passenger side door was open. Sione looked left, through the front passenger window.

His heart dropped.

Across the road, he saw Spencer.

Ben was forcing her into the trees...

57

A'arotanga, South Pacific

Spencer went ice cold.

"You didn't think I knew about the baby, did you?" Ben led them down into a shallow ditch and then pushed aside several large, waxy leaves, heading into the forest. "I would congratulate you, but it's not exactly a blessing. At least not for the child. I feel sorry for the kid. Having a treacherous bitch for a mother."

"How did you find out?" Spencer asked, struggling to keep up with him as they walked down a narrow path, bordered by a thick wall of trees and bushes.

"The woman who took you was given strict orders not to mistreat you," Ben said. "But she had proved herself to be difficult to control and was prone to disobedience, so I was watching to make sure she complied with my wishes."

"You were watching me?" Spencer asked, feeling violated, even though Moana had told her about the cameras.

"I saw you holding your stomach and talking to yourself," Ben said. "Soon, I realized you were talking to your 'little one,' telling him that everything would be okay."

"Now that you know I'm pregnant, will you please let me go?" Spencer begged. "I don't want anything to happen to my baby. I need to see a doctor to make sure the baby is okay."

"I'm sure the baby's fine," Ben said, continuing along the path. "But, just in case, once we get off the island and make it to our next destination, I'll drop you off at a hospital."

"Where are you taking me?"

Ben said nothing.

"Why are you doing this?" she asked, wiping sweat from her forehead, praying for a breeze to somehow make it through the humidity. "You have the envelope. You have what you wanted."

"Not quite, sweet girl," Ben said, his smile wry. "Don't quite have everything I wanted."

"What do you want that you don't have?" she asked.

"I don't have…" Ben stopped, his body rigid.

Wary, she glanced up at him. "What is it?"

Frowning, he shushed her. Tightening his hold on her arm, Ben pulled her off the path and behind a large elephant tree.

"Ben?" Her heart slammed.

"Be quiet," he whispered, lowering one of the leaves with a finger, peering through the space.

Spencer moved her head, squinting to see through the leaves. Seconds passed, and then she saw two men emerge from the bushes on the other side of the path they'd been walking on.

Voice lowered, Spencer asked, "Who are those men?"

"Keep your mouth shut," Ben whispered. "Don't say another—"

Several muffled thuds whizzed through the air, and the wide, waxy leaf near Ben's head exploded. Cursing, he crouched, forcing

Spencer to the ground with him. Peeking between the tangled branches of a hibiscus bush, he said, "Stay down."

Ben rose to a defensive crouch, using the barrel of his gun to move the leaves of the trees they hid behind. Freed from his oppressive grasp, Spencer took a step back. Ben was distracted. She had to take advantage of his preoccupation with the men who'd shot at them. Richard's mercenary minions, she thought, but she wasn't sure. The men were dressed in dark suits. Taking another step back, she alternately watched Ben and scanned the ground, looking for a weapon. Spying a fallen branch about the size of a baseball bat, lying beneath a bush, put a dangerous idea in her head. One she wasn't sure would work.

Bullets pierced two more elephant leaves, and Ben jerked and ducked. Spencer had to do something. She couldn't wait to accidentally be shot to death. With a careful sidestep to her left, she picked up the branch, and then screamed. "Help me! Please! Ben—"

"You devious bitch!" Ben roared, turning as he started to rise.

Spencer swung the branch toward him, smashing it against the side of his face. Dropping the branch, she turned and ran into the trees.

58

A'arotanga, South Pacific

Crying, Spencer lurched to the left, following a different path. Struggling to breathe, she forced herself to keep going. Though terrified of seeing Ben right on her heels, Spencer looked back.

Ben wasn't chasing her.

Confused, Spencer continued to run. Blades slashed and nicked her skin, and every now and then, she got winded and had to slow her pace. Once or twice, she nearly fell, but she was determined to stay on her feet. Her body screamed at her to stop. But if she stopped, Ben would catch up to her. If Ben caught her, he would kill her. No, no that wasn't right, was it? He couldn't kill her because he needed her.

Hurrying through ankle-high grass, Spencer skirted around a group of bushes. She ran through clusters of trees spaced apart at intervals. A banana grove, she realized when she stopped to catch her breath, noting the clusters of small, green bananas hanging from the top of the trees. *You, sweet girl, are my ticket off this island.* Ben needed a hostage, or he wasn't getting off the island alive.

Sadness threatened to overwhelm her, and the urge to sink to her knees and sob was tempting. She couldn't give up. John needed her. Somehow, she had to find her way back to him. She had to call an ambulance so he could get the medical attention he needed. She remembered the blood streaming down his face, and prayed he would be okay. She couldn't give up. The baby was depending on her. She couldn't let her little one down. Not now. Not ever. She owed her little boy the chance to come into the world, to grow and thrive, and be loved. She had to be for her little one the mother she'd never had. She had to be fierce and determined. She had to fight to make sure she, John and the baby would have the chance to be together.

Unable to run anymore, Spencer pushed herself to walk as fast as she could. Through the jungle vines, she saw something large and white up ahead, the end of it peeking between wide, fat leaves. Eyes trained on the object, she ran toward it and found herself in front of an old, overturned speedboat, abandoned between two large elephant trees.

Spencer ran around to the opposite side and crouched down, leaning against the rusted, paint-flecked stern to get her bearings. Trembling, she tried to catch her breath and figure out what to do next. She wished it wasn't so damn hot and muggy. Her hair hung around her shoulders, the strands limp and damp. Sweat rolled from her neck, down her back, and between her breasts.

Something crawled up her leg, and she slapped it.

Hysteria threatened to overwhelm her. She didn't know how to fight the panic and terror. She was lost in the tropical forest. Lost in unfamiliar surroundings with no one to hear her screams. She'd tried to find her way back to the road, but she'd gotten confused and disoriented in the twists and turns between trees and bushes, trying to follow dirt paths that snaked and curved, with sharp turns.

A sob escaped, but she bit her lip and rubbed her eyes, refusing to cry.

Was anyone looking for her? Ben? Richard's minions? Or were they too busy shooting at each other? What if no one found her? What if she died out here in the middle of the rainforest? She would never see John again. Never hold her precious little boy in her arms for the first time.

59

A'arotanga, South Pacific

Sione stared at the two dead bodies sprawled across the dirt path stretching before him.

It was balmy, the humidity smothering and suffocating, the breeze lost in the trees.

Heart pounding, he focused on the black, custom-tailored suits, the Italian leather shoes, and the bullet holes between each man's eyes. Compliments of Ben Chang, Sione was sure of it. Two of Richard's guys. Ice filled his veins, chilling him to the core despite the oppressive heat. Richard was in the middle of the situation with Ben, where he didn't belong, where Sione didn't need or want him.

Sione dragged a hand down his face. He didn't know what to think or how to feel. All he knew was he would have to see his father. Sione would have to deal with him, but he didn't know how the hell he would survive the encounter.

Looking down the path, a thin ribbon of dirt through thick

trees, Sione realized he and Ben were both in the same regrettable predicament. Both would have to face their fears of Richard, and neither of them would escape unscathed.

Taking off, Sione ran along the path, slapping away broad leaves and outstretched branches. Skirting a group of trees, he saw a flash of movement ahead of him to the right. Was it Spencer? Or Ben? More of Richard's men?

Sione took off in that direction, pushing through the dense foliage.

60

A'arotanga, South Pacific

Spencer couldn't stop the tears. A bug landed on her shoulder, and as she slapped it away, she felt like that scared, lonely, seven-year-old girl again. Curled in a ball beneath her bed, she hid from her mother. Crying because of the pain from punches and kicks, she was careful not to sob too loud, or her mother would get mad and beat her again.

As sad and tragic as her childhood was, being a teenager was even worse. By that time, her mother no longer beat her, no longer screamed and yelled. Instead, she tolerated abuse as the much scarier sycophantic Stepford version of herself that Spencer secretly thought of as "that wife."

Once, when she was fourteen, she found her mother in the bathroom, furiously trying to cover up a black eye with makeup. She'd asked her mother if she was okay, and her mother had told her "Beautiful girls have to suffer. We're both desired and despised. Beauty is useful but causes a lot of problems."

Spencer, at the time, had assumed her mother wasn't taking the medication her therapist had prescribed. Now, she wondered if maybe her mother was right. Was she suffering because she was beautiful? No, not because of her beauty, but because she'd tried to use it to deceive. She was pretty enough to trick men she'd assumed were stupid enough to believe her lies.

But she hadn't fooled Ben. He wasn't stupid. He was a psychotic criminal obsessed with revenge. She'd made the mistake of underestimating Ben, not realizing how dangerous he was, and now, she might not live to—

"Hey."

The whispered voice to her left sent confusion and relief surging through her.

"Spencer."

She felt a hand close over hers, fingers slipping between her fingers, and everything within her started to lift.

"John," she whispered, afraid it might not really be him, but then he put his arm around her, helping her up, and when he pulled her close to him, all the doubts and hesitation vanished.

Crying, she pressed her face against his chest and wrapped her arms around him.

"It's okay." He rubbed a hand up and down her back, kissing the top of her head, soothing her. "You're going to be okay. I'm here now."

Trembling and dizzy with relief and happiness, Spencer tilted her head back to look up at him. "How did you find me?"

"I kept thinking I was catching glimpses of you, but when I thought I was close, I would lose sight," he said. "When I saw the old speedboat, I decided to stop and get my bearings, figuring it would be a good reference point, if nothing else."

"I'm so glad you did." She hugged him, holding on to him, never wanting him to let her go.

"Where is Ben?" John asked. "Did he get away? Did he leave you?"

"I got away from him," she said. "He wanted to take me so he could get off the island. He wouldn't tell me where we were going. We were headed down this path, and then two guys started shooting at us. We hid behind some trees. I found a branch, and I hit Ben with it and ran off. I think the guys worked for your father."

"Yeah," he said, his tone grim. "They did."

"They did?"

"They're dead," he said. "Shot twice between the eyes."

"Ben killed them?"

Nodding, John took a small cell phone from the front pocket of his pants. "We need to call my cousin Roy and let him know that—"

A thud against the other side of the boat sent Spencer's pulse racing as she clutched his arms. "Was that a—"

Another thud and then one more.

"Bullets," John said, cursing as he grabbed her. Pulling her with him, he crouched low, using the boat for cover.

"Ben's shooting at us," Spencer whispered, her hands trembling as she held on to his shoulders.

Two more thuds.

Flinching, Spencer clutched him tighter. "He's going to kill us."

"Listen to me." John held her face in his hands, stared at her. "I want you to run behind those trees and over to that path. It leads back to the road. Once you get to the street—"

"And what are you going to do?" Spencer asked. "Stay here and get shot?"

"Spencer—"

"Why can't we run back to the road together?" she asked, her voice tremulous. "I don't want to leave you alone. I don't want anything bad to happen to you."

"You can't stay here, not with Ben shooting at us," John said. "Nothing bad can happen to you or the baby."

Nodding, Spencer blinked back tears. "Okay."

"Get back to the road," John said, handing her the cell phone. "Call Roy. His number is in the contacts. Tell him you left me by Nonu's old boat."

"Nonu's old boat?"

"He'll know what I'm talking about," he said.

"Okay, John." She kissed him and then said, "I love you."

"I love you, too," he said, his gaze an expression of his feelings and emotions. "I always will."

"Promise that nothing bad will happen to you," she said, desperate and terrified. "Promise you'll be okay."

"I promise," he said and then kissed her forehead, her eyes, and her lips. "Now go. Hurry."

61

Spencer ran off down the path, crouched low.

Sione kept his eyes on her until she blended in with the trees, and he could no longer see her moving. He didn't like sending her off alone, but he needed to keep her and the baby away from Ben.

Sione rose a bit, just enough to peer over the bottom of the overturned speedboat, looking toward the muddy path, trees obstructing his view.

The wind had picked up, carrying the scent of rain, and in the distance, thunder rumbled.

Staying low, he made his way toward the stern, stopping near the outboard motor. From there, he dashed across a small clearing to a line of trees, scanning the dirt path through gaps in the leaves and bushes, looking for Ben.

Moving to the opposite side of the boat, Sione stared at the hull, counting the bullet holes. Why had the shooting ceased? Was Ben reloading? Sione didn't think so. Ben was clever, a good hunter with the ability to quickly analyze his prey. He used to tell Sione you have to get into people's heads, understand their motives, find out what their fears were, what was important to them, and then you had them. You could bring them down, quick and easy.

Worried, Sione walked toward the path, hurrying through grass and weeds.

Something snapped, a branch to his left, but when he looked that way, he saw nothing, only trees clustered together.

"Old friend." Ben's voice came from behind him. "We meet again."

Sione spun around and lunged at Ben before he could say another word, slamming his right fist into Ben's jaw.

"Well, it's nice to see you, too." Ben staggered back into a banana tree, clutching his jaw and smiling.

"Why did you drug me and lock me up?" Sione hit him again, catching him in the chin. Sione hit him in the chest and then in the gut, sending Ben to the ground, gasping and coughing. "We had a deal. The envelope for Spencer."

On his knees, looking up, eyes furious, Ben said, "You think I didn't hold up my end of the bargain?"

"If you had kept your word, then—"

Ben grabbed Sione's forearm, yanked and twisted it, and then hit Sione in the side. Doubled over, Sione felt a sharp pain in his knee before his legs were swept from under him, and he ended up on his ass in the dirt. Ben sprawled over him, panting and bleeding.

"You want to know why I didn't keep my word?" Ben growled the words through gritted teeth stained with blood from Sione's first blow. "Because I couldn't. Because you called your father. You didn't keep your word!"

"I didn't bring Richard into this!" Sione shoved Ben off him, getting to his feet. "You think I want him involved? You think I want him thinking he can come back into my life?"

"Well, he's here now." Ben grunted as he half-crawled, half-dragged himself up from the dirt and staggered to his feet. "And he's not going to let me leave this island alive. Unless…"

Furious, Sione pressed him. "Unless what? That's what you meant by insurance, right?"

"I have to get off this island, old friend," Ben said. "And you're coming with me."

"Oh, am I?" Scoffing, Sione shook his head. "One of your guards told me about your ridiculous plan to run away with me and Spencer. Somehow, you thought you would be able to force us to fly to Australia with you. You thought, if you had us, as a shield, that you could get away without my father putting a bullet in your back."

Sighing, Ben said, "You just can't get good help these days."

"They didn't even tie me up," Sione said.

Ben shrugged. "Well, it was not my intent to treat you like an animal."

"But it is your intent to use me to cover your ass."

"Once we're in Sydney," Ben said, "You and I can go our separate ways."

Sione shook his head. "That's not going to happen."

"You owe me," Ben said.

"What the hell do I owe you?" Sione said, wary, his pulse racing.

"You owe me a life," Ben said. "Don't forget, I have killed for you. The least you could do is help me stay alive."

"I never asked you to take a life for me," Sione said, wary of Ben's cold, appraising scrutiny, feeling he was falling short and somehow didn't measure up.

"You didn't stop me. You didn't tell me not to," Ben reminded him. "You cried and said you couldn't do it. You were so scared of what Richard would do to you when he found out, so I promised you that he wouldn't find out. When we lied to Richard, you didn't expose me."

Sione looked away and tried to think over the pounding in his head.

"You were exposed as a coward and a fraud that night, old friend," Ben said. "I was your protector, your saving grace. Because of me, your father never knew that you didn't have the guts to be what he expected you to be. And then you ran away to this Godforsaken island. You weren't trying to escape to some better life your uncle offered you. That night, you realized that you weren't good enough."

Sione turned his head, staring at Nonu's old boat. Ben was trying to take him back in time, back to that horrible night when everything had gone to hell, but Sione wasn't going to the past.

He refused to let Ben trick him into reliving old nightmares.

"Looks like we got company," Ben said.

Sione turned. Across the path, about fifteen feet away, leaves rustled, twigs cracked, and then a man in a custom-tailored suit, impeccable despite the heat and humidity, came out of the dense thicket of trees and bushes. Two more men followed forming a trio of well-dressed thugs. And then Richard pushed his way out.

Sione stared and stepped back. Spooked, as though he'd seen a ghost, he fought the urge to run, fought to forget all those lessons Richard had taught him.

Always be prepared for the enemy to strike.

Anxious, Sione felt his muscles clench. His body anticipated a fight even though Richard appeared to pose no immediate threat.

Prepare…stay ready…don't underestimate your opponent, don't get caught off guard…the war is won when the enemy is defeated. Never take prisoners, they'll find a way to overcome you because they have nothing to lose and everything to gain. Always be prepared for the enemy to strike.

Sione would be a fool not to, knowing his father. Richard would attack him. Not with bullets or a blade. With the chance for restoration. And revenge. His father wanted to repair their fractured relationship. What better way to heal the rift between them than to offer Sione an opportunity to finally get back at Ben for all the hell he'd unleashed in Sione's life.

Richard's attack would be emotional, not physical, and Sione knew he might be tempted to accept Richard's offer, but he wouldn't take the bait. He couldn't take it. His father might appear to be extending an olive branch, but it would actually be a clinging vine, winding around him, trapping him in an unbreakable bond.

"Richard Tuiali'i, as I live and breathe," Ben called out, a hearty greeting devoid of any goodwill, full of fake cheer.

"Ben Chang, always testing the limits of my patience and compassion," Richard said. "How did we get to this point?"

"Ask your son," Ben said.

Sione glared at Ben and then at his father, a quick glance before looking away.

"Sione," Richard addressed him, his booming voice dripping with possessive pride. "It's very good to see you. How are you?"

"Why are you here?" Sione asked. "What do you want?"

"I'm here to, hopefully, facilitate a truce between you and Ben," Richard said.

Frowning, Sione said, "A truce?"

Ben scoffed and leaned against the hull of the boat, arms crossed, regarding Richard with amusement.

Richard said, "It is my sincere wish that the two of you treat each other with loyalty and respect, like the brothers you were raised to be."

"Only problem with that is, we're not brothers," Ben said.

"And we never will be," Sione agreed. "And you shouldn't be here, Dad."

"Your mother thought you needed my help," Richard said.

"She was wrong." Sione stepped toward his father. "I don't need your help. I don't want you here."

"I think your uncle Siosi would be very disappointed by how ungrateful you're being," Richard said. "If not for me, Spencer might have been killed."

"Spencer was never in any danger," Ben disputed. "You know how I feel about her. You know I wouldn't hurt her."

"You left her with Moana," Richard said. "You might as well have put her in the care of some wild, rabid animal. Do you really think you could have controlled that deceitful whore?"

"That's why you killed her?" Sione asked.

"He killed her because you couldn't," Ben mocked.

"Shut up," Richard told him and then focused on Sione again. "Son, why do you seem upset? Moana was a sinful, deplorable bitch. She got what she deserved. She's the reason for the animosity and strife between you and Ben. It was time for her to pay for her sins."

Sione asked, "And when are you going to pay for your sins? When are you going to stop hiding behind your supposedly legitimate businesses? These men you travel with are not your bodyguards. They kill people for you."

"Son, you are going off on tangents," Richard said. "What you must understand is that Moana would have killed Spencer. And my grandson."

Sione sucked in a breath, feeling as though he'd been sucker punched. "You know about the baby?"

"Your mother told me," Richard said, aggressive pride in his voice. "It's a blessing. I can't wait to meet him."

Shaking his head, Sione said, "You're not going to have anything to do with my son."

"The child is my grandson," Richard said, frowning. "You have to let me be in his life."

"Speaking of going off on tangents," Ben interjected. "You two can argue about diaper duty later. We have more important matters to deal with."

"There's nothing more important than my grandson," Richard snapped.

"There's nothing more important to me than getting the hell off this island," Ben countered.

"You think you're getting off this island alive? You kidnapped my son. You think I'm going to let your shameful behavior go unpunished? There are consequences for bad decisions."

"You getting involved in matters that don't concern you was a bad decision, Richard," Ben said. "That's why I kidnapped your son."

"You should have stayed out of it, Dad," Sione said. "Ben and I had a deal."

"But we wouldn't have had to negotiate if your son hadn't stolen my envelope," Ben said and then shook his head. "But I don't blame Sione. I blame you, Richard. You set all this in motion when you told Moana to steal my envelope. You started it."

Richard smiled. "And I will end it."

62

———

A'arotanga, South Pacific

Terrified, but determined, Spencer hurried through a thick throng of trees, following the path John had told her to take, which would lead her back to the road.

No longer able to run, she walked faster, clutching John's cell phone. A thousand questions and worries swirled in her mind. One thought prevailed, demanding her attention.

What if something bad did happen to John?

Panting, gulping air, but unwilling to stop, Spencer kept going, propelled by fear and desperation as the question haunted her. John had promised he would be okay, but there was no guarantee he would make it out of the forest alive. Ben had a gun. He was probably going to kill John. Or worse, force John to leave the island with him to make sure Richard didn't kill him.

The path snaked right. Ahead, Spencer saw a slight space between the trees. Quickening her pace, she continued until she pushed through leaves. Out of the forest, she walked down into the shallow ditch and up onto the shoulder. Crossing the road, she headed back to the car, abandoned in the ditch where it had crashed. Leaning against the trunk, Spencer used John's cell phone to call his cousin Roy Collins, whose number she was finally able to find in the contacts. Shaking hands and trembling fingers thwarted her attempts more than once, but eventually, she had him on the line.

With surprisingly cool detachment, she introduced herself and then explained the situation, in chilling detail.

Roy Collins arrived on the scene almost immediately, backed up by nine other police officers, half his force, he told her.

John's cousin was aware of Nonu's old boat. Roy told her the location of the boat was well known to the locals, particularly the youth, who used it as a place to congregate for wild parties featuring drugs and sex.

"I'm coming with you," Spencer told Roy Collins, moments after he'd given his officers the command to head into the forest. As the cops crossed the road, Spencer wiped her damp forehead and fought the dizzying panic.

"No, you're not." The stocky islander, who vaguely resembled John, shook his head. "Something happens to you, my cousin will kill me."

63

———————

A'arotanga, South Pacific

Richard spoke to his men in Tongan, issuing a shockingly vicious command.

Disturbed by the words, Sione tried to force the English translation from his mind, but it played over and over, an ominous broken record. *Kill him. Make sure he's dead. Cut him up and burn him alive.* Richard had to know his men weren't capable of obeying his demands. Why would he ask them to attempt a feat they couldn't accomplish? Did he want Ben to get away?

Two of Richard's debonair hit men grabbed Ben, trying to hustle him off the path into the trees to carry out Richard's orders. Ben resisted. The assassins looked nervous. They had been trained by Richard but as servants. Ben had been trained as Sione had, as a son. There was a profound difference. The gentlemen assassins, as his father like to call them, didn't know all of Richard's secret tricks. They wouldn't know how to beat Richard, if they were ever put in the position to try. Ben could bring Richard to his knees. Richard had made sure of it. *Once you can overtake me, subdue me, and make me succumb, then you'll be ready.*

"So it's come to this, Richard?" Ben laughed heartily, wrestling against the men struggling to contain him. "You treat me like I mean shit to you."

"You mean more to me than you know, than you'll probably ever realize," Richard said. "But I can't tolerate the way you treated Sione. You drugged him. Locked him in a room."

"You forced me to do that," Ben said. "I never meant to—"

"But you did," Richard said. "That was a terrible mistake you made. Actions have consequences."

"Yeah, you're right," Ben said. "They do ..."

Seconds later, Ben slammed his heel against the shin of the guy holding him. Sione recognized the moves. The gentlemen assassins would end up on their asses in the dirt, wondering what the hell had just happened. As if on cue, Ben's foot slammed down on top of the second assassin's foot. With both men stunned, off guard, and in pain, Ben executed a series of defensive maneuvers in lightning quick succession.

After ramming his elbow into the gut of the guy on his left, Ben grabbed the arm of the guy on his right. Forcing the man's arm backward, he dislocated the man's shoulder and then pushed his head down. Two knee strikes to the face, and the guy was on his knees, wailing and holding his useless arm.

The guy on the left stumbled to his feet and threw a wild punch. Ben countered with an elbow strike to the guy's head, followed by a palm-heel strike to the chin and a knife-hand strike to the side of his neck. Wobbling, the assassin tried another punch, but Ben blocked it and delivered another elbow strike, this time to the guy's face before he grabbed the assassin's head with both hands, pushed his head down, and then brought his knee up, smashing the guy in the face.

"Shit," Richard muttered. "He's good."

Irritated and grudgingly impressed, Sione said, "You taught him well."

"Taught him better than I taught these pussies," Richard said, disgusted, shaking his head as Ben took on the third assassin, who was steadily losing the battle against Ben's powerful left hooks and right jabs.

"When you want something done right." Richard shook his head and took a step, as though he was about to head into the chaotic melee fifteen feet away.

Alarmed, Sione grabbed Richard's arm.

"What?" Richard glanced back at him, slight confusion in his hazel eyes.

"Dad, wait," Sione said, though he wasn't sure why he didn't want his father to get involved. "Don't—"

Gunshots rang out like suppressed fireworks. Whizzing and popping, bullets blew large chunks of bark off the tree Richard stood next to.

"Dad, get down!" Sione pushed Richard to the ground as Ben and the assassin wrestled for control of the gun, grappling in a haphazard circle, grunting and straining, while Ben managed to squeeze the trigger a few more times. A fine spray of dust flew toward Sione as a bullet slammed into the dirt, inches from where he crouched down.

"Come on, this way," Sione told Richard, his eyes on a narrow clearing to the right, a place where they could hide from the spray of wild bullets. Staying low, Sione ran toward the path, glancing back.

Behind him, Richard rose a few inches from his crouch, reaching beneath the hem of his trousers, his gaze focused on the fight.

"Dad, come on," Sione implored, angered by Richard's dogged persistence. "Don't—"

Richard grunted and then cursed, clutching his side. "I'm hit!"

Sione pulled Richard off the path and into a small clearing surrounded by bushes. Helping Richard ease to the ground, Sione unbuttoned the jacket, terrified by the blood steadily soaking his father's shirt.

"I'm okay." Richard grimaced, sweat beading his forehead. "Bullet just grazed me. Flesh wound."

Unconvinced, desperate to see for himself, and wanting to make sure his father was okay, Sione yanked the dress shirt open, popping platinum buttons, searching for the wound.

The mangled, bloodied flesh looked worse than he'd expected. Enraged, Sione looked over his shoulder where Ben was still wrestling with the third assassin, who was barely holding on. Standing, Sione turned, his mind screaming with crazy thoughts and ideas, propelling him toward something dangerous and yet inevitable.

"Sione, don't…" Richard said behind him, his voice weak and whispery. "You can't kill him."

"Don't I have to?" Sione glanced at his father, lying in the grass, bleeding. "Aren't we Cain and Abel? It's just like Uncle Siosi said. One of us has to die. One of us has to kill the other."

"George was wrong about you," Richard said, panting. "You two are like Jacob and Esau. There is strife and anger between you now, but one day, you will forgive each other."

Turning from his father, Sione headed toward the fray he'd tried to stop Richard from entering. Why? He wasn't sure. Or maybe he did know and wasn't ready to face the truth. Now was not the time for reflective introspection. Ignoring Richard's pleas to stop, Sione stalked toward Ben. Heart slamming, his mind swam with images of his hands around Ben's throat as he thought about all the ways Ben had made his life a living hell.

Ben slammed the butt of the gun against the third assassin's head. The man stumbled back. Ben shot him two times and then turned, pointing the gun at Sione.

Stopping abruptly, Sione glared at Ben, looking for some sort of weakness to exploit. Trying to think of a way to get the advantage, Sione saw a flash of something to the right of Ben, something moving through the leaves.

Raising the gun, holding it steady with both hands, Ben smiled. "Well, old friend, I'm not surprised it's come to this."

Behind Ben, the trees rustled slightly.

"So now what?" Sione asked. "Are you going to shoot me? Kill me?"

"I should," Ben said, an almost imperceptible tremor in his hands, as though the gun suddenly weighed more than he was able to bear. "But…"

"But…" Sione took a step toward Ben, recognizing the hesitation in his dark gaze. "What?"

Eyes narrowed, Ben tightened his grip on the gun. "But, I—"

Without warning, Ben pivoted, turning from Sione and pointing his weapon toward the trees. A gunshot roared. Unsure of where the bullet had come from, Sione dropped to one knee.

"Freeze! Nobody move!"

Confused, Sione scanned the clearing. Ben was sprawled on the ground, face-down in the dirt. Obeying the directives of the familiar voice, Sione stared at Ben's unmoving form, wondering if he was dead, wondering why so many conflicting emotions seemed to be churning in his gut.

"I mean it! Do not move!" Roy stepped out of the bushes. An instant later, too many cops emerged from the trees in all directions, surrounding the scene. "Especially not you, Uncle Rich!"

Richard half-scoffed, half-wheezed. "Do I look like I can fucking move, Roy?"

"You look like you're about to try, but I would not advise it," Roy said. "Mom wouldn't want me to shoot you, but I will."

"I'm not going anywhere," Richard said. "So, do your uncle a favor, and call me a damn ambulance before I bleed to death."

64

─────

A'arotanga, South Pacific

Pacing from one side of the street to the other, Spencer felt like she was losing her mind.

Clouds crowded the sky, blocking the sun, and an ocean breeze wafted through the sea grape trees bordering the road. She was hot and dizzy, slightly nauseated, feeling as though she might come out of her skin.

Where was John? What was happening? Had the police caught Ben? Was he being handcuffed right now? How much time had passed since Roy and his officers had disappeared into the trees? An hour? A few minutes? Forever? Walking toward the car, Spencer wiped sweat from her face and took a deep breath. Praying she wouldn't go insane, she leaned against the trunk and cradled her stomach, mouthing assurances to the baby. Daddy would come back to them. Daddy loved them too much for anything bad to happen to him. Swiping a tear from her cheek, she pressed a hand against her mouth so she wouldn't wail the anguish churning within her. John had to come back to her. After everything they'd been through, all the hell and damnation they'd suffered and survived, they could not have made their way back to each other only to be separated by—

No, she would not think the worse. John would come back to her. Nothing bad would happen to him. It couldn't. She wouldn't be able to survive if—

A sound, faint and yet unmistakable in the distance, rattled her. Sirens. More police? She turned. Her heart slammed when she saw the ambulance speeding down the road. The closer the ambulance came, the faster her pulse raced until the loud blaring seemed to be coming from within her, trying to escape from her mouth. She was screaming, she realized, as the ambulance screeched to a halt on the opposite shoulder.

Two paramedics jumped out. Trembling and confused, Spencer watched the EMS workers remove a stretcher from the back of the ambulance.

"What's happened?" she whispered, taking several halting steps away from the car. Why was an ambulance here? Was someone hurt? Was it John? Please, God, no. Not John. He promised he would come back to her.

Carrying the stretcher, the paramedics headed into the forest. Spencer wanted to follow them. The only thing stopping her was fatigue and dizziness. Watching the trees, she panicked and prayed and panicked again for what seemed like hours. She'd just about made up her mind to head back into the forest when two A'arotangan officers came out of the woods, followed by three men in dark suits, all of whom were handcuffed and seemed to be sporting black eyes, bruises, and various other facial traumas.

Spencer's heart sped up when Richard Tuiali'i was escorted out of the forest by two officers who had a firm grip of each of his arms. The shirt beneath his jacket was opened and was stained with a large, dark splotch. Blood, she thought, her pulse jumping. Walking gingerly, he seemed to be favoring his left side and had a hand pressed against his abdomen. Next came the paramedics, carrying a man on the stretcher. Straining to see, she couldn't determine who was strapped to the gurney. Spencer cried out and ran toward the back of the ambulance, where the EMS workers were headed, praying it wasn't—

"Spencer!"

Flooded with relief and joy, she turned.

John walked toward her, smiling. As everything within her started to lift, Spencer rushed to him, crying, collapsing into his embrace as he put an arm around her waist, pulling her close and holding her tight.

65

A'arotanga, South Pacific
The Tuiali'i Estate

Standing in the large foyer of the home where he'd spent two of the most promising and profound years of his life, Sione hesitated and took a deep breath. Memories washed over him, taking him back to the first time he'd stepped foot in the sprawling, grand mansion, which belonged to Uncle Siosi, his father's older, and infinitely more wiser, brother.

For a moment, as the smell of pineapple, frangipani, and coconut swirled around him, he was sixteen again, far from home. Anxious to start a new life, relived to be away from the demoralizing expectations of his father, he'd tried to focus on his new opportunities. Tried to forget about the secrets of his life in Belize, the pressure no one knew about, except for his mother and Ben.

Once in A'arotanga, Sione had resolved to forget his father. And

Ben, too, he supposed. Initially, he did miss Ben, their friendship and fraternal camaraderie, but in order to move on with his life and be the kind of man his mother and uncle could be proud of, he could have no lingering ties to the violence he'd barely escaped. Uncle Siosi always told him he'd been snatched from the fire. Sione wondered if those flames had burned the bridge between him and Ben.

Ben had said he'd been left behind, suggesting he might have embraced the chance of a better life, a less terrorizing existence. Selfishness and fear had kept him from inviting Ben to embark on the new journey with him. The first year in A'arotanga had been exciting but also jarring and sometimes lonely even though the Tuiali'i family was large and there seemed to be another cousin to meet every other day. At times, Sione had wanted to contact Ben, but he worried his father would find some way to exploit and manipulate Ben, using Ben to invade his life. Richard was a magician at times, casting spells, using misdirection to overwhelm and overpower. Sione worried he'd be fooled and enticed into giving his father control over his life.

Looking back, Sione supposed he should have made an effort to sustain the friendship with Ben. Maybe if he had, things would have been different between them.

"John, is that you?"

"It's me," he called out, buoyed by Spencer's voice. Out of the foyer, he followed the wide hallway to the large den, where he found her waiting, still wearing the grass-stained, fabric-snagged sundress she'd had on when he saw her walking into the bank. From the wall of windows where she'd been standing, Spencer hurried across the room toward him.

Three, maybe four, hours had passed since the shootout at Nonu's boat. After the police had surrounded the area, everything happened in a blur of slow motion. Time passed quickly but not quite fast enough, as Richard and his three assassins were arrested and marched out of the forest. The paramedics stabilized Ben, who'd been shot in the back by one of the cops, and then strapped him on a stretcher. With Ben headed to the hospital, Richard and his crew had been taken to the police station. Roy had driven Sione and Spencer to the station, where they'd given statements separately. Spencer spent two hours with one of the detectives and went to the hospital to be examined.

Sione stayed behind, confident she would be competently and thoroughly taken care of by the resident ob-gyn, his cousin Winnie.

"You okay?" Sione asked. "What about the baby?"

Nodding and cradling her abdomen, Spencer said, "I'm fine. The baby is fine despite everything this precious little guy went through because Mama was running from crazy people. I hate what he had to go through because of me."

Sione put an arm around her and led her to one of the four couches positioned in a square around a rectangular coffee table. They sat, and he pulled her as close as possible, entwining his fingers with hers. Holding hands, they cradled her abdomen together.

Spencer was wrong. It was his fault. He was the reason why both Spencer and the baby had gone through torment—traumatic circumstances that could have been disastrously life changing. And unforgivable. If anything horrible had happened to Spencer and the baby, he wouldn't have forgiven himself. Wouldn't have been able to—

He stopped the thoughts, pushing away the grim reminders of unforeseen tragedy. He would never forget the hell they'd suffered because of his strange selfishness. Whatever had compelled him to steal Ben's envelope remained a mystery. Some malevolent force had taken over him on that humid night in October, when he'd confronted Ben. Influencing his thoughts, whatever had possessed him had compelled his actions.

Or maybe the anger had guided his fatal choices. It was easy to blame everything on the devil, but he had to take responsibility for bringing Ben back into their lives, allowing the bastard to wreak so much havoc on their dreams and hopes, their future.

"John?"

He looked away for a moment, fearing some strange look was reflected in his gaze, and then focused on Spencer again. Mesmerized by her lovely face, and the baby bump, which seemed to have become more noticeable to him, he pushed away all thoughts of his uncertain motives.

"You've been at the police station all this time?" Spencer asked, resting her head on his shoulder.

"I was talking to Roy and some of my other cousins on the force," he explained. "Just trying to figure out what happens now that my father has been arrested and Ben…"

"Is Ben dead?" Spencer asked.

"No," Sione said, worried, wondering if he'd heard a hint of concern in her tone. "He had emergency surgery to remove the bullet. Caught him in the back, near his right kidney. He's expected to recover. My cousin Cora was the nurse on duty during the surgery. Ben is in ICU now. Handcuffed to the bed with a cop outside the door."

"So, he'll be arrested when he wakes up?"

"As soon as he wakes up," Sione said, thinking he'd imagined the concern and hoping he had, though secretly, when Ben had been shot, he'd been bothered by the sight of his lifeless form. He told himself he'd been frazzled by the heightened emotions and drama of the moment, but he wasn't so sure. He'd always believed he wanted Ben dead, had believed he wanted to kill him.

"Is there enough evidence against Ben to make the charges stick?"

"Two of Roy's officers caught one of the guards Ben had watching me," Sione said. "Local guy. Ben gave him a few hundred bucks to watch the outside of the house where I was being kept. He's spilling his guts. The guards inside the house were Triad guys, and they have disappeared, not surprisingly."

After moment of silence, Spencer asked, "What about Richard?"

"Still sitting in jail as we speak," Sione said. "Roy doesn't think any charges will stick. His guys will not rat. They'll eat a bullet before they snitch. Roy can hold him for forty-eight hours, then, if there's nothing to charge him with, Richard and his guys will be released."

"Your father shouldn't be released from jail."

"I don't like it either," Sione said and then exhaled. "But my father is claiming he came to the island to rescue me from Ben, and that Ben ambushed him and his men, and they were just trying to defend themselves."

"Does your cousin believe that?"

"I doubt it," Sione said. "There's just no evidence to the contrary."

"John," Spencer started, haltingly, before going on, "After the detective took my statement, your cousin Roy came into the room to ask me how I was, and he wanted to know what I'd told the detective."

"He told me he talked to you."

"Did he tell you that I told him something I didn't tell the detective."

Sione nodded, and his heart started to race. "You told Roy that Richard killed Moana."

"I'm sorry," Spencer said. "Maybe I shouldn't have—"

"I'm glad you told him," Sione said, hoping to reassure her, even though he wasn't quite sure how he felt about her confession of his father's crime, one that was unsubstantiated.

"But your cousin can arrest him for that, can't he?"

"My father killed Moana in Belize," Sione said, revolted and relieved by his father's actions. The hypocrisy of his feelings, however, was not lost on him. How could he throw stones at Richard for finishing what he'd started, accomplishing what he'd failed at but had wanted to do. "Belize has jurisdiction over the crime, which Roy knew, and I figured, but we called my cousin Jared, and he confirmed it."

"So, you told Jared?" Spencer asked, hope in her voice.

"I did, and he's going to look into it," Sione said. "Honestly, I don't think much will come from his investigation. My father is very good at covering his tracks. After we got off the phone with Jared, Roy and I talked to Richard. Of course, he was shocked and dismayed that you had falsely accused him, considering that he'd rescued you, saved your life."

"Maybe he did save my life, John." Spencer sat up and put a bit of space between them. "But he killed Moana, too. And I know she was no saint, but..."

"Richard claims he rescued you from Ben's beach house and that you were alone and unattended," Sione said, recounting his father's inaccurate but compelling narrative. "He claims you had been abandoned by your kidnappers."

"But, that's not true," Spencer insisted. "I told Roy what really happened."

"I know, but Richard's guys are telling the story the same way he is, the way he instructed them to tell it," Sione said. "According to them, Moana was never there."

"So there's no evidence that Richard killed Moana," Spencer said, shaking her head. "There's only my word, which Jared probably doesn't even believe because he thinks I'm a liar and—"

"Come on, don't get upset," he said, pulling her back into his arms. "Jared believes your story. He's going to look for evidence against Richard."

"But you don't think he'll find any, do you?" Spencer said. "And I guess I don't either. After Richard killed Moana, he told his guys to get rid of her body and make it appear as if she never existed."

"My father will be brought to justice," Sione said with more confidence than he felt. "One way or the other."

"And Ben?" Spencer moved her head to look up at him. "Is he going to get away, too?"

"Not likely," Sione said. "Roy has him on kidnapping and murdering the two guys from Richard's crew."

"But will Ben go to jail?" Spencer asked. "Or will he get away somehow?"

"Ben is not going to get away with what he did to us," Sione said, and again, the confidence in his voice contrasted with his true beliefs, which worried him. "Trust me, he's going to jail for a long damn time…"

66

A'arotanga, South Pacific
The Tuiali'i Estate

"Spencer okay?" Roy asked, taking a seat at the table in the large kitchen.

Several hours had passed since the last time they'd talked in Roy's office at the police station. The chaos surrounding the arrest of Richard and the transport of Ben to the hospital had precluded Roy from finding a moment to talk with Sione, who had waited around to get a word with his cousin. Roy had promised to stop by the house once things calmed down.

Sione grabbed two beers from the refrigerator. "Yeah, she's upstairs resting."

"Winnie said the baby is okay," said Roy, accepting the beer Sione handed him.

"Thank God," Sione said, thankful his little boy had survived the nightmare Spencer had endured. A nightmare he'd put in motion and had been lucky to have escaped.

Roy nodded, took a swig of beer, and said, "Funny."

"What?" Sione sat across from Roy, confused by his cousin's teasing smirk.

Shaking his head, Roy said, "You gonna be a father."

"Is that so surprising?"

"Guess not. Maybe." Roy shrugged. "You excited?"

Sione smiled. "I actually can't wait. Part of me wishes he was already here, but then I feel like I need time to get ready, you know. I need to prepare."

"Trust me, I do know what you mean," Roy said. "But even after having two, I still don't know if I was really ready. I don't think it's something you can fully prepare for. You just have to do it because once the baby comes, it's too late to change your mind."

Sione frowned. "Now you're starting to scare me."

"Relax," Roy said. "You'll be fine. I can tell how much you already love that kid."

"I really do," Sione said. "As soon as Spencer told me she was pregnant, I felt like he became my world, you know?"

"I do know," Roy said. "I felt the same way when I found out my wife was expecting."

"I just want to be a good father," Sione confessed. "I want to be like Uncle Siosi."

"And unlike Uncle Rich, huh?" Roy gave him a sympathetic look.

"Can't imagine subjecting my son to what my father put me through," Sione said. "Thinking about it now, it was child abuse."

Roy said, "Uncle Rich is a complicated man."

"Complicated?" Sione scoffed. "There's nothing complicated about it, Roy. He kills people."

"Well, that's never been proven," Roy said. Sione rubbed his eyes. "Look, I know Uncle Rich is a bad dude, and that's a gross understatement, but he loves you. You're *his* world."

Sione looked away. He didn't like the idea of being Richard's world. Meaning everything to his father required too much sacrifice. It was too high of a price, costing him his mind, body, and soul. He could never be what Richard expected him to be or what his father wanted him to be. He could never live up to his father's hopes and dreams and schemes.

Still, part of him wanted his father to be proud of him. Part of him liked the idea of meaning so much to Richard. He liked the idea of his father always being on his side and having his back, looking out for him. Maybe Roy was right. Maybe the relationship with his father was too complicated. Maybe he wasn't quite sure how he felt.

"I don't want to talk about Richard."

"Well, too bad," Roy said. "Because I came to tell you that Richard is still behind bars."

Relieved, and yet strangely suspicious, Sione said, "Yeah, but not for long."

"Maybe longer than you think," Roy said. "He's facing a few charges. The most serious being possession of unlicensed firearms which is illegal in A'arotanga."

Dismissive, Sione said, "As soon as he makes bail, he'll disappear."

"If he makes bail," Roy said. "He went before the magistrate judge who set bail at fifty thousand dollars, which I thought would be no problem for your dad, but he couldn't pay it."

"You're kidding."

Roy shook his head. "Surprised he didn't call you."

"I would not have answered."

"Is Uncle Rich really broke?"

"I don't know and I don't care," Sione said. "Probably not. May just be having a problem getting access to funds. I'm glad to hear he's got to sit in jail for a while. Maybe it'll give him time to think about his life."

"Maybe," Roy said and stood. "But I doubt it. Before I go, you know anything about this?"

"What?" Sione asked.

Roy dropped something on the table. Sione stared at it in disbelief. What the hell?

Ben's envelope.

Grass-stained and frayed around the edges and at the corners, it was stained and streaked with dried mud splotches. Had Ben accidentally dropped the envelope? Or had the damn thing fallen out of his pocket? Somehow, Ben's envelope had left his possession after Spencer had given it to him.

Sione's heart pounded as he picked up the envelope, pretending to examine it, making sure to frown, and hoping he seemed confused. "What is it?"

"Appears to be an envelope."

"I don't know what this is," Sione said, holding Roy's gaze, which was more curious than suspicious. "I've never seen it before."

"One of the officers found it in the area where Uncle Rich's guys and Ben had their little skirmish," said Roy. "Took a look inside. Strange. A bunch of animal symbols on a piece of paper. Might have been hand-drawn. Maybe made with some kind of stamp."

Rubbing his jaw, Sione shook his head. "I don't know, Roy."

"Think it might belong to Uncle Rich?" Roy picked up the envelope.

Sione shrugged. "You have to ask him."

"Maybe I will," said Roy. "Or maybe I'll just lock it up in the evidence room for safekeeping until someone comes to claim it."

"You know," Sione said, staring at the dirty, torn envelope in his cousin's hand. "I think that might be the best thing to do."

67

———————

A'arotanga, South Pacific
The Tuiali'i Estate

ONE MONTH LATER

Spencer's heart pounded with joy and exhilaration as she basked in the beautiful summer day on the island of A'arotanga.

Walking through the grove of palm trees, Spencer clutched her bouquet of frangipani flowers. The soft petals were the same white as the wedding dress she wore as she headed down a wide path cut through a grove of tall hibiscus bushes. Making her way across the expansive lawn behind the mansion on the enormous, sprawling estate of John's late uncle, Siosi Tuiali'i, Spencer walked with a measured pace. She forced herself to keep time with the romantic processional music even though she really wanted to race down the aisle and into John's arms.

Stepping onto the strip of white silk on the grass, Spencer

walked between the rows of white chairs where her wedding guests sat, smiling and crying. In addition to the entire Tuiali'i family and John's Belizean relatives, Spencer's grandmother and a few of her cousins had been flown in from Houston for the ceremony.

With each step, her relationship with John flashed before her eyes.

She remembered meeting him for the first time...their first kiss...the first time they'd made love...and many of the other intimate times they'd shared after that first explosive encounter... their horrible breakup...the passionate reunion...and then the proposal she'd never expected.

With each step, the story unfolded of a troubled woman involved with a dangerous man. A woman who should have been dead or in jail but had somehow, through the grace of God, found love instead.

Walking down the aisle seemed to take forever, but soon Spencer was at the altar holding hands with John, standing before God and all their guests and the minister, moments away from becoming John's wife.

Each step had been worth it. Each step had been a testament to the trials and tribulations. Each step reminded her that everything they'd suffered had not been in vain but had been so they would appreciate and be forever thankful for the joy they were experiencing right now.

Spencer handed the bouquet to Rae, who smiled and mouthed "You're so beautiful. I'm so happy for you." Spencer smiled back and after a deep, fortifying breath, Spencer turned. It was all she could do not to gasp.

When she looked up at John, it was as though she had gone back into the past and was seeing him for the first time. Her reaction was the same as it had been then. He was still the most handsome man she'd ever seen. That he was tall and muscular made it even better. And knowing what was in store for her in those tuxedo trousers made it beyond phenomenal.

John took her hands and smiled at her.

She smiled back, hypnotized by those hazel eyes gazing at her, giving her butterflies.

The minister began with the reason for the ceremony: to join together Spencer T. Edwards and Sione D. Tuiali'i. He made pastoral comments about the union of marriage and how it should not be entered into lightly but with sincerity and an intention to honor God.

"And now at this moment in the ceremony," the minister said, "the groom has some sentiments he would like to express."

Nonplussed, Spencer stared at the minister and then at John, wondering what was going on. During all their wedding rehearsals, they had never practiced the moment when the groom expressed sentiments. Why was he rewriting the script?

John stared at her and said, "I know we said we would do the traditional vows and we will, but I want to tell you something, and I want everyone to hear it, as well."

There was a slight cough.

Spencer cut her eyes toward the groom's side and saw Carmen staring at them with pursed lips.

"John," Spencer half-whispered, half-mouthed. "You don't have to—"

"Yes," he whispered, "I do."

Giddy and yet slightly apprehensive Spencer nodded.

Clearing his throat, he said, "You once asked me what kind of woman I wanted Mrs. Tuiali'i to be, and I told you I wanted my wife to be selfless and compassionate and a woman who would help me be a better person. Well, I realize now I was describing the woman I thought I was supposed to want and should be with because that was the kind of woman my family would accept. But now I know that Mrs. Tuiali'i is loyal, tenacious, encouraging, supportive, and most of all she loves me as much as I love her. Spencer, you are all those things and so much more. You are the woman I hoped and prayed and wished for, and I love you and I don't care what anybody else thinks. Don't think you have to be a certain kind of person to make me happy because you make me happy just being who you are. I don't want you to be anything except what you are to me, the woman I want to spend the rest of my life with."

Speechless, Spencer stared at him, moved beyond words by his public declaration of love for her. His acceptance of her meant more than she could say, more than he would ever know.

John's heartfelt profession deserved a response, and despite the tears threatening to ruin her makeup, Spencer took a breath and said, "John, I remember that conversation, and I also remember thinking that I could never be that woman no matter how hard I tried. I'll admit I was a little upset because I knew even then that whoever got to be Mrs. Tuiali'i was going to be so blessed to have a wonderful man like you to love her and protect her and be with her forever. You could have had your pick of all the kind, compassionate girls in the world, but you chose me to love and—"

Spencer stopped to blink the tears away and then said, "I really love you, and you have made all my dreams come true. I'm so happy that I'm the girl who gets to be with you forever. I can't wait to spend the rest of my life with you."

John smiled at her as the minister continued, and Spencer couldn't help but think of how they had finally arrived at this moment—happily ever after.

Despite the mistakes, the danger, and the betrayal, she and John had withstood all the setbacks and the threats to their happiness.

They'd overcome the treachery, deceit, and violence inflicted upon them by Ben and Richard. Neither adversary could hurt or hinder them anymore. Ben remained comatose and Richard incarcerated—the future grim for both men.

As the ceremony continued with the exchange of rings, the minister's blessing, and the reading of Scripture by Shady, Spencer stared at John, hardly able to believe she was really marrying him. John looked so perfect and gorgeous. He was everything she would ever want for the rest of her life.

"The Bible states that two are better than one. They receive a good reward for their toil, because, if one fails, the other can help the companion up," the minister continued. "With the blessings of God, it is my pleasure to now pronounce you husband and wife."

Weak-kneed, Spencer reeled from the sensations of a million butterflies set loose within her as John stared at her, his gaze an expression of love and bliss.

"You may now kiss the bride!"

ALSO BY RACHEL WOODS

REPORTER ROLAND BEAN COZY MYSTERIES

Roland "Beanie" Bean, husband and loving father, finds himself the unwitting participant in solving crimes as he seeks to make a name for himself as a reporter for the *Palmchat Gazette*.

HAPPY BIRTHDAY MURDER

EASTER EGG HUNT MURDER

MERRY CHRISTMAS MURDER

TRICK OR TREAT MURDER

GOBBLE GOBBLE MURDER

HAPPY 4TH OF JULY MURDER

PALMCHAT ISLANDS MYSTERIES

Married journalists, Vivian and Leo, manage the island newspaper while solving crimes as they chase leads for their next story.

UNTIL DEATH DO US PART

NO ONE WILL FIND YOU

YOU WILL DIE FOR THIS

DON'T MAKE ME HURT YOU

THE PALMCHAT ISLANDS MYSTERIES BOX SET: BOOKS 1 - 4

SPENCER & SIONE SERIES

Gripping romantic suspense series with steamy romance, unpredictable plot twists and devastating consequences of deceit.

HER DEADLY MISTAKE

HER DEADLY DECEPTION

HER DEADLY THREAT

HER DEADLY BETRAYAL

MURDER IN PARADISE SERIES

A series of stand-alone women sleuth mysteries with murder, mayhem and a dash of romance, set against the backdrop of turquoise waters and swaying palm trees of the fictional Palmchat Islands.

THE UNWORTHY WIFE

THE PERFECT LIAR

THE SILENT ENEMY

ABOUT THE AUTHOR

Rachel Woods studied journalism and graduated from the University of Houston where she published articles in the Daily Cougar. She is a legal assistant by day and a freelance writer and blogger with a penchant for melodrama by night. Many of her stories take place on the islands, which she has visited around the world. Rachel resides in Houston, Texas with her three sock monkeys.

For more information:
www.therachelwoods.com
rachel@therachelwoods.com

facebook.com/therachelwoodsauthor
instagram.com/therachelwoodsauthor
bookbub.com/authors/rachel-woods
amazon.com/author/therachelwoods

ABOUT THE PUBLISHER

BonzaiMoon Books is a family-run, artisanal publishing company created in the summer of 2014. We publish works of fiction in various genres. Our passion and focus is working with authors who write the books you want to read, and giving those authors the opportunity to have more direct input in the publishing of their work.

For more information:
www.bonzaimoonbooks.com
info@bonzaimoonbooks.com

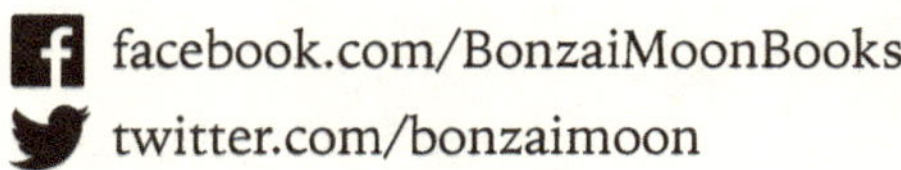